SOMEWHERE TO CALL OUR HOME

BLUEY ROGERS

DEDICATION

This book is dedicated to Stephen.

CONTENTS

ACKNOWLEDGEMENTS

Thank you to my family and friends who, in one way or another, helped and encouraged me along the way to completing this book.

In particular, a special thanks to Lee who gave so much of his time with editing and help with my technological challenges.

Chapter 1

Rohan and Ruby Connors were orphans. Their parents had both been killed in the same car accident that had badly injured the two children. By the time the children had come out of their comas, the funerals were over and they did not have a chance to say good-bye to their parents. Their mother's parents had also passed away, but on their father's side, they had a very kind Nanna who offered to take care of them when they were well enough to go home. Rohan was fourteen and Ruby was only seven so Rohan felt responsible for her. Nanna was seventy-five, but she was quite active and, after some delay and arguing with various representatives, she received approval from the Department of Children, Youth Justice and Multicultural Affairs to have temporary custody of them while she remained in good health. Her home was a large old-fashioned house with lots of rooms and a large veranda that wrapped around three sides. Nanna knew that she would not be able to care for them until Ruby was old enough to look after herself, so she used every opportunity to teach them how to cook and do all the house-hold chores. Rohan enjoyed mowing the lawn and doing all the manly jobs while Ruby loved helping with the cooking, the shopping and even the ironing and vacuuming.

They missed their parents very much and they often talked about them but Nanna helped them to stay happy. She looked after them and they looked after her. Nanna often told her friends how much she was enjoying the company of these two delightful young people. Rohan was a strong and sensible boy and he soon became quite a handyman around the house, doing all the heavy work and saving Nanna from employing someone to do the lawn and other work that she could no longer do herself. Ruby was a tremendous help with the housework and her happy loving chatter always amused Nanna who had previously felt quite lonely. The children had been living with her for nearly two years when Ruby noticed that occasionally Nanna did some strange things. She sometimes put strange groceries in the trolley—groceries they would never use, and once she could not remember her address when they caught a taxi home. A few times she tried to catch the wrong bus and Ruby had to argue with her to convince her that it didn't go anywhere near their house. Ruby did not know what was happening to her precious Nanna who would sometimes be quite angry with her when she tried to stop her from doing such strange things. She often left the iron on and once she nearly caused a fire, but Nanna blamed Ruby and was very cross when Ruby argued with her and said that she had been using the iron herself.

Because Rohan understood that older people sometimes lost their memory, he decided to ring his Aunty Patricia to get her advice. Aunty Pat was Nanna's only child now. The children's father Greg was her brother and he had been killed but Pat didn't visit her mother or try to help her in any way, especially after the children moved in because she was extremely jealous of them, and didn't like them living with her mother. Rohan knew that she didn't like them, but he didn't know what else to do.

Aunty Pat arrived one Friday afternoon without any warning and, although Nanna was unhappy about the sudden visit, she tried to make her welcome. The first thing she did was to strip all the linen off one of the spare beds and make it up again with clean sheets and pillowcases. That was completely unnecessary because, like the rest of her house, everything in the bedrooms was kept very neat and clean. Nanna cooked a delicious meal which they all enjoyed, and then Rohan and Ruby cleaned the dishes and packed them away while the two ladies watched television and caught up on some talk. Later the children joined their grandma and aunty, and they all had a pleasant evening together, until Nanna excused herself, then went off to the same bedroom and stripped down the same bed and started to remake it with fresh linen. When Aunty Pat found what she was doing, she was furious, and she started shouting at Nanna. "You stupid old woman" she shouted. "What are you doing? Have you gone completely mad?' Ruby had never heard adults shouting at each other in such an angry way and she was terrified. She began to cry as she ran into Nanna's arms and cuddled into her. Rohan was stunned too and he went to Nanna and put his arms around her shoulders and turned to face his Aunty.

"She might be old," he said, "and she might forget some things, but she is not stupid and you have no right to talk to our Nanna like that. She is the kindest woman I know. You don't deserve to have a mother like her, and I wish I didn't ring you for help."

Aunty Pat's mouth dropped open as though she was going to speak but for a moment, she was speechless. Then she exploded "How dare you speak to me like that, you can forget about her kindness because she won't be wearing herself out any longer, trying to look after you pair. She will be going into a home where she can be looked after properly."

Nanna's mind had recovered again because her temporary lapse of memory had passed. She looked straight at her daughter and said very firmly, "Just stop right there. The children have been a great comfort to me, and they do not wear me out. They help me and I help them." Nanna's anger was raised to such a pitch that she went very red in the face and suddenly her legs buckled under her, and she almost fell, but Rohan quickly held her firmly and helped her to a chair. Little Ruby ran to a side table and grabbed Nanna's fan and took it to her, and then she ran to the kitchen and returned with a glass of water. Even Aunty Pat was impressed with how the children reacted, but she didn't say anything. Nanna asked for her blood pressure spray which the children had seen her use occasionally and Rohan went to her bed-side table and brought it to her. While he stayed with her and talked quietly to her, Ruby went to the kitchen and made her a cup of tea.

Nanna soon relaxed completely and after about fifteen minutes she was feeling much better. Aunty Pat had sat down in a chair near her but she didn't say a word to her mother or to the children. When Nanna recovered, she looked at her daughter and sadly said "I would like you to leave now. I have all the help that I need right here with me." Without any sign of emotion Aunty Pat stood up, went to the bedroom, and returned almost immediately with her suitcase which had not been unpacked, and as she reached the door she looked back and said, "This is not the end of it. You will be hearing from me." Then she walked through the door and closed it behind her.

Chapter 2

The little family had a very restless night. Ruby didn't like her Aunty Pat and she knew that she was going to cause trouble, but she had no idea of how serious the situation was and how her life was about to be turned upside down again. Rohan understood that it was a very serious situation because he knew now that his Nanna's mind was sick, but he was hoping that he would be allowed to look after her and also Ruby.

They had been living together for nearly two years and he was almost sixteen. He could leave school and get a job, and when Nanna had to go into a nursing home sometime in the future, he would go on looking after Ruby in this house and visit Nanna every week. Nanna knew that she had an incurable illness and her doctor had already warned her that she would not be able to manage much longer. He had told her to put all of her affairs in order while he could still certify that her mind was sound enough for her to be capable of making difficult decisions. She had spoken to a close friend who had promised to help her cope with all of the arrangements when the final decisions had to be made. Nanna also knew her daughter would not be any help and she realised that she was about to lose her precious grandchildren, and after that, she would not be able to live in the house on her own.

First thing the next morning, she rang her friend and asked her whether she would be able to come and visit her straight away. She told Mrs White briefly what had happened without going into great detail, because she didn't want the children to hear her plans a little bit at a time. She wanted to be able to explain the whole situation carefully and answer all of their questions. It was going to be a difficult and sad morning.

When Mrs White arrived, Nanna had a large plate of sandwiches ready and cups of coffee for her and her friend and flavoured milk for the children so they all sat down in the large living room. It was difficult for her to know where to start, but finally she explained about her daughter's behaviour on the previous night and the threats that she had made. She knew that at least the children already knew that much.

Then Nanna turned to the children and explained that the doctor had warned her that her memory would gradually worsen until she was not capable of caring for herself. She had tried to put it off for as long as she could, but now that Pat knew, she would contact the authorities and they would insist on placing Ruby in some other home. Ruby didn't understand but she was frightened and she began to cry. Rohan insisted that he could look after her and he wanted her to stay with him, but Nanna had already checked the law with the Children's services to see whether that was possible and they had made it very clear that it would not be allowed. She asked the children to listen patiently to her whole plan before they began to panic. Things would not be as bad as they feared.

She would have to go into a home herself, because she would not be safe trying to care for herself and, even if Rohan left school, he could not be with her all the time. She told them which nursing home she had booked herself into and it wasn't very far away.

Next, she faced Rohan and said that he was too old to go into a home for children but she did not want him to be all on his own. Mr and Mrs White were happy to have him live with them but they didn't have room in their house so she had already bought a big caravan and it was in the White's back yard. He would have company but at the same time, he would have his own little home. She had also placed twenty thousand dollars in his bank account so that when he was old enough to drive, he could buy a reliable car. Both children gave a little gasp, but Nanna put her finger on her lips to signal them to be quiet, still. Then she turned to Ruby. "Darling you have been my greatest worry, but Mrs White and I have visited the home and the children seem to be well cared for and it won't be for very long. Rohan will be able to visit you every weekend and when he is eighteen, he will be allowed to look after you. You will be in a dormitory with five little girls about your age. It will be like having a lot of sisters."

Ruby's eyes filled with tears as she listened to her grandmother but she didn't say anything. She just sat and looked at her. "Don't be sad" Nanna said. "The time will go by quickly, and then you will be together again and you are both going to have a wonderful future. That is something that I can help you with. I have put the same amount of money in your account Ruby, but of course it will be a long time before you need a car.

This house will be sold and all my furniture and other bits and pieces will be stored in a new shed which I have already had built on Mrs White's farm. When you are old enough to buy your own homes all of this will be yours."

Both children struggled to understand what was happening to their lives and both ladies tried to comfort them and convince them that, after a short time they would have a very bright future.

Rohan quietly thanked Mrs White for allowing him to live in a caravan on her property and for allowing Nanna to have a shed there where she could store her furniture and other precious things. However, he was completely surprised when Mrs White explained that his grandmother actually owned the farm and she and her husband were leasing it from her. Rohan knew that his Nanna was too wealthy to receive a government pension, but he had absolutely no idea how wealthy she actually was.

After Mrs White went home, their grandmother decided to tell them how many properties she owned and where the properties were. She also said that someday most of it would be theirs. The conversation created a new interest for the children and they began to look forward to a better future. There was a lot of talk that day about many things that Ruby did not understand. Sometimes Nanna's memory faded and Rohan began to wonder how much of what she had told them was true, but he didn't put any doubt in Ruby's mind because the whole business seemed to be capturing her imagination and some of her sadness and fear was being dispelled.

Chapter 3

It was three months after the little family had been dispersed in three different directions. Nanna was in the nursing home and Rohan visited her every week and he was shocked at how quickly her mind had deteriorated. Sometimes she did not know him at all. On other occasions, she thought that he was her son, Gregory, Rohan's father. Sometimes when she recognised him when he arrived, she would soon forget and then casually say, "I'm all right now Doctor. You can go". It was sad and frustrating for Rohan but he had continued to persevere, hoping that her mind would improve.

Rohan's own life was very good. He had an interesting job at a car wrecking yard where he had already learnt a lot about cars and the value of their spare parts. He earned a good wage and had no expenses, so he banked most of it each week. Nanna had provided for his board at the White's by lowering their rent to such a trivial amount that they paid no more than a token rent so that the contract remained as a business deal.

Ruby had settled into the orphanage after a month. Rohan had visited her on Saturdays and Sundays for the first month because the Director of the home would not allow her to go home with her brother until she had fully settled in to her new life. For the past eight weeks she had been allowed to spend the whole weekend with Rohan. At first, she was extremely happy to be with him and always appeared to be happy to return to the orphanage on Sunday night. Then her attitude changed. She frequently cried for nothing and when it was time for her to go back to the home she dallied as much as she could and even appeared to be afraid. Both Rohan and Mrs White tried to find the problem but Ruby refused to tell them what was worrying her. Rohan considered asking Mrs

Mullens, the dormitory mother, if she knew what was making Ruby so unhappy, but he remembered how much trouble he had caused by asking Aunty Pat for help when his Nanna had a problem so he decided to try to solve it on his own.

On her next visit, when he found her with her face buried in the pillow and sobbing for no obvious reason, he tried once again to talk her into confiding in him, but she just cried more and said that she did not want to go back there again. She had lost weight and was very pale. She cried for most of the weekend, and Rohan was so upset, he rang for a doctor to come and check her out.

The doctor was very gentle with her, but the only symptom of any illness that he could find, was a slight fever which, he said she had probably brought on by crying so much...

However, he agreed with Rohan that she could not go on as she was or she would really become ill. He prescribed for her, a medication which had a mild sedative in it, and promised to ring Mrs Mullens and ask her to keep a special eye on Ruby until they solved the problem. He also suggested that it might be necessary to have some blood tests taken if the cause was not found very soon. The following week when Rohan went to collect her, he made up his mind that, one way or another, he was going to make her talk to him. Ruby didn't look at all well, but she was still on the medication so she was very quiet and did not cry all the time. He said to Mrs White, "Although Ruby is not crying, I think she looks worse. I am sure she is much thinner and she is not interested in having any fun at all. I feel like crying myself now." After lunch, he said quite firmly to Ruby, "Ruby you have to help me. You are not being fair by causing so much worry and not letting me help you." He took two fifty dollar notes out of his wallet and showed them to her, then he said, "If you will talk to me, and tell me a believable reason why you are so sad, we will go shopping and buy a nice present for each of your friends." He was sure that it would have more effect offering to buy something for the other girls than it would if he just offered to buy something for her. She looked at him with sad eyes and then she said "You won't believe me. You will think that I am being silly."

"Of course I won't" he said, "If it makes you as sad as you have been for several weeks, it is a major problem and we will solve it"

"You can't," she almost shouted, and Rohan put out his arms and cuddled her to him "We will and we will make your friends happy too," he assured her.

"Promise?" she asked

"I promise." he replied "Now tell me.".

As she sat there Ruby held the hem of her frock and twisted it around in her fingers while she stared down at the floor. Rohan waited quietly for her to start with her story and finally she said, "Well, do you know Kylie and Tiffany? They are really my best friends. Every Tuesday afternoon, Kylie has to go around to Mr Robinson's room. Then on Friday afternoon he sends for Tiffany and they always cry and they don't want to go, but they have to. It is not because they have done anything wrong because they always come back with chocolates and lollies for all of us. Sometimes when we are playing outside, he puts his arms around them and tells them that they are his special girls. One day he put his arms around me and he said that I go home too often and I could be his special girl too." Ruby stopped talking and started to cry. Then she burst out, "What will I do if he stops me from coming home so that I can be one of his special girls?"

Rohan pulled his little sister close to him and held her firmly, and then he said angrily through tight lips, "He won't stop you from coming home and you will not become one of his special girls. I said that I would solve whatever was making you sad, and l will".

When Rohan took Ruby back to the home that afternoon, he reminded her again that she did not have to be afraid anymore because he was going to look after her. He also made her promise that she would not talk to anyone else, not even her friends, about their conversation, and she quietly said, "I won't. I feel better now."

Chapter 4

As Rohan travelled home on the bus, he had a seat to himself and he quietly planned what he was going to do. Of one thing he was quite certain and that was, that he had to take Ruby away. He would have to plan very carefully, because if they were found, Ruby would be sent back to the home and would never be allowed to come home at week-ends again. Robinson might even stop him from visiting her and then he could easily make her his special girl, just like Kylie and Tiffany.

He had just turned seventeen and he had been planning to buy a car with the money that Nanna had banked for him, but that could wait. He would still draw all of his money out of the bank because he would have to change his name, and then he wouldn't be able to operate his account under his original name. Besides the twenty thousand dollars which Nanna had given him to buy a car, he also had at least another four thousand which he had saved, so they could travel a long way and hide for months, if necessary.

He had lived in Brisbane all his life, and except for an occasional holiday at a near beach resort, when he was a child and his parents were alive, he had absolutely no experience with travelling.

The memory of his parents made him sad for a moment, but then he became even more determined to rescue his little sister.

During the months that he had been living with the Whites, he and Robert White had become very good friends and Rohan knew that he would need his help if he was going to make a success of his frightening plan. Robert was twenty-two and he had worked at a variety of jobs and travelled around much of Australia.

That night he asked Robert to come over to his van after dinner and then he told him everything. Robert knew that Ruby had been sad and causing his mother and Rohan a considerable amount of worry, and when Rohan told him his suspicions about Robinson's behaviour he was stunned. He agreed that they had to move her before they could do anything for the other girls, so the two young men set about making very careful plans.

First Rohan should withdraw all of his money and keep it in cash. It would be dangerous but if no one knew that he had it, it shouldn't be a serious problem

Second, Robert asked him to prepare two letters; one for the police to assure them that he was intending to look after his little sister and also to tell them why he felt that he had to rescue her. He hoped that they would start an investigation and that should help the other girls too. The other letter he should write to the Children's Services, and tell them everything also. Then Robert said "When you are safely away, I'll send them enclosed in a larger envelope, to my friend in Melbourne. I'll ask him to post them at the Melbourne Post Shop, and hopefully that will make the authorities think that you are hiding down there and send them on a wild goose chase."

"But I was considering going to Melbourne," Rohan said, "and that would bring them straight to me."

"Well, I have a good friend who travels between Brisbane and Longreach, twice a week and if he will help you, I think it will be the best for both you and Ruby. It really scares me thinking of you two kids down in Melbourne. He is a good fellow and he has a couple of girls a bit older than Ruby. I know he won't help unless he knows the whole story because he will be wary of being part of anything that is illegal. His wife is a school teacher at a little three teacher school out near Winton, and she also does a lot of welfare work for country children, so she would certainly know how best to help. Whatever happens, you will both be in good hands, and far safer than trying to make it on your own in Melbourne or Sydney."

Rohan agreed that it sounded like an excellent idea but first he would like to meet Robert's friend, the truck driver. Robert told him that his name was Jack and he assured him that even if Jack wouldn't help them, he was certain that he would not report them and spoil their chance of hiding somewhere.

Another thing that Rohan would have to see to before the weekend was to buy a supply of clothing for Ruby, because she would not be able to bring any of her clothes from the home. The two young men sat down and made a list of all of the things that Rohan should buy, including sleeping bags, a tent, and some camp cooking utensils. It all had to be ready before he picked Ruby up on Friday afternoon.

Chapter 5

Rohan's and Robert's meeting with Jack went very well. He heard their story and agreed to help them but there were certain conditions on which he insisted. He let them know that he was completely disgusted with what they had told him and, therefore he felt compelled to do more than just rescue Ruby. He had to help the other girls too as soon as they had taken Ruby away. He told them that he would be confiding everything to his wife because she had dealt with similar situations before.

He also told Rohan that he knew of a Motel and Truck Stop, near Longreach where the elderly owners were looking for workers and because of its isolation, they were not having much success. He said that the owners lived at the motel but the old farm house was still on the property and, so far as he knew, it was not occupied. He said that it looked rather shabby from the highway but if he was willing to clean it up, it might make a safe hide-away for him and Ruby.

Rohan was very excited about the idea and made it clear that he would work hard to make it a home if he was given the opportunity. Jack warned him that things didn't always turn out the way that one hoped they would, and if this plan didn't succeed, he would take them home to Longreach with him and look after the two of them at his home until better arrangements could be made. He hadn't asked his wife but he assured them that she would agree because they had fostered many children who had been in need of a home, and it was a normal part of their life. Jack told them where he would be leaving from at about eight o'clock on Friday night, and told them to be there about thirty minutes before then. Rohan was so excited that he could barely conceal his emotions. He still had most of Thursday and all of Friday before he had to pick up Ruby from the home. He had told his boss that he was sick because he was afraid to let anyone other than Robert, know what he was planning to do. If anything went wrong at that stage he would have been devastated. He and Robert checked and rechecked their list of things to do, and he felt as though he was thoroughly prepared.

When he went to collect Ruby, he was surprised to find her already waiting in the little vestibule at the entrance to the home. She said that she was ready to go, but he asked her to pick out a few more of her best frocks and to bring them with her because they had both been invited to a wedding on the Saturday and a party on Sunday. It was a fib but he couldn't tell her the truth without a lot of explanation and as he wanted her to bring as many of her good clothes as he dared to ask for, he hoped that he would be forgiven. "You had better bring a few he said and we can choose the most suitable when we are at home."

Mrs Mullens appeared at the door just as Ruby was dashing back for her little port and Rohan gave her the same explanation. He also reminded Ruby, to bring Shirley with her. Shirley was a beautiful doll which their parents had given Ruby at the last Christmas that they shared before their parents were killed. He explained to Mrs Mullens that their friend, Mrs White was going to make Shirley some new clothes to cheer Ruby up because she had been so sad lately. It was another fib but he knew that Ruby would be very upset if she lost her doll by leaving it at the home.

Ruby was excited about the wedding and the party and she asked so many questions while they were on their way home that Rohan was beginning to worry that she might be disappointed when she heard the real reason why she had to bring the extra things. He waited until they were in the caravan before he tried to explain what they were about to do.

When they entered the van, Ruby gasped and put her hand to her mouth when she saw a pile of new clothes for herself, numerous books and board games, and a complete set of school books for her year level and for the following year. Rohan's clothes and other things were already packed and an empty port was sitting on the table ready for Ruby's clothes and books "What's all this for?" She exclaimed. "Shh!" Rohan whispered. Then he began his explanation while Ruby stared at him in utter shock. He talked for some time and Ruby didn't say a word, she just sat there staring at him until he stopped and said, "Are you alright? Are you happy to go away or are you frightened?' "What if they catch us?" She whispered.

"I don't think they will" Rohan said "and Jack is a really nice fellow and he has said that we can stay with him if we can't find anywhere suitable. His wife has had lots of foster children and she will help us."

Ruby gradually started to smile, then a huge smile spread over her face and she threw her arms around Rohan's neck and thanked him over and over. She was suddenly over the moon with happiness and all her fear was replaced with excitement.

"There is still one thing we have to deal with," he told her. "We each have to choose new names. I have decided that I want to become Jeffrey. Who do you want to be?" Once again fear showed in her eyes and it was a moment before she replied, "I like Chloe. Can I pretend that I am Chloe?"

"Yes, that's a pretty name, but remember it is more than just pretending. We have to be Jeffrey and Chloe Hamilton all the time and never make a mistake." Rohan helped Ruby to pack her things into her port then they had a drink of strawberry milk and a slice of cake. They packed a few eats into a small lunchbox, tidied up the rest of the van and waited for Robert who told them to be ready by seven o'clock. They were sad that they could not say good-bye to Mr and Mrs White because they wanted to thank them for all the kindness and help that they had given them since their Nanna had been placed in a nursing home. However, Rohan was sure that the adults would try to stop them from running away, and he also didn't want to involve them in anything illegal.

Instead, he had written a letter assuring them that he would take good care of his sister and also explaining to them why Ruby had been so unhappy. He thanked them over and over for their care and told them how much he and Ruby appreciated everything that they had done for them. He also promised to contact them as soon as he felt that it would be safe to do so.

Chapter 6

Jack had told Robert that he would park his truck in the last parking space, near the brick fence and leave just enough room for him to slip in beside his truck with his little van. As Robert drove in beside the huge semi-trailer, he said.

"This is perfect. No one can see us as we pack your things in the back, and Jack would have been watching for us to arrive because we are right on time, so he will be out soon." Ruby was stunned by the size of it, and she whispered to her brother, "I know you said that it was big, but this is the biggest truck that I have ever seen".

They had just stepped out of the van when Jack came around the back of the truck. He looked at Ruby and being experienced with children, he realised that she was feeling shy and perhaps a little frightened. "You must be young Ruby," he said as he tapped her on the head in a friendly manner. "My name is Jack, and I believe that you have chosen a new name for yourself, so what would you like me to call you now?"

"I am Chloe," she said as she held out her hand to shake hands with him. "Can I call you Jack or Mr Jack?"

"Jack is my name," he laughed. "If you call me Mr Jack you will make me feel old."

It didn't take long to pack their things into the back of the truck. Jack went back to the restaurant to have another cup of coffee and he told the children to climb into the cabin and keep out of sight as soon as they had said good-bye to Robert.

It was a farewell of mixed feelings. All three were happy, excited and also a bit afraid. Robert said that he half envied them setting out on their adventure, but he wished that it was under different circumstances.

Several times he made a point of calling them by their new names, Jeffrey and Chloe Hamilton. He reminded them that they must never make a mistake and use their real names.

After a final, "Good luck," from Robert, he stepped into his car and was starting the motor as Jack came around the back of the truck. They spoke a few words to each other and then Robert drove away.

Jack had hamburgers and flavoured milk for the children and he joked as he handed it to them, "I hope neither of you suffer from travel sickness."

They assured him that neither of them had ever had any trouble with car sickness, but as it was still only a quarter to eight; he gave them time to eat their meal before starting his motor. They even had time to run across to the restroom before they moved off.

Jack asked them many questions as they travelled along. Where they lived before the accident; which school they went to, what was their Nanna's name, what other relatives they had and where they lived. For the first hour he kept them busy answering questions and always making sure that Chloe was included in the conversation and that she had to answer some of the questions too. However, he avoided asking anything about the children's home because he was trying to make the children relax and enjoy the trip.

It was after nine o'clock when Chloe began to yawn and as she leaned against Jeffrey, she soon fell fast asleep. Jack was not surprised and after Jeffrey assured him that they were both comfortable, he said that he would be stopping for a break in about another hour, and then they could move her up into the sleeping cabin.

Chloe slept through all of the stops during the night but Jeffrey was awake and he stayed near the truck, while Jack put in fuel or bought some food. Sometimes Jack was away for an hour because he needed a good break before he went any further. At every other stop they both dosed off for an hour or two until Jack felt revived and ready to drive on for a couple more hours. When it was daylight, Chloe joined them back in the cabin, and at the next stop, they all stretched their legs, went to the restroom and then had a good breakfast.

There didn't appear to be anyone else around because it was very early in the morning, so the three of them sat at a picnic table and bench, and enjoyed a feast of bacon and eggs and hash-browns. Jeffrey had a second helping with a cup of coffee, but Jack had a second huge plate full with some toast on the side plus a couple of cups of coffee. Chloe was more than satisfied with a glass of orange juice to finish off her meal.

The two young people were feeling quite relaxed and enjoying the trip along the country highway where they had never been before, but Jack reminded them to avoid attracting any attention to themselves. He said that if there was a report in the paper on Monday morning someone might recall having seen them travelling west during the weekend. Jack had been careful to stay strictly within the limits of the law with his speed and rest periods, carefully filling in his log book at each stop. It made the trip slow but it was best to be safe.

During the journey, they had plenty of time to make their plans and create a story that Jeffrey could tell the owners of the motel when he applied for the job. He would not tell them about Chloe but he would try to talk them into allowing him to live in the old farm house. If they insisted that he had to live at the motel, he would not be able to accept the job because it was too soon to confide in strangers.

If he was allowed to live in the house, they would have to manage with their sleeping bags and the camping equipment that he had brought with him until Jack returned on his next trip. Jeffrey told Jack that he had enough cash that he could give him to buy some suitable second-hand furniture. They warned Chloe that she would have to hide in the sleeping compartment until they had sorted everything out.

Again, Jack parked his truck at the far end of the parking lot that was set aside for trucks and buses. From there they had a good view of the old farm house which was built on very high stumps, and Jeffrey commented on how flat everywhere else was, except for the house and the motel which were built on hills. He also noticed a row of trees that appeared to be growing on much higher land. Jack explained that behind the trees there was a river. He said that they were man-made hills to protect the buildings from floods.

Both Jeffrey and Chloe were excited about what they could see and began to imagine how they could make it into their home. They were anxious to hear what Mr and Mrs Harris would say and whether Jeffrey would get the job, but they had noticed as they passed the front of the motel that the sign was still in the window.

Chloe crawled into the sleeping compartment and Jack and Jeffrey went over to the motel restaurant to find either Mr or Mrs Harris.

Chapter 7

Fortunately, they were both there and there were no other customers in the shop at that moment so Jack immediately explained that his young friend, Jeffrey, was interested in applying for the job that was advertised in the window.

"How old are you, Lad?' Mr Harris asked Jeffrey as he looked straight at him.

"I am seventeen," he replied. It took him a bit by surprise because he and Jack hadn't discussed whether he should change his age in case a newspaper report mentioned a seventeen-year-old brother, but he didn't like telling outright lies. He felt sure that they would not be missed yet because Chloe was not due back at the home until the next afternoon, so there wouldn't be any reports yet.

"You are a big boy for your age," Mrs Harris commented "so you should be able to handle the work easily enough. Where have you worked before?'

"I have done a lot of handyman work and I have worked in a car wrecking yard" he answered honestly.

"Well, I am willing to give you a try, if you think you can handle the loneliness out here. Not many young people can. That is why we have so much trouble finding employees, "Mr Harris said. "You will receive full board and $500 a week. There are three very nice rooms at the back of the restaurant for employees. You will have your own room for now, but as we add more staff, you will have to share with one other lad. You will have your meals in the back of the restaurant but you will be responsible for your own laundry."

Jeffrey was trying to think of a way to ask about the house, but Jack spoke up first. He said that as they parked, they had noticed the old house and Jeffrey was hoping that he would be able to rent it.

"Oh!" Mrs Harris said, "That house hasn't been lived in for two years. It would be full of dust and there is very little furniture in it anymore. It is very shabby but we haven't had the heart to knock it down because it was our home for forty years and before that George's family lived in it for about sixty years. It is over one hundred years old."

"I'd look after it and you can deduct a fair rent for it from my wage. I just love old houses and I don't mind cleaning it, and sometime later I would be happy to paint it in my own time." Jeffrey begged.

The Harris couple both looked at each other, then George Harris said, "Well if you are that keen, I can't see why you shouldn't try it. It is a bit cold in winter. There is a good ceiling in it though so it is a cool house in summer. We didn't realise how cold it was until we moved in here, and then we noticed the difference. There is an old 'Crown' wood stove in it and the tank water will be clean because we have been letting it run into a trough for the cattle so it won't be stagnant. We can turn that off because there are plenty of other drinking troughs for them."

Another car pulled up so Jack took the opportunity to suggest that they should grab a few packets of sandwiches and some drinks and go on up to the house to put Jeffrey's things there. Then they could make a list of what he would need and he said that he would pick up some furniture and bring it back on his next trip.

"If I know Lexie, she will be chasing me back with a truck load on Monday," he laughed. They bought sandwiches, milk, cereal, eggs sugar, bread and butter and cheese, and some cream biscuits.

The Harris's lent Jeffrey an ice box that he could use until he was able to get a refrigerator. George handed Jeffrey a huge door key, and when he saw the surprised look on Jeffrey's face, he laughed, "Don't lose it." Then he added, "I'll catch up with you soon, after I see to these people. I will have to turn the generator on for you and show you which fire wood you can use."

Jack drove into the small fenced off yard and parked near the side steps. The truck was so long that part of the trailer was still sticking out through the gate when he stopped.

The house was higher than normal as an extra protection from floods and it was closed in underneath with batons, although some of them were missing or broken and they all needed to be painted. The shrubs around the fence that hadn't been eaten by the cattle, were high and straggly, and helped to provide some privacy for them to unload and for Chloe to run up the stairs without fear of being seen.

Chapter 8

As Mrs Harris had predicted the inside was very dusty and there was a musty stuffy smell so the two men went around opening up windows to let some fresh air in. "It is not nearly as derelict as I feared. Most of the windows open and close quite easily and none of the glass is broken." 'Jack said.

"Yes. It is very liveable. Obviously, it was well cared for when it was occupied and there are no vandals out here to destroy it." Jeffrey added. "Even the old floor coverings look as though they only need a good cleaning. You are very quiet Chloe. So, what do you think?' There was a short silence then Chloe, who had tears in her eyes, asked "Are you sure we are going to be allowed to live here?'

"Definitely, it is all arranged." Jeffrey answered and he reminded her that they had been given a key. "I love it," she said, "and I will help you clean it. I'll be able to do some while you are at work because no one can see me in here."

They had brought all of their things upstairs and had a feed of sandwiches and drinks. Jack and Jeffrey were making a list of the furniture and other things that were needed when Chloe suddenly exclaimed, "There's somebody coming from the motel in a little truck.

Where can l hide?" In their excitement they had both forgotten that George had said that he was going to catch up with them after he had served the customer. "Quick. climb into my sleeping bag and face the wall" Jeffrey said. Then he put their rolled-up bed, a couple of back packs and the two ports in front of the sleeping bag. He stood one port up and the other one he lay flat on the floor and opened it and left the lid up to create a private look so that George was less likely to go near it.

Before the truck had reached the house, he quickly counted out two thousand dollars and handed it to a very surprised Jack, saying, "Quickly take this to buy the stuff we need. Put it out of sight before George is here." Then he added "Don't look so surprised. I didn't rob a bank, but I drew every cent I own out of the bank while I could." Jeffrey felt sure that Jack did not notice the huge bundle of notes which he had slipped back into his port. Each thousand was rolled up separately and held with a rubber band.

"Lad, you have only known me for a day. You should wait until I buy the stuff before you go handing out so much". They heard the motor stop and the door slammed, so there was no time to argue but Jack took a note book out of his pocket and quickly scribbled a receipt and put it into Jeffrey's hand.

They met George at the door and he said casually, "So, you have found your way in all right. How do you like it now?"

"Fantastic! It is not nearly as shabby on the inside as it looks from the outside." Jeffrey answered. "I really will look after it for you and I would love to completely restore it if I can. I really would like to pay rent so that I feel that I have a right to be here." At that moment Jack interrupted and suggested that if the young fellow was planning to buy a lot of furniture and put his own money and time into restoring the house, it might be fairest, if he had a written contract for a definite amount of time.

George agreed and said that he would be happy to set up a lease for possibly two years, but he would want to put some conditions in it. "I will need a few days to organise it," he said, "because I will have it set up correctly by our solicitor."

There were dark clouds gathering on the horizon and Jack was anxious to get on home, so he told Jeffrey that if he didn't need him anymore, he would be off and he would be back with some furniture at the first opportunity.

They said goodbye and then George and Jeffrey went under the house to turn the generator on and sort out some of the fire wood that was still stored there. George showed him how to cut the kindling to start the fire and then they went back upstairs. With some old newspaper that he had brought with him, the old man soon had a strong fire going in the stove. There was a small water container attached to the side of the stove which he filled with clean water. Then he explained that it would keep him in hot water for washing, but it would not be clean enough for tea or coffee. He would have to boil that water in a saucepan or a billycan. It looked as though it was about to rain so George invited Jeffrey to go back over to the motel with him to get a couple of burgers and chips, and he said that there was a bicycle there that he could use to ride to work. For the rest of the afternoon, he said that he should rest and settle in as much as he could without furniture, and he would like him to start work at seven o'clock the following morning.

Jeffrey felt slightly uncomfortable going across to the motel to eat and leaving his little sister in this house on her own but he knew that it would often happen in the future if she was to remain in hiding, so he thanked George and climbed into the front seat of the utility with him.

George did not pry into Jeffrey's story. Instead, he talked about the work that he would be doing and told him a little bit of the farm's history. Jeffrey hurried through the meal and he was very surprised when Mrs Harris handed him a large carton packed full of groceries, including bacon, sausages, hams, bread, eggs, milk, sugar and a few salad vegetables so that he could make his own burgers if he needed more to eat. He also had the makings of a good healthy breakfast. With a wide smile of gratitude and delight Jeffrey thanked her, and she gave him an affectionate hug and with misty eyes she said, "You remind me of my own boy and I wish I could do the same for him".

The bicycle had a large metal trailer attached just behind the seat and had obviously been used before for carrying similar loads.

Chapter 9

Chloe had already unpacked the kitchen utensils and swept the floor of the kitchen and one bedroom with an old broom that she found under the house. The bedroom was quite large and she asked Jeffrey if she could sleep in the same room as he had chosen because she was feeling a bit nervous. He readily agreed because until everyone respected his privacy, and didn't feel that they could wander freely though his house, they might ask why he needed two bedrooms.

They sat down together and Chloe had a meal from the food that Jeffrey had just brought home. They were both extremely tired but they were also excited and talked about their plans for the future. It seemed too good to be true. Here they were, together, in a lovely big house. The house needed a lot of work, but they would enjoy working on it and that would make it feel like their own home. Jeffrey had a job and Chloe felt safe from Robinson.

Nanna had taught Chloe well and she was excited about being a house keeper. She would do her best to make Jeffrey proud by keeping the house clean and by cooking their meals.

Chapter 10

The children slept well in their sleeping bags and Jeffrey woke early to the sound of a cow bellowing just outside their little house yard. It was a strange sound for a city kid but a very homely one and his mind quickly raced through the events of the previous day. It was still early but he was wide awake so he rose and went out to the kitchen to start the wood stove and warm up some water for a bath. Chloe was also awake so she began to prepare breakfast. What a feast they could have with cereal and then some bacon, eggs and sausages.

Jeffrey reminded Chloe that she had to keep out of sight all day, but he also assured her that he would have a clear view of the house and everywhere around it from the motel and he would be home in an instant if he saw anything that could cause trouble.

Before leaving for work, he closed the old curtains and reminded Chloe to lock the doors and not to answer a knock or any call that someone might make. The house was about two hundred metres from the motel but there were no buildings or bush to block the view so Jeffrey assured her that he would be watching as much as he possibly could.

He arrived at work a few minutes early and George was pleased to note his enthusiasm. Chloe immediately set about cleaning the camp dishes which they had brought with them but she could only put them up on a fixed shelf in the kitchen until Jack arrived with the furniture. She was almost ten years old now and Nanna had taught her well. Next, she took the old broom which she had found the previous day and swept the kitchen again, then she started slowly sweeping each room. It was a big house—even bigger than Nanna's and as she swept, she began to dream of how lovely they could make it. One room had lots of shelves built on each wall and it reminded her of the school library. Perhaps that's exactly what it was, and she began to dream of all of the shelves being stacked with books and a couple of comfortable chairs in the room so that she could just sit and read for hours.

The next room had two big glass doors that opened onto a sunny veranda and she would have loved to go through them but she remembered Jeffrey's warning and she knew that if anyone saw her, she would lose all of it. Suddenly a shudder went through her as she thought of Robinson.

During his lunch break Jeffrey dashed home on his bike to be with her and see that she was coping with the loneliness, and he was surprised at how clean she had made the house and how excited she was about their new home. He thought to himself what a fantastic kid his little sister was. Chloe was just like a little housekeeper.

They sat down to lunch together but Chloe was too busy chatting to eat very much. She was full of ideas, and could hardly wait for Jack to bring their furniture. However, it was only Sunday so she would have to control her curiosity for at least one more day.

Jeffrey returned to work and Chloe tidied the kitchen again and then sat down on the floor in a sunny spot near the front door to read one of the many books that they had brought with them. She loved reading and she was a very good student at school, so she would soon have to start looking at some of the workbooks that Jeffrey had bought for her.

It was after dark when Jeffrey arrived home. Once again, he was loaded with burgers and sandwiches because Mary knew that he had no refrigeration to keep some of the food from the previous day fresh. Chloe was surprised at how dark it was outside but there was no electricity here to reflect any light across the paddock. The house was securely locked so she was not afraid but she was pleased when she had finally seen her brother's bike light weaving its way up the path.

They enjoyed their unusual dinner together. Nanna didn't like take-away dinners but during this weekend they had a real feast. This time it was Jeffrey who did all the talking. He liked his job and he also liked George and Mary. He said that they seemed to be very nice people, not just to him, but to the customers too, and also to each other. It was a very busy shop, but the sign was still in the window, so he hoped that they would soon find another lad to help him.

Jeffrey told Chloe that the radio was turned on all day and he had listened every time he had a chance to hear whether anything was said about their disappearance. So far there was no report but that didn't surprise him because she wouldn't be missed until she was due to return in the afternoon, unless Mrs White had reported them. He didn't fear that Mrs White would do that, because Robert would tell her enough so that she knew that they were together and that they were safe. Jeffrey had also written her a letter which he left on the table in the caravan. Robert would talk to his mother about Robinson, and as she already knew how upset and frightened Ruby had been she would understand. Jeffrey said that he had heard most of the 6 o'clock news before he left work and there was still no mention of any missing children.

Chapter 11

On the following morning Jack arrived at about 11 o'clock and when Jeffrey saw him pull into their driveway, followed by a small car, he asked George whether he could have an early lunch hour so he could go home and help with the unloading. George immediately agreed and told Jeffrey to stay until it was finished and if he had a chance himself, he would also go over and help but Jeffrey assured him that they would be able to cope on their own and it seemed that Jack had brought some extra help with him.

Chloe also saw the truck and recognised it but she was shocked when she saw the little car and quickly ran and hid in Jeffrey's room. She was feeling disappointed because she had been looking forward to Jack's visit as well as looking forward to having a lot of furniture for their home, and now she would have to stay in her sleeping bag. She had just finished disguising herself when she heard Jack knock on the door and call out, "Come on out Chloe. It's okay! You're safe! There's someone here that I want you to meet!" She trusted Jack completely and she scrambled out of the bag and raced to the door to meet him.

Standing next to him was a very pretty lady who had such a friendly magnetic smile on her face that Chloe immediately liked her.

"This is my wife Lexie," Jack said, "and she is eager to meet you." Lexie stepped forward and gave Chloe a long hug and kissed her on the forehead. It was just what Chloe needed, and she felt comfortable and safe as she stood there held in this pretty lady's arms.

The tears began to roll down her cheeks just as Jeffrey came around the corner of the house and Chloe excitedly called out to her brother, "Jeffrey, this is Lexie and she is our friend." Then they began to unload.

A refrigerator a table and six chairs, a kitchen cupboard for crockery and another for groceries, a lounge suite and two other soft comfortable chairs, also a china cabinet with beautiful glass doors. Then there was bedroom furniture, beds, dressing tables, wardrobes

and two extra storage cupboards for linen and any other bits and pieces. Last of all was a twin tub washing machine. Among the furniture that was unloaded there were also two very large cartons and Chloe could not contain her curiosity any longer so she tried to pull the folded lid open but her little hands were not strong enough and Lexie had to help her. As the contents were revealed she gave a squeal of delight. There were blankets, bed spreads and every piece of linen that they could possibly need, and packed through the linen there were lots and lots of crockery and cutlery, and, just to add a little homely touch there were a few pretty ornaments.

Chapter 12

While Chloe was dancing around the cartons and giving her familiar little clap of her fingers and then putting her hands up to her mouth, Jeffrey was trying to estimate the cost. He quietly said to Jack, "You have done extremely well with two thousand dollars, I must owe you another thousand."

'No Lad. The owner of the shop is an old mate and when I told him that it was for a young couple just trying to get started, he was pleased to help you.

You see, these days it is so easy to buy new furniture without even a deposit, and second-hand shops are really struggling. Believe me, this was the best sale that he has had in a long time. He did give you the china cabinet and all of the crockery and ornaments for nothing. I think he is on the verge of closing his shop so he was happy to get rid of a lot of it for a good cause.'

Chloe was struggling with a chair which she was trying to carry up the high stairs when Lexie called out, "Come on you two. "Are you going to talk all day or are you going to take this furniture upstairs.?"

Chloe returned and was ready to pick up another chair when George came around the corner of the house. Lexie glanced at Chloe and saw the startled look on her face, but she was a quick thinker and she immediately put her arms around her and whispered, "Don't try to hide. It is too late." then she called out to George, "Hi George. I hope you are feeling strong because we can really do with some help here. I even brought my daughter Chloe with me to help." It was a perfect disguise for Chloe because, although George knew that Jack and Lexie had some daughters, he had never met any of them.

Finally, all of the furniture was upstairs and placed in the correct room and George had returned to the motel.

Chapter 13

They were all very tired so Lexie boiled the kettle on the wood stove and set out some lunch on the table so that Jack could have a good meal before he went on his journey to Brisbane.

As they sat there eating, Lexie said, "Now kids I would like to hear your whole story, going right back to your accident, and Chloe, I especially would like to hear everything about the Children's Home and Mr Robinson."

Jeffrey was the first to start speaking. He explained how the family was returning from a holiday at Redcliffe near Brisbane when a car had tried to pass a bus that was coming towards them but was unable to move back into its own lane and hit their car head-on at a very high speed. Their parents were killed and also the driver and passenger in the other car. He said that he and Chloe were badly injured and they were in a coma for several days and when they were brought out of the coma their parents' funerals were over. He told her how happy they had been when they lived with their Nanna and how nasty and jealous their Aunty had been. He also explained in every detail how Nanna and Mrs White had arranged for their care.

Lexie looked at Chloe and said, "I know it will be hard for you to talk about the Children's Home but if I am going to help you, I really need to know everything that you can tell me."

Chloe started talking and she talked quickly and she sounded almost excited as she raced through her story telling Lexie more than she had told Jeffrey, because she was so frightened then but now, she felt safe. She started from the day that she had to leave her Nanna's house and the memory of that day made tears well up in her eyes. She poured out all her feelings from good days with her new friends and her visits with Jeffrey then she began to cry as she talked about Robinson. Lexie was stunned into silence as she listened to this brave and intelligent little girl. Jeffrey was silent and angry as he heard more about how Robinson had behaved, and he was so pleased that he had rescued his little sister and now they were going to get some real help and be able to help the other little girls too.

Lexie was silent for a moment, then she said "I will help your little friends Chloe and have an investigation into Robinson's behaviour started immediately. That man should not be allowed to be near children."

When Lexie was saying goodbye to the two children, she looked concerned and worried as she told them to be very careful. She said that as soon as the authorities started questioning Robinson he would soon realise that they had reported him and he would be trying to find them. She said that he would employ private investigators who would question the Whites and check every possible transport that they could have used to leave Brisbane.

It was a sickening and disappointing feeling for the children who were beginning to feel safe.

Chapter 14

On the following Friday Jack visited them very early in the morning on his way to Brisbane and he had a special present with him. He had brought two young German shepherd dogs. They were not tiny puppies but they were quite young and full of energy and love. The children were pleased to see Jack but the pups soon took all of their attention. Chloe was so excited that she started running around the yard with them and completely forgot about staying out of sight until Jeffrey gave her a sharp call.

The pups were enjoying all the attention too. They were ready to join in any game that these new playmates might like to invent.

Jeffrey, who always thought ahead said to Jack, "What do you think George and Mary will say? Do you think they will mind?"

"No. I have already cleared it with them, but you will have to make sure that they can't get out of your house yard and chase the cows.

They also said that you were welcome to take home any suitable scraps for their food each afternoon."

Jeffrey thanked Jack and said he was very pleased that Chloe would have the extra company during the day and even at their young age they would be an extra insurance for him and Chloe if anyone was sneaking around their house at night. Before Jack left Jeffrey gave him some more money to buy a few boxes of good canned dog food and a large bag of dry dog food. They will be our family and they will be living in the house with us," he added.

Jack called in as often as he could until the puppies were very obedient and quickly responded to either Jeffrey's or Chloe's instructions. They taught them to guard but stopped them from biting. Chloe enjoyed their company and they were never very far away from her. They had named their new pets Heidi and Champ.

She read her stories aloud and they appeared to listen to her. She talked to them all through the day and she really loved them like two very special little friends. She would have enjoyed running around their back yard and playing with them but, of course that was too dangerous. She never knew when someone from the motel might be looking towards the house.

When Jeffrey came home each afternoon, he played with them until the three of them were exhausted, and ready for a big dinner.

Chapter 15

Time went by very quickly. Two more boys were employed to work at the motel and Jeffrey 's hours were shortened so that he had more time at home. Chloe was pleased to have more company and he was still earning enough money to add a little more to his savings. He used his extra spare time to do little renovations and he had replaced all of the missing batons under the house. He just needed to tidy up a few more areas and he would be ready to begin painting. The new boys, Dean and Sam, soon became friends with Jeffrey, and they introduced him to other local boys and girls.

They sometimes went fishing together or Dean took them for a country drive in his new car.

Chloe was not forgotten. Jeffrey was not ready to share their secret with his new friends so he didn't invite any of them to his home, but Lexie's girls had met Chloe and they had been told the whole story. They often visited her with their mother and some weekends she stayed with them for a sleep-over.

Pamela, Wendy and Christine gave Chloe three boxes of books and helped her to stack them on the shelves in her little home library. Her dream of having her own little library with a few comfortable chairs was coming true. She was very happy.

Before their mother and father were killed in the accident the family was very happy. She missed her parents every day and sometimes she would cry for them, but she never allowed her brother to see her crying, because he had been so kind to her and she thought that he might think that she was ungrateful.

After they had left Nanna's home Jeffrey had moved into his own caravan on the White's farm and had a good job at a wrecking yard. He had enough money to buy a nice car and he had many good friends. He had planned to get an apprenticeship with a mechanic but, instead, he gave it all up to rescue Chloe from Robinson's clutches. Although she missed her parents as any little girl would, she was happy with her new life.

Heidi and Champ had grown into two very big and intelligent dogs who were never far away from Chloe. She was still limited in where she could go, but when the girls visited her, she felt safe playing out in the yard with them and the dogs because, even if someone from the motel saw them, they wouldn't know that she was living there.

Time had gone by so quickly and it was almost one year since they had run away from Brisbane and Chloe wanted to do something special for Jeffrey to show him how much she appreciated everything that he had done for her.

From his first wage, Jeffrey had given Chloe a small allowance that she could save or spend on anything that she wanted. She didn't have many opportunities to shop so over the twelve months she had saved a nice amount in her money box.

She told Lexie that she wanted to cook a special roast dinner for their anniversary and that she would like to turn it into a party. She hoped that their whole family would be able to have dinner with them. As she was speaking, she held out a bundle of notes and a shopping list and asked Lexie whether she would have time to do some shopping for her.

With a smile Lexie gently pushed her hand back and said, "I will do more than that. How about if the four of us come around on Saturday morning and then the five of us will cook all day. I have plenty of recipes from China, Thailand, India, Japan and Italy. Chloe was so delighted that she jumped up and down, clapping her hands and saying, "Yes, yes, yes. That would be wonderful."

Chapter 16

They agreed that Jack would have to be told, but they would not tell Jeffrey. It would be another secret. Chloe was so excited that she was afraid that she might accidentally tell him, but she had a lot of practice at keeping secrets so she locked it out of her mind and kept herself busy with school work whenever Jeffrey was at home.

On the Saturday morning, she told him that the family would be visiting her and she would have heaps of company so it would be a good opportunity for him to have lunch at work with his friends. He had often wanted to stay with them, "Because," he told Chloe, "When they are together, they are a laugh a minute. They are so funny. I really do like them. In fact, I think they are the best friends that I have ever had."

It pleased her to hear that he had made some good friends but, once again she was taking up his time each day when he would probably prefer to be with them.

The family arrived in the mid-morning as had been arranged and Chloe had already made the house spotless. Lexie knew that Chloe didn't have many cooking utensils or large food bowls, so she packed up her own and bought a few extra bowls for Chloe. She had also bought all of the necessary ingredients to make enough food to feed an army.

The girls had been busy too. They had selected some bright decorations to set a party atmosphere. A few quick decisions were made and then the five of them set about decorating the kitchen and dining room. It didn't take up too much time and the result absolutely focused their mood on the party.

The first job was to set some of the sweets which needed to sit in the freezer or refrigerator for some hours, then they concentrated on the main dishes.

They all worked hard all morning and again after a quick lunch preparing bowls of steaming hot colourful food and it filled the kitchen with a mouth -watering aroma. Jack was the first to arrive. He had driven through the night but he had stopped for a few naps in the sleeping compartment of his huge semi-trailer.

Pamela made him a cup of coffee and handed him a plate full of freshly made small cakes.

He was still tired so, after enjoying his snack and admiring the girls' work, he went out onto the veranda and lay down on the hammock to have some more sleep.

Before Jeffrey arrived home, all of the girls had a quick wash and changed into fresh clean clothes. Chloe apologised because the level in the water tank was low and they couldn't have a full bath.

They woke Jack up and then brought out some presents for Jeffrey and Chloe.

Chloe had given Lexie some money to buy her brother some car magazines and some mechanic's books previously and she had wrapped them neatly and hidden them away. Now it was time to give them to him.

Jeffrey had also remembered to buy something for his little sister. He had bought her a mobile phone. He had one of his own and whenever he was away, he left it with her so she could ring for help if it was necessary. However, they could not ring each other, but now he could ring her whenever he was worried about her.

They were both delighted with their gifts and affectionately hugged each other.

It was, however, an unexpected surprise, when Pamela, Wendy and Christine handed a small parcel to each of them. For Chloe, they had each chosen another book, and she giggled and hugged the books to her chest as she excitedly thanked them.

For Jeffrey, they had each chosen a hand tool which Jack had suggested.

Jeffrey thanked them profusely. He had left his tools at the White's place, but he had bought himself a tool box and was gradually filling it. That was not the end of the surprises. Now it was Lexie's turn, and she leaned into a box on the floor and pulled out a parcel for each of them.

For Jeffrey, it was a new shirt and shorts, and for Chloe, the prettiest frock that she had ever seen and a pair of white sandals. The material was a floral cotton with bright flowers, which were a brilliant red, lilac yellow and pink, and bright green ferns. Lexie had made the frock herself.

It was sleeveless with a wide white collar, a gathered skirt with two neatly trimmed pockets and a belt with an attractive buckle. As Chloe held it up, she had a broad smile on her face, but at the same time tears of happiness were rolling down her face and she threw her arms around Lexie and thanked her over and over.

Now that the presents had been given to the children, it was time to eat. Chloe quickly slipped into her bedroom and came back looking beautiful in her new frock and sandals.

Chapter 17

Everyone was keen to taste this appetising food that was steaming away and sending off such tantalising aromas.

"If it tastes half as good as it looks and smells, I am ready to eat the lot," Jack said.

There was plenty of joking and light conversation as they all eagerly helped themselves to a variety of food from different countries. As Lexie looked around the table a wave of happiness swept over her. These two young people had been through so much and now they looked so happy and relaxed. They had all been hungry and the food was delicious but after nearly an hour everyone was slowing down and the bowls still had a considerable amount of food in them. Pamela reminded them that they should leave some room for dessert, and then Wendy, Christine and Chloe stood up and started clearing the plates away.

The conversation went on as they all had a short break before the desserts were brought out.

Suddenly Champ and Heidi, who had been lying quietly on the floor pricked up their ears and gave low growls.

Jeffrey stood up quickly and hurried across to bolt the door, but before he reached it, it was flung open and seven young people burst in, shouting "Surprise.!"

Everyone sprang to their feet and the girls screamed. Jeffrey instinctively raised his hand ready to swing a punch but checked himself just in time. Jack was angry and let the newcomers know by shouting at them in some strong colourful language. Chloe dropped back into her chair and her face went completely white.

Lexie was also shocked but she recognised the children and she even knew their parents. She had taught some of them and the others she had met at church. She quietly asked Jeffrey to take the three boys with him and go down under the house and bring up the two old long wooden stools that George had stored there.

The visitors were all loaded with food so she asked them to put any cold food in the refrigerator and place the rest anywhere that they could find room on the bench.

After the boys had brought the stools up, she asked the visitors to sit down. Chloe's reaction was worrying her so she made up her mind to bring her back into the group.

She looked at the visitors and said, "Now that you have arrived so dramatically, there is something which, with Jeffrey's and Chloe's permission, I must tell you."

Jeffrey was nodding keenly, but Chloe was still pale and motionless, just staring at the floor and rubbing the hem of her new frock between her fingers.

She added in a serious voice, 'You must never repeat a word of what I am about to tell you. Don't even joke or hint about it. If you do, I will personally skin you alive."

They knew that she was not about to take out a knife and carve them up, but they also knew that she was very serious.

She started by telling them the children's story from the tragic day when they lost both of their parents, also their Nanna, Robinson, how they met Jack and their life in the house. Occasionally she reminded them that they must never repeat what she was telling them. She finished by saying, "I am sure you can understand how dangerous it would be for Chloe, if Robinson found her."

Two of the girls stood up and went to Chloe and then they were followed by the other two. They crouched down beside her and one at a time they put their arm around her shoulder, and gave her a hug and a kiss on the cheek and promised her that they would never break her secret, and that they would help Jeffrey to look after her. The boys also mumbled their promises.

"Well, now that we have sorted that out, let's eat", she said. Chloe had lifted her eyes to look at the girls and whisper a quiet thank you and a faint smile spread across her face.

The visitors were invited to finish off the main dishes after they had washed plates for themselves, and the rest started on the desserts. The lively chatter and joking went on for another hour until everyone had eaten as much as they could. Finally, Pamela stood up and asked Chloe where her parents could have a rest while the young ones cleared the remainder of the food away and tidied the kitchen. Jack and Lexie were taken to the library where they happily settled down on a couple of soft comfortable chairs with foot rests and then they were handed cushions and a warm rug each. Soon afterwards Wendy and Christine came in with cups of tea for each of them.

With everyone helping, it didn't take long to return the kitchen to a spotless condition.

Jack was tired and he was troubled when he realised that the new visitors had brought their sleeping bags and intended to stay the night.

Jeffrey had a simple solution. He and Chloe would sleep in their sleeping bags and Jack and Lexie could sleep in their beds. His solution was gratefully accepted. The twelve young friends then moved downstairs where they could make as much noise as they liked.

During the year when George could see that Jeffrey was serious about renovating the old home, he installed a new and stronger electricity plant, so there was ample lighting for dancing and party games, and, of course, music.

They played and nibbled their way through most of the left-over food and time flew by. Two of the boys had to start work at 8:30 the following morning, so, soon after 3 a. m. they began to wind down.

The following morning Jeffrey was the first to stir. As he lay in his sleeping bag thinking of the previous night, he suddenly realised that he had fourteen guests for breakfast and there would not be anywhere near enough food to feed them.

He quietly climbed out of his bag and went out to the kitchen and lit the wood stove, then he rode his bicycle down to the motel. George met him as he was walking out of the shop and laughed at his large basket of food. He had eggs, bacon, bread, cereal, milk, sugar, coffee and sausages.

"I could hear your visitors last night, but I didn't realise that you were entertaining the Australian army," he laughed. Jeffrey explained who his visitors were but he didn't mention Chloe. George knew that Sam and Dean were due to start work at 8:30, so he told Jeffrey to tell them that he would keep the night staff there until 9:30 so the boys could have an extra hour to wake up and get themselves together.

As Jeffrey rode home he was thinking of how lucky he and Chloe had been since they met Jack. George was a wonderful old man and he and Mary had been like grandparents to him. Jack and Lexie had been like parents to both of them. Now that his friends knew about Chloe, they would all be able to spend more time together.

There were not enough plates for everyone to eat at the same time, so the girls offered to cook the bacon and eggs and sausages while the boys had their cereal, then the boys could wash their plates for the girls, and then eat their hot food. The girls put some of the hot food aside for themselves and threatened the boys with death by torture if they dared to touch it. Once again there was a lot of laughter and fun as they ate breakfast.

Chapter 18

The girls were true to their word and often called in to visit Chloe. There were only six cows left now. They were too old for milking or calving so Mary insisted that they must be allowed to stay on the farm where they could just graze until they died. The other cows had been moved to the neighbour's farm on the condition that they would be sent back to retire on their home pasture.

As there was so much green pasture not being used, the girls asked whether they could put their ponies in the paddock and George and Mary happily agreed. They had one extra pony so they were able to take Chloe with them on Saturday mornings. Chloe's life would never be boring again.

The girls were all older than Chloe and they were very protective of her. She was such a nice little kid that they all became very fond of her. When they went riding, Ellen, who was the oldest of the group, taught Chloe how to put the harness on her pony and how to mount and dismount a horse. She also taught her how to sit when the horse trotted and cantered and eventually, how to gallop.

Sometimes they rode around the boundary fence to check it for any damage and sometimes they took a picnic lunch and their bathers and rode along the banks of the river to a safe swimming spot.

Lexie and her daughters continued to help Chloe with her schoolwork, and her new friends who were high school and university students also took an interest in her lessons. She was on her own during most week days and she loved learning so she made excellent progress, and Lexie brought her some year seven test papers and found that Chloe was certainly ready for high school.

Eighteen months passed by very quickly and she enjoyed her new freedom. Sometimes Chloe went shopping with her friends. She also went to church and joined the church youth group. Sometimes the twelve young friends went to the movies together. The only people that they really avoided were George and Mary and the motel customers. Life was so normal that both of the children became careless.

Chapter 19

One day as Jeffrey and Dean were cleaning a semi-trailer, Dean suddenly shouted to Jeffrey, "Hey Jeff, a big four-wheel drive has just pulled up near your gate."

Jeffrey quickly looked around from the other side of the semi-trailer just as the driver stepped out, and, leaving the car door open, walked towards the gate. He immediately recognised the man and shouted, "It's Robinson" and he ran towards his bicycle. As he ran past Dean, Dean held out his keys and said "Here. Take my car. "There was no time to discuss it, so Jeffrey grabbed the keys with a quick "Thanks" and jumped in. The car started immediately and he sped up the hill just as Chloe ran through the gate and ran as fast as she could towards him. Robinson was not far behind Chloe, and Heidi and Champ were right behind him. Robinson slammed the gate in front of the two dogs but they cleared the fence and knocked him to the ground. However, they were still young and they were confused because their young mistress was running away. Robinson was confident that they would not attack him, so he inched towards his open door until he was right under it then, he suddenly sprang up and into his vehicle and slammed the door on the dogs. They barked savagely at the window but he started the motor and raced down the hill at a deadly speed. Chloe was in the car and Jeffrey was turning it around to take her back to the motel and safety. Sadly, Robinson was there before they could complete the turn and he crashed straight into the side of the little car.

It rolled over and over while the big vehicle continued on through the motel garden, making the startled witnesses jump out of its way.

Everyone had their mobiles out. Some were calling the police; some were calling the ambulance and some photographed the back of that deadly vehicle. Dean was calling Lexie.

Most of the stunned people ran to the smashed vehicle to get the children out because it had left a trail of petrol on the grass but fortunately the motor was not hot and it didn't ignite. The car was still on its side so a couple of men gently pushed it back onto its wheels. Jeffrey's door fell off and he rolled out onto the grass and stood up, and, although he didn't appear to be badly injured a couple of men grabbed him to steady him on his feet. He was ghostly white and he didn't say a word, he just stared into space.

At that moment Mary and two of the motel maids arrived with blankets and pillows. He was helped to a large gum tree where he sat down with his back to it and also with his back to the mangled car. Others were trying to release Chloe's legs from the tangled metal. She was unconscious and by the look of a nasty bend in her leg and her arm they were almost certainly broken. She was also bleeding badly in two places.so, although they knew that they had to be careful, they were anxious to get her out so that they could stem the bleeding. There was no doctor available but one of the truck drivers had an advanced certificate in first-aid and he took charge of the rescue. As they removed the last piece of bent metal that was trapping her little body two men arrived with a large flat plank that they had pulled off a garden seat and she was gently and carefully moved onto it.

She was still quite unconscious but alive and as they worked on her open wounds, the wail of sirens could be heard in the distance. The first ambulance arrived soon afterwards and the two paramedics were directed to Chloe who seemed to be the most in need. The second ambulance arrived from the other direction at almost the same time, and it was followed by two police cars.

The second pair of paramedics went straight to Jeffrey who was still ashen white and not speaking or listening to anyone. Dean had raced over to him as soon as he finished his phone call to Lexie and tried to make a conversation but it was very clear that something was seriously wrong with him.

As soon as the two paramedics that were attending to Jeffrey had checked him for physical injuries, they placed him on a stretcher and wheeled him into the ambulance. As it went slowly through the motel garden and out on to the highway, Lexie drove in.

Her heart was pounding as she looked around. It was beating so wildly that she felt weak. She had cared for many foster children while they were going through a rough patch in their life, and while they lived with her, she always became fond of them, but she had never felt the same way about them as she had felt about these two children. She simply loved them. She could see the other ambulance further up the hill and there was a large crowd standing around it while the paramedics were treating someone on the ground. Which child had been taken to hospital and why were they taking so much longer with the other one? Was one of the children already dead? As these thoughts were running through her head the tears that were welling up in her eyes overflowed and streamed down her face. Dean had seen the car come in and he recognised Lexie and ran towards her. When she saw him coming from the direction of the garden and not from the crowd, she was sure that Jeffrey had been taken in the first ambulance, and her thoughts turned to little Chloe. Dean told her all about Jeffrey but he didn't know much about Chloe. They had fallen into each other's arms and stood there talking and crying, then they started moving towards the ambulance. She was pleased that she was already on her way to visit them when she received the phone call so she was able to get there quickly.

The paramedics had Chloe on a stretcher and were wheeling her towards the ambulance door as Lexie and Dean reached her. They pushed through the crowd and Lexie took hold of her little hand and said, "Hang in there Sweetheart. I'll be right here with you." Until then no-one knew who the little girl was and the paramedics were keen to hear more.

Lexie didn't want to start telling the whole story so she simply told them that she was Chloe's foster mother. They were anxious to get Chloe into hospital but also keen to collect more of her personal details and Lexie said that she and Dean would be following them and she would meet them at the hospital.

More police had arrived and more cars were out on the highway looking for the vehicle that had caused this tragedy. When an officer heard Lexie say that she was the little girl's foster mother he intercepted her as she was hurrying towards her car, and said that he would like to ask her a few questions.

She had to think quickly, and she decided to tell him who they are but not to spend time going right back to their parents' accident and their life with their Nanna.

She told him that Chloe is the little girl that ran away from an orphanage in Brisbane about eighteen months ago, and Jeffrey is her brother. The director of the orphanage has been stood down and is currently being investigated. He has guessed who has complained about him and has just tried to kill her. She also told him that their real names are Ruby and Rohan Connors.

"How do you know that he was the driver who tried to kill them?" he asked.

Dean spoke up and said that Jeffrey saw him walk towards the gate and shouted out "It's Robinson." He also told him that Jeffrey was running to his bike but he had handed Jeffrey his car keys and that it was his car that was smashed. Dean said "I don't regret that I gave him my car because both of them would have been dead if they were on the bike, but it is still new.

The officer said, "Good work young lad. I am sure you did save their lives and when we catch this fiend, he can replace it for you."

Lexie and Dean had given him more valuable information in a few minutes than any of the other witnesses knew, and he agreed to let them follow the ambulance and speak to him again at the hospital.

Dean ran over to Mary and George and asked them whether he could go with Lexie and they quietly agreed but reminded him that they needed to know what had caused this tragedy. Dean promised them that he would tell them all about it later.

As they sped along the highway, Dean turned on the radio and found that every station was telling the same story, and saying that the police have been unable to find the vehicle. Then, suddenly there was a breaking message. Tom Briggs, a local farmer had gone up in his crop duster and had quickly located the vehicle at the end of a bush track down near the river and the driver was trying to disguise it with bushes. Tom Briggs was circling above it and directing the police to it.

He turned the radio off and started ringing his mates and asking them to spread the word. Lexie asked him to ring Jack and her girls. He had just finished making all of the phone calls when they arrived at the hospital gate. Poor Dean was exhausted and he felt that he just wanted to get away on his own somewhere and cry and cry until he felt relieved.

Lexie was kind and always sensitive to other peoples' feelings, especially when they were only children. Dean had just turned seventeen. She parked the car and when she stepped out she put her arms around him and once more they both had a good cry before they went into the hospital.

It was a small hospital and as she entered the door and went to the main desk, the paramedic who had spoken to her at the accident immediately approached her. He had no personal information about the children, especially Chloe, and he was anxious to complete his report. Now that they were in a more private situation, without reporters standing nearby she was quite happy to give him more details. She told him their real names and their current names and also that Chloe had run away from an orphanage in Brisbane. She still claimed to be their foster mother because there was no other adult to fill that role.

She also told him about Robinson and why he had tried to kill her. He didn't need any more information and both she and Dean went to find out what was happening to Jeffrey and Chloe. It took them a few minutes to find anyone who would talk to them but eventually they found a doctor who was just as anxious to speak to them as they were to speak to him.

He told them that Jeffrey would be staying at that hospital but Chloe's condition was very serious and she was being prepared for a flight to Brisbane to the Princess Alexandra Hospital. Lexie immediately asked whether she would be allowed to travel with her. He thought it would be possible but he went away to check.

While he was away, she rang Jack and the girls to let them know what was happening and also to tell them that she was hoping to go with Chloe. She then rang George to ask him to come and pick up Dean. The doctor still wasn't back so she rang Mrs White because she was sure that she would have been listening to the news and would be very worried about them.

Mrs White and Lexie met at the cafeteria in the P A Hospital as had been previously arranged. They were not allowed to be with Chloe so they filled in the time completing each other's story. Mrs White knew a lot about their younger life and Lexie was able to tell her where they had been and what they had been doing during the last eighteen months. They were told that they would not be allowed to see Chloe that night so Mrs White invited Lexie to go home with her, and she gratefully accepted.

The following day it was the same, she could only see
 Chloe through a glass wall. Her condition was very dangerous and she was not allowed to have any visitors.

Unfortunately, Lexie could not wait any longer, so she tearfully said good-bye to the little unconscious girl from outside the window and went off to meet Jack and go home with him. While she waited a couple of hours for Jack, she made use of the time and did some shopping to relieve some of her tension. She and her daughters seldom had a chance to shop in the city so this was a good opportunity to inject just a little bit of happiness into a sad stressful situation.

In the meantime, all of Jeffrey's friends had been trying to visit him but he had been placed in a coma and they were told that it would be a couple of days before he was allowed to have visitors.

Everyday some of his friends would go to the hospital in hope of being able to speak to him but it was the same answer each time. His bed-side table was full of magazines and boxes of chocolates all waiting for him to wake up. After three days, that time came. Jack was there when he woke and Jeffrey's first thoughts were for Chloe. The doctors and Jack were able to assure him that, although she was still in a coma, her doctors were very happy with her progress. Jeffrey spent three more days in hospital before he was given an appointment for the following Thursday and allowed to go home. He was told not to return to work until after that appointment.

Chapter 20

George had taken on an extra lad, Corey, to help Dean and Sam while Jeffrey was recovering and Dean and Sam had moved into the old house to look after Heidi and Champ.

One day while Corey and Dean were working in the yard cleaning rigs, they saw two well-dressed middle-aged men walk over to George and start speaking to him. Then they saw the three of them go into George's office. Jeffrey didn't like speaking to reporters and police and the boys guessed that these men were either reporters or detectives so they rang Jeffrey to warn him. The men were with George for about half an hour, then the boys saw Jeffrey coming down the hill on his bike. As he rode past them, he gave them a cheeky wave and a smile and then walked into George's office.

The three men stood up to meet him and George introduced them to each other. They were James and Richard Bennet, solicitors from Brisbane. Richard was the first to speak. He said, "We have read quite a lot about you recently, and George has told us more. Too much of it is a sad story for two young people to have to endure, so I am sure that you are over-due for some really good news, and we are happy to be the ones to bring it to you".

Jeffrey gave a faint smile and nodded his head as he thought of Chloe and all of the pain that she was going through and wondering what her future would be.

"I am not going to drag my news out. I am going to tell you our whole story and then you or George can ask any question that is sure to be buzzing about in your minds. I have asked George to stay with you as an adult witness.

First, a little bit of sad news, but I am sure that you have been expecting it. Soon after you disappeared your Nanna died. It had nothing to do with your disappearance. It was simply her time to go, and she went very peacefully in her sleep. He gave them time to absorb that and then he added, "Now, do you remember your Grandpa? "

"I don't remember him because I was young when he died, but Nanna often talked about him," Jeffrey said.

"Well even Nanna didn't know all about him," Richard said. "Your Grandpa was a very clever man. He started working in our father's real estate business when he was a young lad like you and soon after he bought a rundown old house at the Gold Coast and he has never sold it. Every year from then onwards he aimed to buy some sort of property. You don't have to be a genius to realise that those properties are worth a fortune now."

Both George and Jeffrey were nodding their head and waiting for Richard to carry on speaking.

"After he had bought three, there was no stopping him, but the bookwork involved, writing leases, supervising renovations and collecting rent, took a lot of time and he often required legal advice, so that is where we came in. He chose the property and we handled the business side. We inspected the properties regularly. We employed the tradesmen to renovate and maintain every building at a very high standard.

Plumbing, electricity, painting and fencing on every building, whether it was on a house, a set of units or a farm shed was maintained in perfect condition. At any time, any one of the properties could be put on the market with one week's notice."

'Wow!" Jeffrey said, "Nanna never said anything about that."

"I doubt whether she knew. "James remarked.

"What a clever man." George added. "That real estate must be worth millions now."

"Hundreds of millions. "James said.

"Now for the important part, "Richard said with a smile," and I would prefer it if you don't interrupt me", he added.

"When your dad and mum got married, your grandpa gave them a house, the one that you lived in before your accident," he said. "Then he gave your Aunt Patricia and her husband one when they were married, and when their marriage ended, she kept the house. Later, when he became ill, he gave each of them another house and a block of units. To provide for your nanna, he arranged for us to deposit the rent from all of the tenants in one block of units into her bank account each month. She could have travelled around the world but she was a very humble person and preferred to live quietly at home. As you know, she lived for another twenty-one years and that money has grown into a huge amount. Your

Nanna has left her house and all of her money to the two of you. Your dad's house and money will also become yours. That will include his and your Mum's insurance money from their accident when it is all finalised. Both of you also have insurance money coming to you." When Richard stopped talking for a moment, Jeffrey and George sighed and looked at each other speechless. Then Richard continued "As clever as he was, I don't think that your grandpa realised how valuable his other properties were going to become, because he left everything else to both of you."

Jeffrey was lost for words. He didn't speak and, for a moment, the men feared that it was too much for him to take in, and that he might go into shock again. Then Jeffrey said "I just can't understand. That is so much, there must be a mistake."

Then James spoke and he said "No Rohan. There is no mistake. I'll put it into a few simple words for you. You and Ruby are multi-millionaires."

George gave a loud laugh as he patted Jeffrey on the back and he said, "Congratulations Lad. Now all of your dreams can come true." There was some chatter and laughter around the table and then Richard said, "Do you have any special dreams that you thought you would never be able to achieve?"

"I have always wanted to be a mechanic and while I had to keep Chloe hidden from Robinson I couldn't go to college, but now I will be able to do that and set up my own workshop." he said. Then he added "I can't wait to tell Chloe. She reads so much and she has huge dreams, even Robinson couldn't dampen them."

George spoke then. He started with a little cough and an apology for what he was about to ask. He said that he and Mary had given up the farm because the work had become too much for them. He said that they both grew up on dairy farms and Mary treated the cows like family pets, so it was very hard to part with them. They gave the milkers to the neighbours on the condition that they were never sent to market. When they were too old to be of any commercial value they would be sent back to graze and live out their life here until they died. The motel has been so successful that the work here is now becoming too much for us. She won't sell out because she is afraid that the old cows will be sent to market and also, the hassle of selling and relocating is a bit daunting. Therefore, he added, "I was wondering if there could possibly be a block of units in the kids' collection of properties that would be about the same value as the farm and motel and everything that goes with it, and we might be able to make a clean swap. It would include a few thousand hectares of good grazing land, all of the sheds and the old house."

Jeffrey looked at the brothers who were looking at each other, then James asked" How would you feel about that Rohan?'

He didn't have to think for long before he said "It would be fantastic and I can say with certainty that Chloe would agree. She already thinks of the old house as her 'forever home.'

"In that case," James said, "I had better start looking into it straight away."

When the conversations had finished George pushed a little button under his desk and a waitress appeared at the door.

"Pauline, would you bring us some menus please?" he asked.

She walked away and soon returned with a handful of menus which she passed around. They each selected a meal and she wrote down their order. The restaurant was not busy at the time so it wasn't long before they each had a delicious meal in front of them.

Chapter 21

Chloe had come out of the coma and her doctors were very pleased with her progress. Many bones were broken or crushed and she had multiple internal injuries and now she had made such excellent progress that they were considering sending her back to the local hospital. She would be one step closer to home. Jeffrey had been talking to one of her doctors on the phone and when he hung up, he looked at Dean, who was waiting for the latest news, and he did a little Chloe dance. First, he ran up and down on the spot as though he was running in a fast race and then he clapped his hands and quickly placed his hand across his mouth the way that Chloe did when she was excited. Dean recognised the sign message and laughed and said, "When?"

"Probably on Friday, her doctors want to watch her for a few more days, but they are very hopeful," he said. He continued, "I spoke to Mrs White last night and she said that Chloe has had loads of visitors, even before she came out of the coma. Many of her Brisbane school friends have visited her because they have followed her story on the news and they were worried about her. Mrs Mullins from the orphanage has also visited her and she took two of Chloe's dormitory friends with her. Tiffany and another little girl that Robinson abused have new foster homes now and they are very happy. Their new mums took them up to visit her and to thank her for her help. Mrs White said that Chloe has a room full of flowers, books and chocolates, and in spite of all of the bandages and tubes she always has a smile for anyone who comes in". As Jeffrey finished speaking his eyes were full of tears as he said, "Isn't she a great little kid?"

Dean quietly added, "She sure is."

Jeffrey sent e mails to all of their friends and invited them to welcome her home, if they wished to, but he would like to have her all to himself on Saturday because they had a lot to talk about.

Jeffrey still hadn't returned to work at the motel so he spent the next two days cleaning and tidying the house just the way that Chloe would like it to be. He also mowed the lawn and swept under the house. He knew that she wasn't coming to the house but he wanted to spend as much time with her as possible once she was back in the local hospital, and he didn't want the distraction of having to catch up on the housework.

Dean's car had been replaced by his insurance company and he offered to drive Jeffrey into the hospital to meet her when she was due to arrive. Jeffrey was very grateful for the offer but he reminded Dean to check with George first to make sure that he could spare both of them. George was quite happy to let both of them go and told Sam that he could also go while Corey and he would cope on their own for a few hours. The three boys set out early on Friday morning to make sure that they were at the hospital in plenty of time.

As they entered the grounds, they were surprised to see that the car park was already quite full and they began to wonder whether there was some special function on that day. Then they saw a bus come in and Lexie stepped out, followed by two more ladies and then several school children.

Very soon afterwards another bus arrived and it was also full of school children from the Longreach School.

"Are these people all here to welcome Chloe?" Sam asked.?

"It looks like it." Jeffrey said as he watched the teachers take the children over towards the helipad.

A crowd was already standing around the perimeter and Lexie had taken her school children to the area near the ramp so the boys also went down to join her.

It wasn't long before one of the children spotted the helicopter in the distance and soon everyone was looking that way.

There was a feeling of excitement as it landed and when the motor was turned   off   three   loud   cheers   went   up. The pilot knew who his little patient was. She was the little girl that some fiend had run down with his murderous four-wheel drive as he tried to kill her, but her small body had fought back and now he had brought her one step closer to home. It made him feel happy to see so many of the town's people come out to welcome her home. so, instead of wheeling her stretcher towards the ramp, he and the other paramedic wheeled her across to the fence, keeping her just out of touching distance, they then wheeled her around the whole perimeter It was a little overwhelming for

Chloe but she managed to give a shy wave as she searched the crowd for a special person, Jeffrey. When she reached the ramp, he was there and he and Lexie walked beside the stretcher as she was wheeled into the hospital.

Sam and Dean stayed behind and mixed with her friends to see who would like to visit Chloe and they broke them into groups of two or three and wrote down an approximate visiting time for them, because a nurse at the hospital had warned Jeffrey that she was still quite ill and she needed a lot of rest.

Lexie only stayed a couple of minutes. She promised Chloe that she would bring the girls in the following afternoon as Jeffrey had promised to reserve that time for them. She and the three girls would visit her in pairs whenever there was a chance in the afternoon.

The women from the church that Chloe had been attending for a few weeks before she was attacked, had been in her room for a couple of hours that morning and had decorated it beautifully. Bunches of balloons were tied to every hook or rod that they could find and large vases of flowers were on every shelf or cupboard. A set of shelves that did not look like hospital furniture stood near the side wall. It was neatly made and painted a pale pink and white. Nearer to the bed there was a matching card display board that was painted a pale lemon and white. Both pieces of furniture were on wheels so that they could be easily moved. When a nurse came into the room, Jeffrey asked where they had come from and he was told that a wardsman had asked for permission to make them when he had heard Chloe's story. They were both amazed at how much kindness she was receiving. When someone brought in a carton of Chloe's gifts from the Brisbane hospital, Jeffrey decided to leave them for Lexie and her girls to unpack and place on the shelves. Chloe had excitedly chatted on about all her visitors in Brisbane and Jeffrey promised her that he would visit her the next day and then they would have a lot of time to talk because he was looking forward to hearing all her news. He had been there for forty-five minutes when a nurse reminded Jeffrey that Chloe had, had a big day and she needed to rest, so he gave her a gentle hug and a kiss and told her that he would be back the following day.

As Jeffrey walked out two nurses came in carrying a container full of flowers that had been professionally packed by a florist back in Brisbane. They put it down on the floor and looked around but they couldn't see anywhere that they could put one more stem. They both gave a little laugh and looked at Chloe as they shrugged their shoulders and said, "Do you have any ideas?"

As usual, Chloe was thinking of others and immediately suggested that she would like them to give the flowers to other patients, especially if they came from a long way away and didn't have any loved ones to visit them. It was a kind thought and soon more happiness was being spread through the hospital.

When Jeffrey went outside, he found Dean and Sam sitting on a seat under the shade of an old gum tree. When they showed him the roster, he was very pleased. He had been wondering how he was going to protect Chloe from swarms of visitors without offending anyone, and his mates had already solved the problem. As he glanced through the roster, he was disappointed that Ellen's name was not on it. He had been watching for her and apparently, she hadn't come. They were the same age and he was becoming quite fond of her.

The three boys returned to the motel where Dean and Sam had to start work, but Jeffrey sat down with George and Mary and told them all about his visit.

He could sense that they were still a bit hurt because they had been excluded from the secret and once again, he apologised and explained how dangerous it would have been for Chloe if one of the customers saw her. He also explained that Jack knew because he had brought them there and Lexie was working with the children's department. Their other friends found out accidentally when they gate crashed their anniversary party.

Dean had told him that he could borrow his car whenever he wanted to visit Chloe so he asked George and Mary whether they would like to go to the hospital with him on Monday. George declined but Mary eagerly accepted. She still hadn't met the little girl who had been living in their house for eighteen months. Jeffrey had already told them how her room was full of gifts and flowers and so he added that he had told her friends that he would give her a big party when she came home.

Chapter 22

As he walked up to the house many thoughts were running through his mind. He realised how much he loved that old couple and, not for the first time, he also realised that they had been like grandparents to him.

At the same time Mary was saying to George how much she loved that polite young lad and how she would be so proud to be his grandmother. George completely agreed and said, "Well now you might have the little granddaughter that you have always wanted too."

The next morning Jeffrey was up early before the other two boys were awake and set off for hospital feeling so happy that he was humming a little tune as he drove along the highway. He stopped humming while he planned exactly what he was going to tell his little sister.

She was clever and mature for her age but she was still only eleven.

years old and she had already been through more drama in her life than most children her age would have to cope with, especially when she didn't have any parents to support her.

He decided that he would tell her about Nanna's house and her money and all of her investments. Nanna had already told them about that when they lived with her. He would also tell her about their parent's insurance and their own house where they once lived. Then he would remind her that they would be receiving insurance from the accident in which they were involved with their parents and also from the attack by Robinson. All of that money would add up to millions and that would be enough on which Chloe could start building her dreams. He knew that she would already be full of dreams that she thought she could never achieve, now she could turn them into real plans. He wouldn't tell her about the multi-millions that would be coming to them from Grandpa's investments. He still found those figures frightening and if he told his little sister, it might turn dreams into nightmares.

With so many thoughts running through his mind he arrived at the hospital gate.

He was too soon for visiting hours so he strolled around the hospital grounds looking for a seat where he and Chloe could have some privacy. It was such a beautiful day that he felt sure that her doctor would allow him to bring her outside in her wheelchair.

Jeffrey went back to the main entrance and walked down the passage to Chloe's room and found her already sitting in a wheelchair and impatiently and excitedly waiting for him. The nurses had anticipated that her brother would want to wheel her outside so two of them had gently lifted her into a chair immediately after her shower.

After the initial greetings the nurses asked him to keep Chloe under a thick shady tree and to bring her back inside in thirty to forty minutes, also to limit the whole visit to about one hour.

Jeffrey had already planned exactly what he was going to tell her, but he also knew that his bubbly little sister would keep interrupting him, so he started by saying, "Now my noisy little magpie, I have a lot to tell you so do you think that you can be quiet for about ten minutes?"

"How about five?" she argued.

He repeated firmly, "Ten."

Chloe teasingly put her fingers over her mouth to gag herself. Jeffrey started by telling her that their Nanna had died soon after they left Brisbane and Chloe frowned but kept her fingers on her mouth. It was not a surprise because they had often talked about it and they had been convinced that she would not be alive still. Then he added that she had left her house and several other investments to them. Chloe just nodded her head but didn't speak. Nanna had already promised them that.

Jeffrey waited a few seconds and then he told her that they also owned their parent's home and any of their investments. As he spoke, he noticed that her eyes were filling with tears and he realised that he was suddenly putting too much pressure on her, so he said quietly

"Are you alright?"

"Yes," she replied quietly, "but that is so much money. How will we look after everything?"

He told her that he had a good solicitor looking after everything until they were ready to use it, and he decided not to mention any of the other money until Chloe had mentally, at least, accepted how rich they had become.

To set her mind in the right direction, he asked her whether she had any dreams about what she would like to do in the future. "We will have a lot of money and you can do anything that you would like to do," he told her.

"I would like to go to university," she said. "I would really like to be a vet and rescue unwanted farm animals. Do you think that George and Mary might sell us the house and some of the land?" she asked.

He knew then that his little sister was starting to dream and her dreams could become true. It was the perfect time to tell her about George's request to swap the whole farm, four thousand hectares, sheds, the old house, and the motel for one of their blocks of units.

As he talked, a broad smile spread over her face. His Chloe was back and she would soon have both of their lives planned out.

Thirty minutes had passed quickly and it was time to go inside. For the next forty minutes she talked non-stop, as she named all her friends and relived their visits. Jeffrey had no doubt that their visits had played a large part in her quick recovery and he wanted to repay them. Many of the people that she named were also his friends and she had some messages to give him. They joked and laughed together until the end of his visit. As he walked down the passage towards the main door, he met Sister Moylan and told her how easily Chloe had become upset, and she reminded him how his moods had fluctuated when he was in shock and then added that Chloe had almost died and it would be a long time before her mental and emotional damage was repaired.

Chapter 23

Jeffrey was feeling ashamed as he thought back over Chloe's moods. How could he have been so insensitive when everyone had been so understanding for him. He had some holidays due when he came out of hospital and George had insisted that he took another three weeks off work to let his nerves settle down and to restore his confidence. His injuries were minor compared with Chloe's. She had been hunted by a monster for eighteen months and then run down and almost killed.

As he was gliding along the highway on his own, his mind was racing through thoughts as quickly as he was travelling across kilometres of flat Australian landscape. Right from that moment he wouldn't stop preparing for her return until he was satisfied that she was going to have the very best care and absolutely the best opportunity to make a full recovery. He wanted his little sister back exactly the same as she had always been.

When he reached his home, he found Dean playing with Heidi and Champ and the three of them stopped playing to greet him. His life was full of friendships.

It was good to have a friend to talk to instead of coming home to an empty house. First, he told Dean about his visit and his talk with nurse Moylan. The two friends then went upstairs where they sat down and had some lunch. While they ate Jeffrey started pouring out his ideas. He had to make life easy for Chloe. He couldn't allow her to be his little house keeper anymore, and he wanted to completely renovate the house before she came home.

He had gradually repaired a few problems but now he was going to employ tradesmen to do it quickly and properly. The swap hadn't been arranged, so he would have to take his ideas to George and enlist his help and advice.

Dean listened as Jeffrey rattled off his ideas one after the other.

A new colonial kitchen would be installed and then a new modern bathroom with tiled walls and floor. Every room in the house would be checked for repairs and then painted and decorated with new floor coverings, blinds and curtains.

He had already replaced the missing batons under the house but some of his repairs were a bit rough so they would be improved if necessary.

They didn't have a laundry, so a modern tiled laundry would be built with fitted cupboards.

He would have a lift installed immediately so that Chloe would not have to be carried up the stairs, and he would have a new polished concrete surface put over the cement under the house.

"When do you hope to do all of this?" an amused Dean asked.

"Starting next week, I hope, hope, Oso that it will be finished before my little sister comes home, because from now on, she is going to be a little girl again, and not my pretend mother," he said.

"I am also going to have a single bitumen car track laid between the house and the motel and another one laid down to the river, where I hope the council will allow me to build a picnic shed, a short jetty and a boat ramp," he added.

"You are aiming high, "Dean said, "but it will be fantastic if you can do it. Do you think that George will approve?"

"That isn't all. I haven't finished yet" Jeffrey laughed.

"So that Chloe can be a little girl again, I need a housekeeper and a nurse to look after her, so I am going to build a unit under the house. I am hoping that you will help me plan it. It will have a double bedroom, a small modern kitchen-dinette, a living room and a toilet and shower."

"Wow!" Dean said. "You have had a brain explosion, but I would love to help you. Let's go down and have a look under the house."

The two friends made a quick sketch on paper and then used some batons that were under the house to mark out the floor plan for the unit and the laundry. When they were satisfied with the layout, they used a tape measure and moved the boards to exact measurements, and then they copied it onto paper. They were both very pleased with the result and with themselves.

When Sam came home, he brought a bag full of hamburgers and other left-over treats so they sat down together and once again Jeffrey repeated his plans. Sam was interested and offered to help wherever he could. He reminded them that he was hoping to visit Chloe the next day and asked Dean whether he could borrow his car. Again, Dean told them that either of them could borrow it anytime they wanted to visit Chloe. He said that it was one way that he could help that brave little kid. He said that he had promised her at the anniversary party that he would help her any way that he could and lending his car was his only opportunity.

The conversation prompted Jeffrey to tell them that he would be buying his own car as soon as the money was in his bank and he was hoping that they would go with him. He also promised Dean that he would repay his generosity with some extra generosity and that they would have a super shopping day.

After dinner, while Sam and Dean watched TV Jeffrey re-wrote his plans and added a few other requests so George and Mary would understand his reasons for attempting such a huge project.

Chapter 24

On the Sunday night Jeffrey went back to work for the first time since the attack. He took his plan and written hopes with him and, with a lengthy explanation, gave it to George as soon as he arrived. George listened carefully to everything that he said and agreed to have a talk to Mary and then both of them would see him later in the night when business had slowed down.

It wasn't a busy night out in the yard and Jeffrey had ample time to re-think all of his plans and there wasn't a thing that he would change. He hoped that the adults would agree. Ellen was still on his mind and he would ask Sam to make more enquiries when he met their friends at the hospital the following day.

It was nearly ten o'clock when George called him into the restaurant and offered him a hot drink and a packet of sandwiches.

Jeffrey was a bit nervous and was wondering whether Mary had gone to bed, but she soon came in with such a bright happy smile that he began to feel confident that they had liked his idea.

She walked straight up to him and put her arms around his shoulders and said "Thank you. Thank you!"

It took him completely by surprise until George said, "She has been worried that you would demolish the old house and put a new modern one there to replace it."

"Never." was Jeffrey's prompt reply.

That was a perfect beginning for the conversation.

"We like everything about your plan," George said, "but we don't think that you can manage it yourself. I supervised the building of this place and it was a full-time job, so I would like to take it on as a foreman. I will have to get the council permits because the property is still in my name, and I will use the same tradesmen that I used here. They will do a good and quick job for you. However, I can't manage the work here and take on another job, so I want you to manage the motel."

Jeffrey didn't see that coming. Having George supervise the construction would be awesome, but he knew nothing about managing the motel and that thought was very daunting.

"You have to learn some time," George reminded him, "and Mary will help you. The most important thing is to make sure that your stock is up to date and that your orders go in, in plenty of time, because it can cause severe problems if you run short of some common·

product," he added.

"I guess it will provide me with some training for the future, and I would be really grateful if you would supervise the construction," he replied.

Jeffrey said that he had talked to the solicitors and they told him that the money from Nanna was ready to be transferred to his bank but the properties would take a bit longer. He already had enough of his own money to make a start and a large deposit should be made early in the week. While they were discussing some of the details, he asked Mary whether she would like to go shopping with Lexie and choose the floor coverings, the curtains and the blinds. He added quickly that he hadn't asked Lexie but he would be ringing her the following morning. Mary was a quiet and shy person and being given such a responsible job made her speechless for a moment.

"I really would like you to help her if you have time," he added.

"There will be decisions to be made in the kitchen too and two women would know more about it than I would. Of course, there are so many choices to be made and I wouldn't know where to start. The tiles, the inside colours and furniture. I hadn't really thought about that before," he added. "The only thing I am sure about is the outside colour, because Chloe and I have always talked about painting it dark and light grey with white trimmings."

When he stopped speaking Mary had regained her voice and she said, "I would love to have a say in the renovation of my old home," and she laughed as she said, "It would be fantastic, shopping for all of the beautiful things that I would have liked to put in my home and using your money to buy them." They all laughed at Mary's expression and just then a car load of customers pulled in to the motel and they were hoping to rent two rooms for the night so the little group dispersed to attend to their needs.

The next time that George was speaking to Jeffrey, he reminded him that he had promised Mary that he would take her into the hospital, and he winked as he added, "to visit her new granddaughter".

Jeffrey laughed as he assured him that he hadn't forgotten.

After work he had a few hours' sleep, some breakfast, and then rang Mary and said that he would pick her up in about forty minutes.

It was a very happy drive along the highway that he had travelled so often during the previous month. Mary surprised him with her animated talking about their history on the farm and how she loved farm life and especially the old house, which was why it was still there, because she couldn't bear to have it knocked down.

She knew that they couldn't go on working forever, but the thought of leaving the district and living somewhere else was very upsetting. As Jeffrey listened a new thought flashed through his mind and he said, "You know, after the swap is finalised, you don't have to leave the motel. You could stay on as managers until you wanted to retire. I know that the solicitors are   taking care of all of the business to do with the units, so why not let them carry on doing that and you can stay where you are for as long as you like."

Once again Mary was speechless. They wouldn't have to worry about their future. It would be assured and when they couldn't cope with work any longer, all they would have to do was pack their ports and move into a unit. They had arrived at the hospital and she just had time to say, "I think that would be absolutely wonderful and I feel certain that George will agree, so I will talk to him as soon as I go home".

Chapter 25

Chloe was already dressed and waiting in her wheelchair. It was hospital policy for long term patients to wear normal day clothes, especially children, and Chloe had chosen the pretty frock that Lexie had given her for her anniversary. It was also the first time that she had been able to wear anything on her feet, and she was wearing her sandals. She knew that she looked pretty because the nurses had made such a fuss about her, and that feeling brought back her charming smile.

Mary had been warned that everyone had to be careful when they hugged Chloe because so much of her body had been crushed. However, she walked straight up to her and gently put her arms around her and they embraced each other lovingly as though they truly were Grandma and Granddaughter.

The nurse reminded Jeffrey that thirty minutes outside would be enough for Chloe and to keep her under a shady tree. He could read his little sister like a book and as he wheeled her down the corridor, he said that she was like a little bubbling volcano that was about to erupt, so when he and Mary were seated on a bench under a shady tree, he said, "Well. What are you so excited about?"

Chloe looked at him and answered "How much land can I have?"

Jeffrey didn't see that coming so he hesitated for a moment and then said "I think you can have about four thousand hectares. Is that enough?"

"Yes. I think so." She took a folded piece of paper out of her pocket and opened it out as she said "This is a plan of where I want to put my pens. I have always liked chickens and I want to collect as many different sizes and colours as I can find, and I want to rescue unwanted farm animals. I know that you want to be a mechanic, so you will need a very big workshop and a couple of hectares to park some of the big rigs that you might have to work on, so I have marked off this area below the motel for you. I want to make a caravan park here," she said as she pointed to the map, "and a smaller area here for people who want to camp in tents. When we have a bigger crowd of customers, there might be a lot of children too, so we will need a playground, won't we?" she asked. "I'd like to have a road down to the river too," she added "and if the council will allow us could we have a boat ramp and perhaps build a little jetty out into the river. It would be nice to have some picnic tables too. "Chloe stopped talking and looked at Jeffrey and Mary and then she asked whether she was planning too much, because she had noticed how they had looked at each other.

"No! No!" Jeffrey protested "We are just surprised and I was thinking what a good idea it would be. Have you thought up all of these wonderful ideas since Saturday?" As he spoke, he gave Mary a gentle nudge with his knee to remind her not to tell Chloe about his big plans.

"No, I started planning my farm a long time ago. Remember Nanna told us that she owned a farm and that it would be ours someday and I started drawing my plan, but I didn't know what our farm would look like so I pretended that George and Mary's farm was ours. There's a plan just like this in the drawer of my dressing table at home." As Chloe was speaking, she gave a little sigh and then she said "I wish I could go home."

"It won't be much longer Dear" Mary said, and she told her how she was looking forward to having her home and how she would like to look after her at the motel until she was really strong.

Jeffrey agreed with Mary and said that they would do everything that they could, to prepare for her, including a lift in the house so that she could go up and down, without help. However, it was extremely important that her bones and all of her injuries must be healed enough so that she wouldn't have any setbacks later.

Chloe was thrilled to hear about the lift and wanted to know where he would put it and how it would work. When she was satisfied, she went back to her plan and pointed to three large pens just past the house and continued with her detailed description of her dream farm.

"This is where I want to have my chickens and these lane ways are here so that the cows and horses can come right up to the house fence because they like to have some contact with people, but they also need a big paddock where they can roam and graze.

There will be a roadway right through the middle of the farm and on the other side I want to have ducks and other webbed feet birds like swans and geese." Chloe stopped speaking and looked up at her visitors to see if they were still following her.

They still looked interested so she continued on and, pointing to a drawing for a small building she said that it would be her veterinary clinic when she was qualified and then she added "Ellen is almost qualified so she might like to open it soon."

"Has she visited you?" Jeffrey asked.

"No. I was a bit disappointed that she didn't come with the others yesterday, but they haven't seen her either. She must be busy studying." Chloe answered.

She moved her map so that they could see the bottom of it and said, "I haven't really planned this part yet because I have to learn more about the larger birds and their habitats. Somewhere here we should put some accommodation for the groundsmen. I have read about that in one of the magazines that Lexie gave me. Some farmers provide little cottages so that their family can be with them, but sometimes they just provide huts and a separate dining hut with a cook."

"There are some huts there already and a big shed where they sheared the sheep," Mary announced.

"I saw them but they are on the other side of the fence, so I thought that they belonged to the neighbours" Chloe explained.

Mary quickly answered her, "No, no that is all part of our farm. You see George had four brothers so there were plenty of workers and his father had a large flock of sheep running in that top paddock. When George bought the farm from the family, he sold the sheep and fenced off the paddock so that the cattle couldn't roam too far away."

"Did George's family have a lot of sheep on the other side of that fence?" Chloe asked in surprise.

"Oh yes. They had quite a large flock, and they had a good yield of wool each year too which made it hard for George to make such a big decision. However, even if he employed a foreman to run it, it would still be a mental burden, and so the neighbour added them to his flock. He has a much bigger run than ours." Mary replied. Chloe immediately turned to Jeffrey and asked, "Do you think we could put some sheep in there?"

"Well, not yet," he answered slowly. "Perhaps someday, but all of this is new to us so let's move slowly for a while."

As they were talking Jeffrey saw an angry nurse come hurrying out of the side door of the hospital and he glanced down at his watch and was shocked when he saw how long they had been outside. They had talked and listened for forty-five minutes and nobody had thought about the time.

Jeffrey hurried to stand up and turn the wheelchair around while apologising for being so slack, but the nurse wasn't listening. She talked over him explaining how dangerous it was to overdo any excitement or activity for Chloe. She accepted that Chloe's visitors were giving her a boost and Chloe was making a remarkable recovery. However, it was important for everyone to understand how badly her body had been crushed and broken and bruised, and so many things could still go wrong. She also said that they hoped they would be able to move her to an open ward where she would have the company of other children but Chloe would need at least another week's rest before that could happen. She was talking quietly and Jeffrey was hoping that Chloe couldn't hear what she was saying. Mary had the same thought and bent over and started making remarks about the beautiful hospital garden.

After they reached the ward, they each gave Chloe a hug and a kiss and once again she was left with the nurses, the doctors and her room full of cards, books and beautiful flowers.

Chapter 26

As Jeffrey drove along the highway, Mary commented on what a bright, lovely little girl Chloe was, and she couldn't understand how that monster could plan to kill her.

"She didn't complain once, except for a little wish that she could go home. When you are talking to her, it is easy to forget how badly she has been injured," she said.

Jeffrey was feeling very guilty once again. In spite of all of her injuries, his little sister was so bright and cheerful that he forgot that she was still trying to recover.

"You are not wrong Mary, "he said. "She tricked me again today. I feel so embarrassed and ashamed because it makes me look as though I don't care, but her excitement and ambition are so contagious that she just blows away any negative thoughts and drags me along with her. It makes it so important to get those repairs and improvements done so that she has something special to come home to."

There wasn't much more small talk during the trip home because they were both deep in thought. Mary was mentally planning all of the wonderful things that she was going to be doing with her old home. She knew every floor and wall in every room and she already knew what she would like to do with the kitchen. It was something that she always dreamt of doing when she lived there.

Jeffrey was also thinking about the house and wondering whether he had forgotten anything. It was a comfort to know that George was going to supervise it because he would soon find any problems and have a solution ready.

The house wasn't Jeffrey's only thoughts. He was also worrying about Ellen. He was surprised that she hadn't visited Chloe. There must be something wrong. Some of the group said that her father was an old grump and they were afraid to approach him but Jeffrey was going to ask Dean to take him over to her house as soon as he could. He knew that her family had a large farm about twenty kilometres out along the highway on the other side of town, but he didn't know her exact address.

Over the last few kilometres, they started chatting again when Mary ran a few of her ideas past Jeffrey for his approval. As he listened to her, his excitement grew. She obviously knew the house well and her ideas were so grand and exactly what he wanted. Now he hoped that she and Lexie would work well together.

When he let her out at the motel, he reminded her about their conversation that they had on the way to the hospital. He wanted her to suggest to George that they should stay on at the motel after the swap was finalised.

He drove up to the house but this time only the dogs would greet him because Dean and Sam were both at work.

Before he went upstairs, he roamed around the yard and backed away to the fence so that he could imagine the final appearance, and he felt very keen to get the job finished.

As he stood at the front of the house. looking at its size, he decided that he would like to close in the right-side veranda and turn it into a long library. He could also solve another problem. At the back he would have another shower and bathroom, with a small hallway leading from the dining room. The closed in veranda would be replaced by a wide-open veranda extension which would run the full distance down the side of the house. It would have a roof covering it, but instead of a wall there would be a railing and batons, painted white.

That night the three boys were home while Corey worked the night shift and Jeffrey brought up the subject of Ellen and her mysterious disappearance from their social scene. Dean was also worried about her so he and Jeffrey agreed to visit her two days later when Jeffrey had the day shift off and Dean didn't have to start work until 2 o'clock in the afternoon.

On Monday George had spent the morning pulling strings to get the necessary permits passed with some urgency. Everyone wanted to help those kids that had been so viciously attacked, so his requests were given top priority. He also personally visited any tradesmen that he knew would do everything in their power to get the job finished in record time. They were all keen to help, and by the end of the day he had a huge team of workers, representing every trade, and promising to spend their whole weekend on the job as soon as the permits were passed and the materials were delivered.

A site foreman, Eric, was selected and he went out to the house and double-checked George's list of materials.

On Tuesday, Mary and Lexie made their shopping list and together they made a rough plan of the kitchen, shower and toilet but they wanted to discuss it with Jeffrey, Jack and George, before they ordered any building materials. Both women were so agreeable that they made detailed lists and plans during one long afternoon's meeting at the house. They would buy most of it locally, but when it wasn't available, they would order it locally and have it brought up from Brisbane.

On Wednesday Dean and Jeffrey left home at 8 o'clock to go out to the Brennan's farm to find Ellen. Jeffrey loved the country drive. The landscape was so flat that there was an uninterrupted view for kilometres. Some farmers had dairy cattle, others had grain fields and sunflowers. Huge patches of different colours spread across to the horizon making it look like an enormous patchwork quilt. After travelling for about an hour they turned off on to a dirt road. Although it wasn't bitumen it still had a hard surface and was wide enough for vehicles to pass.

"We are not quite there yet," Dean said, "but this is part of Brennan's farm."

As Jeffrey looked across the colourful land, he said in surprise "Wow! They must be wealthy."

"Wait until you see the house," Dean said, "I'll let you be the judge. "As he spoke a three-storey white building appeared in the middle of the quilt.

"There it is," Dean said and he slowed his car down to a mere crawl so that they could have a good look. Jeffrey was very quiet as they drove through a huge wooden entrance with the words BRENNAN'S FARM built into the overhead structure. There was no gate. Instead, there was a grid to stop the animals from walking through the open gateway. He drove along a concrete roadway which was lined on either side with fruit trees that were laden with ripe fruit. The roadway led to a round-about that encircled a pretty cottage garden. Dean parked his car on a space under a covered area which was clearly marked 'PARKING'.

They both stepped out and walked a little nervously towards a set of polished concrete stairs. Dean pressed an elaborate door bell and heard the chimes ring inside. It was answered promptly by an elderly lady. "Good morning Mam" they said politely, but they were not sure how they should address this very formal lady.

"We are friends of Ellen. I am Jeffrey, and I am Dean". The boys said, "and we were wondering whether we would be able to speak to her."

"I'll ask the mistress." she said and walked away, leaving the boys outside. It wasn't long before an older version of Ellen, came to the door and wearing a beautiful charming smile, she said "I am so pleased to meet both of you because I have heard so much about you, and you must be Chloe's brother", she said as she shook Jeffrey's hand. "How is your little sister?"

Her friendliness and sudden question took Jeffrey by surprise but he was already feeling more relaxed and he gave a happy description of how Chloe was recovering. As they were talking Ellen came into the hallway and walked towards them.

"Oh, there you are Dear. I was hoping that you would come down. You have two nice young visitors here and I hope they can cheer you up." After speaking to Ellen, Mrs Brennan walked away and left the three young people together.

"Let's go outside," Ellen said as she walked between them and led them to a picnic setting under a shady tree.

Both boys spoke together as they told her that everyone was worried about her.

Then the tears flowed down her face as she blurted out, "They have sold the farm. I don't know what to do. I don't know where to go and how can I save my little family?"

Jeffrey put his arm around her and she sobbed onto his shoulder. He held her tightly as he said, "Ellen, I promise you I can solve all of it for you." Ellen lifted her face and looked a little bit angry because she thought he was making her enormous problem into nothing and tormenting her. He quickly realised what she was thinking and hurriedly said "Your little family that Chloe has told me about can move into our very comfortable cow yard and shelter in the bails until we can build a real pen for them, and you can move into our very comfortable motel until the house is renovated, and then you can move in with us." He then turned to Dean and said, "Ellen has a pig, a sheep, and a goat that she has raised from tiny babies and even they are confused," he laughed, "and they don't know what they are anymore".

She slowly dried her eyes as she looked up and said "Are you serious? What will George say?"

Jeffrey explained how he and Chloe had received a large inheritance from their parents and their Nanna. He also told her that the solicitor had told them that there would be a very large payment due to them from their original accident and from Robinson's attack on them.

She looked at Dean for reassurance and he said, "It's true. They are buying the farm and the motel".

"Oh Jeffrey, that will be fantastic. I have been so worried and so frightened that I couldn't talk to anyone, but what a difference it would have made if I had talked to you. Poor Dad had to sell because he can't work anymore and he has to have a serious operation and I have been adding to their worry because I have been so upset. Some foreign company has bought it and they wouldn't care about a few pets, and they would probably send them to the markets. That is just too horrible to even think about." Ellen was still crying as she spoke, and she seemed to be in shock so Jeffrey and Dean continued to reassure her.

However, time had moved along quickly and Dean reminded them that he had to go to work that afternoon, so they started heading back towards the house.

"Would you like us to talk to your mum?" Jeffrey asked.

"No, no," she said, I will tell both of them. They will be relieved and Dad will bring the family over in the cattle truck. I think Mum might like to come too, just to see where I will be living, and she will probably want to talk to George and Mary."

"Well as soon as you like and any time that you like. It is all ready," he said.

Ellen kissed each of them on the cheek and gave them an affectionate hug, but she gave Dean an extra firm and long hug, because he had been waiting so patiently and she knew that if he hadn't brought Jeffrey over, this miracle would not have happened.

Chapter 27

Dean felt the warmth of the hug and it relieved some of the tension and jealousy that had been building up in him as he watched Ellen and Jeffrey embracing and kissing. They reached the car and drove out along the concrete lane that was lined on either side with fruit trees.

Then Dean commented, "Ellen is beautiful. Isn't she?"

"She is absolutely gorgeous." Jeffrey said in agreement.

Then after a short silence he said, "Dean, I know that the insurance replaced your car that Robinson crushed, with this car, but Sam and I have driven all of the new shine off it and I want to replace it with one that is better. Perhaps one that you liked but you couldn't afford at that time."

"No. No." Dean said, "You don't have to do that. This car is still perfect."

"I have to." Jeffrey argued. "Don't be worried that I am being foolish with my money. I know exactly what I am doing and I have thought about it very carefully. There are three people or families that I must repay. If it wasn't for their help and kindness, neither Chloe nor I would be here, so surely that is worth a lot. When Chloe finally told me what Robinson was doing, she was too young to understand what was really happening, she was just frightened that he might stop her from coming home to me at the weekend so that she could be a special girl, but I knew that I had to rescue her and get her away from that home,

but I didn't know how. Would you believe I actually bought a tent and camping gear, then Robert White introduced me to Jack, and if Jack had refused to bring us out here, I shudder to think what would have happened to us. Jack also bought our furniture for us. Of course, I paid for it, but I had no way of going into town to buy it. Lexie has been a tremendous comfort for Chloe. She and the girls have been like a family for us. Therefore, I am going to buy her a nice new car and she can hand her other one on to Pamela.

George and Mary have been like grandparents to me, and now that Mary knows about Chloe, she has already claimed her as a little granddaughter. If they hadn't agreed to my strange request to live in the old farm house, our lives would have been very different too. Jack had already told us that Chloe could live with them if I had to live in a motel room, but then we would have been separated.

George and Mary have their old ute to drive around and that might suit George but I am sure Mary would like a nice new car, so I am going to buy one for them too. And then, of course there is Dean," and he turned and looked at him as he spoke. "If you even hesitated before you threw your car keys to me that day, there is absolutely no doubt in anyone's mind that Chloe and I would both have been killed. No amount of money can ever repay that debt."

"If you are as determined as that I do have a dream car that I would like. I have always wanted a good four-wheel drive" he said. However, this car does have some sentimental value and I am fond of it. Instead of a car would you consider giving me a small block of land?"

"Absolutely, if that is what you would rather have, but I must repay my debt."

For the rest of the trip home the two friends talked about their dreams for the future and Jeffrey, who had always wanted to be a mechanic, knew that his dream could come true now that he had inherited so much money. As they talked, he realised that Dean shared the same dream and he saw another way by which he could repay the enormous debt that he felt that he owed him. He laughed as he told Dean how Chloe, in her typical organising manner, had allocated him a large area of land on the other side of the motel where he could have his workshop. She wanted him to build sheds big enough to house the longest rigs while he was working on them, and space to park them while they were waiting for his attention.

"I am not going to wait until I am qualified as a mechanic before I have the sheds built and get the business started," he said. "I will get it built and buy the necessary equipment as soon as it comes up on my list of 'to do's'. There are a few other things higher in priority but it will happen", he said. Jeffrey continued speaking. He knew where his story was leading and he watched Dean to see his reaction.

"I will employ at least one mechanic to begin with and I will start a mechanic's course myself and hopefully be apprenticed to him, and I would like you to do the same. It would be fun to study and work together and eventually when we are both qualified, we will have a job waiting for us. "Then he quickly added, "Naturally I will pay for your course. Then once we are in a business together, I might start to feel as though I have repaid some of my debt."

Dean took his eyes off the road for a brief moment while he glanced sideways at his friend.

"I know that I have told you about my little twin sisters, but I have never told you much about my family, "he said. "Well, I grew up on a little dairy farm about twenty kilometres on the other side of town, in the opposite direction from Ellen's place. Mum is the farmer in the family, and Dad was a mechanic, and that is what I have always wanted to be. Dad died suddenly two years ago and the only income we had then was from the farm, and that wasn't very much. I was still at school, a state school, but the twins were at a private school and they also learnt dancing. They liked their school and were very good at dancing but there just wasn't enough money to pay for everything, so I decided to leave school and get a job. The job at the motel is the first real job that I have had, although I sometimes worked for Dad. We don't get a big pay but it is better than an apprentice's pay and I couldn't afford to pay for the course. I don't spend very much and I have full board as well, so each month I take as much as I can save, home to Mum. Mate, if you do what you have just offered to do for me, you have more than repaid your debt."

Jeffrey had listened without interrupting and then he said, "I am sorry to hear about your dad. That must have been very hard for you, but I definitely mean what I said, every word of it. Now it has even more meaning for me than what it had before. How did you manage to save up for a car? Do you owe very much on it?"

"No. When I turned ten, Dad gave me a bank account with one hundred dollars in it. I had full control over it and I could have withdrawn the money and had a spending spree. As you can imagine that was very tempting for a ten-year-old, and Dad knew that. He was testing me. He said that when I was old enough to get my licence, he would match my money dollar for dollar, so I deposited every cent that I earned or received as a present or pocket money into that account and I was soon given the nick-name of Scrooge. Dad died just before my birthday so Uncle James added enough money to my savings so that I could buy the little car that I had, but if Dad had been alive, I would have been able to buy a nice four-wheel drive."

As he was speaking, they passed the old farm house and then they were at the entrance to the motel. They were home.

Chapter 28

On Thursday morning, Sam and Dean went to work, but Jeffrey had the day off so that he could go to town with George and Mary to set up an account that they and Lexie could work from as they paid for the purchases that they would be making for the renovations.

He sat down with his computer and opened up at his bank accounts and went to his new account that he had opened for him and Chloe. As he stared at the balance, he felt dizzy. He knew that the money from his parents and his Nanna had been deposited the previous day. He even had a close idea of how much it would be, but when he saw the actual figure in his account, his mind went into a temporary shock.

All of that money represented his parents and his Nanna and it was because they were dead that it was his and Chloe's now. At that moment, he promised himself that he would never waste one cent of it, no matter how much they received. He would still repay his debts. He would fulfil Chloe's dreams and build his workshops, but after that he would earn every dollar that he wanted to spend.

George, Mary and Jeffrey all fitted comfortably on the seat of the utility and during the drive to town, it was a golden opportunity for Jeffrey to steer the conversation around to four-wheel drives. He told them that he was going to buy one for Dean and he kept asking questions about the different models, their value, and their good and bad points until he asked George directly which one he preferred. He was quite surprised when both George and Mary announced together that they were planning to buy one. They had already chosen the model that they wanted but they wanted to save a few more dollars towards it because they were too old to take on such a huge debt.

Jeffrey showed a real interest in his choice, pretending that he might consider buying it for Dean, but George advised him against that, telling him that there were many models much cheaper that he could give his friend and he would still be giving him a fantastic gift. However, he did suggest that Jeffrey might consider buying one for himself and if he looked after it and kept it for many years it would give him good service.

Strangely, Jeffrey had been so busy thinking about which vehicles he would buy for others, he hadn't given much thought as to which one he preferred. He had a vague idea, but he had been planning to go shopping with Sam and Dean and make up his mind after he had looked at a few. Suddenly he had this elderly man for whom he had so much respect giving him advice.

Jeffrey said, "Dad kept his car for many years. I was fourteen when he was killed and he had the same car all my life until the previous year when he bought the new one. He was driving the new car when we had the accident. We were all excited when he bought the new car but the old one was still in perfect condition because he always kept it so well maintained.

"That's the point Lad". George said. "If you attend to the little problems when they occur, they won't develop into expensive trouble."

As they travelled over the last few kilometres, they discussed the many varieties that Jeffrey would be able to choose from, and once again he found himself being grateful for his friendship with this elderly man.

Their first stop was at the bank where Jeffrey set up an account which his three helpers could use. He would pay the wages and the larger bills such as the kitchen, which the ladies had ordered, but for some purchases it was much more convenient if his helpers could pay for items and materials as they chose them.

After they had finished that business, they went into a cafe and had some tea and cake. They were feeling refreshed so Mary went on her own way, arranging to meet the men at the old cafe next to the Supermarket in approximately two hours' time. The men went car hunting.

George took Jeffrey to the biggest four-wheel drive dealer where he knew the manager, and after introducing him to Graham he explained that Jeffrey was looking for his first car. Jeffrey was interested for himself now, but he was also listening to, and watching George very carefully. Graham glanced around the large display area and then his eyes wandered outside and he started slowly walking towards one particular vehicle and George and Jeffrey followed him. Suddenly, Jeffrey felt quite overwhelmed as the reality of what he was doing hit him. He was actually about to choose his first car although he didn't intend to buy it during this trip. Graham opened the door and invited him to sit in the driver's seat. The dashboard looked so impressive that it would not look out of place in an aeroplane and once again Jeffrey was feeling nervous and overwhelmed, and he began to feel emotional and, for a moment, he was afraid that he was going to cry.

George noticed his slight hesitation and his pale face. He knew this quiet and gentle boy well and immediately realised he was feeling out of his depth, so he suggested to Graham that it might be a good idea to show the lad a few vehicles that could be suitable and then let him choose one. He reminded Graham that Jeffrey was very inexperienced and had only held a licence for a few months.

"Well, still hop in and sit behind the wheel of this one and see how comfortable you feel," he said. "Fortunately, you are quite tall, so you won't have any trouble seeing over the steering wheel," he added. Then he began to point to some of the knobs on the dashboard and to explain the purpose of each one.

"Do you have any particular model in mind?" Graham asked.

"No". Jeffrey replied. "They all look fantastic."

"Well, then I suppose we are just looking at the price?" Graham asked with a question in his tone.

"No, not necessarily Graham. I would like you to explain the good and the bad points of each one to the lad, bearing in mind that at present, as I said, he is very inexperienced but he does intend to keep it for a long time. Is that right, Mate?" George asked Jeffrey.

". Absolutely. We'll talk about the prices after I have chosen one, or perhaps narrowed it down to two."

Now Graham had a much clearer idea of what his new customers wanted and also felt sure that they were ready to buy a vehicle and not just dreaming of something in the future. He led them around the yard and explained clearly any difference.

Occasionally, he had to leave them and speak to other customers. but he always returned to them because he felt sure that they were genuine buyers. After about an hour and a half, they had tried out every vehicle and Jeffrey was sure that he knew exactly what he wanted for himself and he would buy the same for Dean. He also knew which vehicle he would buy for George. It was the one that George and Mary had been saving up to buy for themselves. It would cost more than he had been planning to spend but how could he put a limit on his and Chloe's life?

Graham was about to leave them once more to attend to a new customer who had walked into the yard so they thanked him for his patience and advice and told him that Jeffrey would be back the following Wednesday to settle the deal, but they didn't tell him how many vehicles he would be buying.

They returned to the utility and George took Jeffrey for a drive around the town to fill in a little more time before they met Mary. He explained to Jeffrey that Mary didn't get many opportunities to shop and he didn't want to rush her. Quite clearly, George was a thoughtful old man and they were a kind and loving couple.

Finally, they found an empty parking spot directly opposite the door of the supermarket and sat there waiting for Mary, but they didn't wait long before she came through the door, pushing a trolley laden with groceries.

Jeffrey hurried to meet her and to push the trolley across the sloping footpath, while George walked around the back of the ute ready to unpack the trolley and put the groceries into a very large esky that always went with them when they went to town.

"Oh, my dear. Did you forget that we live in a motel now?" he asked.

In the same tone, Mary replied, "No my dear. I have had the urge to do some cooking lately and I don't have any of the ingredients that I need, so I decided to restock my pantry."

"Yum!" George said as he winked at Jeffrey. "Mary is a fantastic cook, but since we have lived at the motel, it is so much easier to put in an order and then half an hour later sit down at the table and have someone else bring it to you."

"And wash the dishes afterwards," Mary added. Then she said, "After Chloe comes home and settles in, I'll cook a special three course dinner for the four of us."

"She would love that". Jeffrey answered. "Actually, she is a very good cook herself, and always interested in new recipes. Nanna was a good cook and she taught Chloe how to follow a recipe and although she was very young, she enjoyed it so much that she seemed to soak up everything that Nanna told her and it wasn't long before she was cooking the evening meal. And, of course she has had a lot of practice since we came out here."

George, who was always thinking of others, moved the utility around to the normal parking area so that a supermarket customer could park in front of the shop. Mary and Jeffrey went ahead to the cafe. It was a typical old cafe with individual stalls, padded seats and very high padded backs. Wherever Jeffrey looked there were photographs and memorabilia from the pioneer days. The whole room was lit up by three beautiful chandeliers but they were not bright lights, the glow that they emitted was more like twilight.

"Do you like it?" Mary whispered as she chose one of the tables.

"Yes." He replied emphatically. "I feel as though I have just stepped back into history."

"You have," George said as he came up behind them. "This cafe was here when I was a kid and nothing has been modernised or changed in it. My dad always said the same thing. It was here when he was a kid. If anything needed repairs, they would hunt around until they could find the same material. A few more photographs have been added as people donated them, and they represent the pioneers and their daily lives."

He pointed to a photograph of a wagon being pulled by two horses and young children walking beside it.

"Dad remembered that family. There were six children in the family. The oldest was eleven and his name was Bill and the youngest was a young baby named Wally. The oldest four had to walk some of the way, and then they could sit on the wagon for a few miles and have a rest. They were in a group of six wagons, and there were four horse riders bringing along a herd of cattle. That often happened. Sometimes they would drive a herd of cattle and sometimes they would drive a flock of sheep, and that is how the west was explored and developed." George continued looking at the photograph as though his mind had slipped back to his childhood.

His thoughts were interrupted when an attractive young waitress handed each of them a menu and waited for their order.

"We'll start with the main course," George said. "You will find that it is such an enormous feed that it is a real challenge. You can have a large succulent piece of steak with roast potatoes, roast pumpkin and the rest of the plate loaded with other vegetables, or instead of the steak you can have lamb chops or the tastiest sausages that you have ever eaten."

Mary chose the lamb chops and Jeffrey said, "I must leave some room for dessert, so I think I will have the sausages."

When the waitress moved away, Mary asked Jeffrey about the early history of Brisbane and Redcliffe. She had remembered learning about them when she was at school, and she knew that the first white settlement in Queensland, was there, but that was all she could remember about them.

Jeffrey had always liked reading Australian history and he was especially impressed by the importance of his own local area, so he began to deliver a short history lesson.

"In 1770 Captain Cook sailed up the east coast of Australia," he began. "He named Moreton Bay, Cape Moreton and the Glass House Mountains. Cook thought that Cape Moreton was on the main land. However, when Matthew Flinders came along in 1799, he discovered that Cape Moreton was at the end of an island and he named the island Moreton Island. He also named Red Cliff Point. Some of the local people think that Flinders named the red cliffs in front of the main city shopping centre, but his journal shows that the compass bearing of the red cliffs goes exactly through a place now called Woody Point. His journal also states that the rocks were impregnated with iron having small pieces of granite and crystal scattered about the shore, so he must have gone ashore. His journal also mentions a green headland about two miles westward and that would be a place that is now called Clontarf Beach. On the west side of the headland, they found a net about fourteen fathoms long. The twine and mesh were very strong and the net was about three feet deep. At each end there was a pointed stick about the same length so it was obviously used to trap fish on the outgoing tide. The branches and sticks of which it was made were set and interwoven so closely that a fish could not pass through. Flinders was so impressed that he took the net back to Sydney. For payment, he left a sharp hatchet and cut down some saplings and trimmed off their branches to show the natives how to use it.

"You seem to know your local history," George said, "but how did it become the first white settlement?" he asked.

"Well," Jeffrey said, "Nothing happened for another twenty-four years, and then John Oxley was sent from Sydney to see if Port Curtis would be suitable for another settlement where they could send the worst convicts. After he examined Port Curtis, he decided that it was not suitable and he sailed on to Moreton Bay. It was December in 1823."

Just as Jeffrey finished speaking a waitress came to the table with their meals and except for a grateful "Thank you," from each of them, there was silence.

Jeffrey was stunned by the size of the plate which was laden with steaming hot food. The aroma had each of them admiring it in their own way. They all began to eat, and for a while the history lesson was put on hold.

Mary then asked between mouthfuls, "Was it John Oxley who chose Redcliffe?"

"Yes", Jeffrey answered. "However, it wasn't until the following September that the new settlers arrived." Then as he ate his meal he continued to talk between mouthfuls.

"When Oxley sailed into Moreton Bay in 1823 he had a huge surprise because, standing there on the beach on Bribie Island there was a white man amongst a tribe of natives. Oxley took him on board and he told an amazing story. Nine months earlier, he and three other convicts had been sent from Port Jackson, in a small open boat to collect some cedar wood from further down the coast, but when they reached the open water, a severe storm came up and blew them off course. They thought that they had been blown further south, so they sailed north to go back to Port Jackson, Sydney. One man, John Thomson died during the journey. Thomas Pamphlet was the man that Oxley had picked up. John Finnegan was also on the island but at that time he was away with a hunting party and he missed Oxley. Richard Parsons had continued to walk north, looking for Port Jackson. Pamphlet told Oxley about a very large river and the following day a small party set out in a rowing boat and found the mouth of the river and over the next two days, they rowed about fifty miles up it. When he returned to Sydney, he named it Brisbane River after the Governor of New South Wales, and recommended Red Cliff Point for the new penal settlement. "Jeffrey stopped talking to take another mouthful.

"These sausages are scrumptious," he said. "But I don't know whether I can eat three of them. Do you think they would give me a doggie bag to take one of them home?"

"Certainly," Mary said. "They will always do that for you."

"Do they sell them separately?" he asked. "Would I be allowed to buy a kilo of them?"

"No." George said, "But the butcher about four shops up the road, sells them, but I don't think we will have time to go there this afternoon. What about the settlement?" George prompted him.

"That is what I want to hear."

Jeffrey gave a little laugh and continued with his history lesson.

"In September, 1824 Lieutenant Miller, the commandant and John Oxley, some soldiers, Alan Cunningham and the first convicts arrived and immediately started building slab huts for shelter. Oxley and Cunningham and a small crew, once again rowed up the Brisbane River. This time they went much further and, on their way, back down the river they went ashore near where the Grey Street Bridge now stands, to look for water. They found several clear, clean ponds where the town hall has been built and they were very impressed with the whole area. Oxley declared that it would be a perfect place for a settlement. They also found a wooded valley with strong straight trees and strong vines that would make excellent building materials. When he returned to Redcliffe, he told Miller about his discovery." Jeffrey stopped talking so that he could have some more to eat, because George and Mary were nearly finished their meal.

"We had better let the lad eat his dinner," George said, "because it will be spoilt if it is cold."

Jeffrey grinned at him and went on eating. It didn't take him long to clean off most of his plate but he left one sausage to be put in a doggie bag.

"That was delicious," he said, "but I have left some room for dessert. Are you going to have some?"

"Of course." Mary answered quickly "I feel as though I haven't had a meal if I don't have dessert."

The waitress came to take their dirty dishes away and then came back to take their orders for dessert. While they were waiting Jeffrey continued with his impromptu history lesson.

"Miller, the Commandant of the Moreton Bay settlement was very pleased and interested in what Oxley was reporting because he was already feeling unhappy with Redcliffe. Two convicts and a soldier had been speared and killed and the water was stagnant   He   sought permission from England and moved the whole settlement up the river. It was three months before they moved and during the three months, they had built huts and store rooms which they left behind. The natives called the buildings *oompie bongs,* later pronounced Humpy Bong, and that name is still used for some clubs and a large state school. Humpybong State School is one of the largest and oldest schools in Queensland. Humpy means hut and bong means dead, so the natives called them dead huts."

"The settlement in Brisbane was very successful. I won't try to tell you its history now but, if you know the streets you might like to know the general lay-out of the huts. The men's huts were along Queen Street. There were a few women and their huts were where the Post Office now stands and the Commandant and the stores were in George Street. There is one more piece of trivia that I will add and then I will finish. In the City Hall there is a small museum and I read an article there that said that Brisbane is the only capital city in the world that stands on a river by the same name."

As they ate their dessert, Mary thanked Jeffrey for such an interesting story and added that both she and George were interested in Australian history but they had concentrated on stories from the outback pioneers because they both had great-grandparents who had been real pioneers. George agreed with Mary but quickly added that time was moving on and he was keen to go home and see whether any of the materials that he had ordered earlier in the week had been delivered. He was also expecting the Brennans to bring Ellen's little family around.

Chapter 29

During their homeward journey they discussed the renovations, Chloe's ambitions, and Jeffrey's job of managing the motel for the following weeks. George also mentioned Mary's idea of staying on at the motel after the swap had been finalised and he told Jeffrey how very happy they would both feel if he would allow them to do that. They were not quite ready to retire because they needed a little more money to set themselves up with a good caravan and a strong vehicle to tow it. They planned to travel around Australia while they were still in good health and they wanted good comfortable and reliable vehicles to travel in.

Jeffrey listened carefully and he was feeling extremely contented and keen to surprise them with their dream car. He told them that he and Chloe would be absolutely honoured if they would manage the business for them.

The distance had passed quickly and they were home again, but George stopped on the side of the road opposite to the house and looked across at it. "Well, Old Lady", he said. "In a month's time, you will be the best dressed and best-looking mansion on this highway."

"That's our plan," Jeffrey laughed.

George drove through the motel driveway and went up to the house to see whether any materials had arrived. However, he wasn't too surprised or disappointed when they were not there. It was only Thursday so there was still time for them to arrive before the weekend.

He assured Jeffrey that he didn't need any help unpacking the groceries, so Jeffrey said good-bye to them and thanked them for a great day which he had enjoyed very much.

Later in the afternoon, Rex and Sylvia Brennan and Ellen arrived with her little family. Jeffrey saw the truck as it passed by on the highway and hurried out to meet them.

George and Mary also saw them as they passed the motel so they followed them in the utility. They all shook hands, but the only ones who needed an introduction, were Rex and Jeffrey.

The crate holding the animals was lifted down by the three men, and Mary was quite surprised when Ellen leaned over it and opened the door. She was expecting them to run towards the fence, but instead they ran straight to Ellen and snuggled into her. legs. She and Jeffrey strolled towards the cow yard and the little pets followed. Jeffrey carried a long trough for their food while the men followed behind with bales of hay and Sylvia carried a bucket full of their favourite dinner which was fruit and vegetables and some special pellets. After the hay was spread over the concrete floor, Ellen was really pleased with their new home and said that it was much bigger than the pen on their farm.

Once the pets were settled and happily eating their dinner, the six people roamed away in pairs. George and Rex were looking around the farm and discussing the renovations and Chloe's big ambitions. Mary and Sylvia went towards the house followed by Ellen and Jeffrey. The house was still very dilapidated and Ellen was coming from a beautiful mansion so Jeffrey had asked Mary to describe, in detail, all of the planned renovations to Sylvia so that she would know that Ellen would be moving into a grand old Queensland pioneer home.

When Ellen was shown her bedroom, she was pleased with the size of it because she had her own furniture and she observed that the room was much bigger than her own. Then Sylvia reminded her that she also had her study furniture and a new lounge suite which would get dirty very quickly. As she spoke, she turned to Mary and told her that they had given Ellen a pretty pink brocade lounge suite for her eighteenth birthday, quickly adding that Ellen also had her own lounge room.

Jeffrey said, "I know exactly where we can put that, and it will be perfectly safe." He then led them to the veranda which he intended to enclose for a library. It would be an unusually long room with four study nooks. Each nook would have enough power points for any office electronic equipment, and he would be depending on Ellen for advice. She would be able to set up her desks and shelves in one of them, and place her lounge chairs in a curve around her area. The library would be a special place and would never be part of an entertainment area, so no one would be sitting on the chairs unless Ellen invited them to do so. Then he excitedly explained that a new open veranda was going to be built beside the library. It would have tables and comfortable chairs, but the only entrance would be through the library so it was for study only. It would be a quiet and peaceful space. A broad smile had spread across Ellen's face, and she looked at her Mum and said, "Doesn't it sound wonderful? I can hardly wait to move here, and remember how distraught I was before yesterday."

Her mother stepped over to her and gave her daughter a hug as she said, "I certainly feel much better now."

Mary had a very tender heart and she was feeling a bit teary as she added, "Remember there will also be a nurse and a house-keeper living here so you should have plenty of time to study."

Jeffrey spoke up and said, "I must start making some serious enquiries, because I have to find them before Chloe comes home."

"I might be able to help you find someone," Sylvia said. "The people from whom we bought our house in Brisbane are retired professionals who are looking for a different life and new experiences. Belinda was a nurse for forty years and is right at the top of her profession and Sebastian was an architect. She certainly would be the perfect help for Chloe unless she thinks that would be too much like her previous work, because they did emphasise that they were looking for new experiences. As for the house-keeping I am sure Sebastian would happily do his share and they could work together. They would probably be in their mid-fifties and are still very active, and they are extremely nice people. I have their phone number if you are interested and they are leaving on Sunday so you would be wise to ring them immediately."

Jeffrey didn't hesitate. He took the number and stepped out on to the veranda to make the call. After a few minutes he went back into the room with a really happy expression on his face and imitated Chloe's little jig on the spot and then put his hands on his mouth while he added a little giggle. "Thank you very much." he said to Sylvia. "They haven't completely accepted the job, but they will be here on Monday afternoon. They have their own big caravan, so accommodation is not a problem, and Belinda said that, even if they decide not to stay permanently, they will stay until I am able to find someone who is suitable."

"Oh. That is marvellous," Mary said. "Once they meet our little girl, they won't want to leave her, and I am sure George will take Sebastian in hand and make a fisherman out of him. Could you think of any better way of starting a 'working' retirement?" Everyone laughed at Mary's enthusiasm, and Ellen said, "That sounds awesome, Jeffrey. I am so really excited and I am looking forward to my new life. Only two days ago I thought that I would never be happy again."

When the three couples met up again, George invited them back to the motel for dinner, and Jeffrey and the Brennans gratefully accepted.

Jeffrey and Ellen walked down the hill to the motel and the adults drove down in their utilities.

Dean and Sam were cleaning an exceptionally large rig at the side of the motel and one of them gave a wolf whistle and they both gave a cheeky wave to the young couple. However, it was Ellen on whom their eyes were set.

The motel restaurant was busy but George and Jeffrey were able to push two tables together and the little group of friends sat down. Immediately, an attractive young waitress stood beside them with a bundle of menus and Ellen was reminded of something that was particularly important to her. She scanned through the menu as she waited for everyone to select their meal while George urged them to choose what they liked and not to worry about the price. It was all 'on the house'.

As the waitress wrote down the orders, she had a pleasant smile for everyone but she saved the biggest for Jeffrey. He was tall handsome and polite and he was exceedingly popular with all of the girls. When Natasha walked away, Ellen looked across at Mary and said, "Mary, I am finishing up at Mc Dowell's Cafe tomorrow night, so I was wondering whether you would have any vacancies for a waitress or a room maid here."

Sylvia interrupted then saying that she had asked Ellen to finish up because she didn't like the idea of her driving home along the highway after a late shift.

"How long have you worked there?" Mary asked.

"Three years. I started when I was fifteen, but Dad has always picked me up when I was on a late shift." Ellen replied.

"I could certainly use you, and with all of that experience you will be a real asset," Mary said. "Bronwyn is getting married next month and, although she hasn't resigned yet, I am not expecting her to work afterwards because they will be living too far away. She is my head girl, so I will be extremely pleased to have you on my staff. If you type out a list of days and times when you are available, and a list of days and times when you are definitely not available, I will work out a roster for you during the week-end."

Ellen thanked Mary, and Sylvia added her thanks too. "That was one thing that was worrying us", she said. "I am amazed at how everything is working out so perfectly. Our house has been a house of horrors and tears ever since the sale was signed and Rex and I felt so guilty because we didn't know how we could save Ellen's little family. I have relatives who own a farm, but they were not much help. They would have accepted them, but they were intending to add them to their flock and let them roam around a huge paddock. It was better than having them sent to the market, but the animals and Ellen would have been exceedingly unhappy. Now I can see that they are going to be thoroughly spoilt again, not only by Ellen, but also by Jeffrey and Chloe."

The mention of Chloe's name brought on a whole new conversation. They all enjoyed a delicious meal followed by several cups of coffee and the conversation went in many directions. After about three hours they all knew each other much better and Ellen's parents were extremely satisfied with the arrangements.

As they were saying good-night, Rex said that he would bring Ellen and her furniture over on Sunday afternoon because they were planning to leave very early on Monday morning.

In spite of all of the conversation that they had, George had forgotten to tell them that Ellen would be living in the staff motel unit for about two weeks and her furniture would be stored in the hay barn. He apologised for being so neglectful but assured them that the barn was completely weather proof and had been hosed out to remove any dust. They had decided to move all of the loose furniture out of the house so that the workers had a clear space. It was going to be a difficult job because the house was so high, but they decided that it was worth the trouble. Rex and Sylvia had enjoyed the company of their new friends and they trusted them completely, so they were not bothered by the different arrangements.

Chapter 30

Friday was a busy day. Jeffrey rang Chloe in the morning to tell her that he wouldn't have time to visit her because Mary was going to show him the motel books and start teaching him how to manage the buying. He felt bad because he thought that his little sister would be disappointed, but she had her own exciting news. She had been moved into a ward with three little girls. They were eight, nine, and eleven years old and they were all best friends already. The little girls were sisters who lived near Redcliffe. They had all been injured in the same accident when their uncle rolled the old truck that they were travelling in. Everyone was hurt but nobody was killed. Some of their family had been taken to the Princess Alexandra Hospital in Brisbane. She had shared some of her treats with them and had told them that they could borrow any of her books that they would like to read. She was also teaching them how to play Ludo, one of her board games, and the nurses had brought in a table and chairs for them to sit at. The little eight-year-old, Carly, was in a wheel chair too but the table was high enough for the chairs to roll under it. Carly's sisters were Rosemary, who was nine and Fiona, who was eleven. Carly's injuries were the most serious but the doctor had promised her that he would keep her sisters in hospital with her until she was ready to go home. Chloe chatted on full of excitement without giving her brother an opportunity to comment. As he listened, he was truly pleased and relieved because he was needed at the house and the motel and he had been afraid that she would be lonely and start asking awkward questions. He listened attentively as Chloe talked until she stopped to take a breath, and then he told her how pleased he was that she had some little friends and he was looking forward to meeting them. She told him how well her own injuries were progressing and she said that her doctor was very pleased with them. However, she was so busy now and enjoying herself so much she didn't mind waiting in hospital a bit longer.

Chapter 31

The timber for the unit and repairs arrived at about ten o'clock and the delivery truck from the hardware arrived soon afterwards. Jeffrey took George's list and checked that everything had been delivered then he rang George who had gone into town to try to use his influence to get a quick approval for the extension. Jeffrey then went down to the motel to have his first lesson on ordering stock.

Jack rang Jeffrey to tell him that he had spoken to a lot of men who were planning to be there the following day so he thought it might be a good idea to hire a barbecue. Lexie would be happy to buy some sausages and steak and his girls would prepare some rice, pasta, and salad dishes.

"That is a great idea," he said. "We will invite their families to come over in the afternoon too. It will go a little way towards showing my appreciation."

"When Mary heard what was happening, she also offered to prepare some side dishes, and Jeffrey told her to add the cost of the ingredients to her account.

On Saturday morning the first team arrived at 6:30 and immediately started constructing the scaffolding. Gradually others arrived and the house and the grounds began filling up with men of all ages and a few women.

Eric, the foreman, had expected that to happen and he had made his own roster for the day. He knew most of the workers and the tradesmen, so he soon found useful work for them to do. He selected other leaders whom he knew would keep the workers busy and organised. Jeffrey had never seen anything like it. Everything was running so smoothly and every person seemed to know exactly what to do. The whole day could have been wasted, but repairs were happening incredibly fast.

Some women arrived with trays of sandwiches and an urn to boil water to make tea and coffee. Some chairs and long stools were placed in shady areas and the workers were encouraged to have a break. However, many of them, although grateful for the sandwiches and a cuppa, had a quick break and then went straight back to work.

Jack arrived with a barbecue and found the most suitable place to set it up, then he wandered around the house admiring the work and passing compliments on how much they had all achieved in one day. As the sun began to set several families arrived, each of them brought plates of food or bottles of drink. George came up from the motel with more tables and chairs. It was going to be a great party. The men kept working until dark and by then every repair had been completed or the problem had been removed. Some windows were too weather -damaged to repair so the window was taken out and would be taken to a glazier who would give it a completely new frame. The biggest jobs were the stairs. It was decided to remove the side stairs and make a completely new set but they couldn't be erected until the extension was completed. The design of the front stairs would be changed. Instead of running down along the front wall, Eric felt that the house was high enough to have a split design. The new stairs would come straight out from the wall. The first section would be wider and stop at a small landing half way down, and from that landing a slightly narrower set would go from it to the left and a similar set would go to the right. "That will look much more interesting. Don't you think?" he asked George and Jeffrey. George slowly nodded his head, but Jeffrey was much more enthusiastic and said, "Yes, I like that idea. It will look quite special."

The barbecue was, as usual, hugely popular. The country people were always ready for a party.

The tables were laden with delicious food and Jack was cooking the steak and sausages to perfection. Some chose a bun and others preferred a plate with a sample of everything, but there was so much to choose that the level on each dish didn't seem to change. The men had healthy appetites and returned for seconds and still the dishes were full. Lexie was a regular caterer and she could see that there was far more food than could be eaten in one afternoon, so she started moving some of the pasta and rice dishes into the refrigerator before they had time to spoil. They would be appreciated for lunch the following day. As the guests reached their food limit, they broke into smaller groups to have a chin-wag with friends whom they hadn't seen for months.

Heidi and Champ were thoroughly enjoying the attention and had eaten more than their share of steak and sausages. The visiting children had chased them around the yard and had thrown the ball for the two dogs, but the two young animals were ready to play on, and didn't give any hint that they were tired.

Eric banged a couple of old pans together to call for silence and then he thanked everyone for their marvellous effort. In one day, they had achieved an incredible goal. He had expected that it would take the whole weekend to repair any damage but instead, it was ready for painting. He held up a booklet and said "Mary has made up a booklet for each family. It records the history of the old house. This house is 132 years old, and back in its younger years, it was the nicest house in this district. When George's ancestors came here, they took up four thousand acres of land and started their sheep station. George and Mary were the most recent tenants and they lived here for forty years.

Now young Jeffrey and his sister Chloe whom you all know were viciously run down and almost killed, will be taking over the farm. Chloe will soon be home from hospital, and it is her dream to turn it into a rescue home for any farm animals that are no longer needed. So, if you have any cows or sheep or fowls or any other animals that are no longer useful, consider contacting Chloe because she will probably want them and they will certainly be given a good home."

There was a quiet mumble through the crowd and some asked questions about Chloe.

It was a full moon which lit up some of the grounds but there were many dark areas and it was not safe for the children to run around, so some of the parents began to pack up. Those who had worked all day were also tired and they were planning to return the following day, so they began to move around among their friends and say good-night.

Chapter 32

Jeffrey had slept at the motel which would be his home for the next two or three weeks, and he was just finishing his breakfast when he saw the first small gang arrive for work. He quickly mounted his bike and rode up the hill to his house.

It was Eric and three other men who were keen to get an early start

"Good morning Jeffrey," Eric said. "I have been able to bring a few extra cans so that each individual can work from his own paint tin instead of having to take turns at dipping. Hopefully it will hurry everything along, without reducing the quality, although I know we will need several more containers".

As they talked two more cars arrived, each carrying four people, and each person had his own can and brush, or roller and tray.

When a group of about thirty had arrived, Eric addressed them.

"The timber in this house hasn't been painted for many years," he said, "and we can't even see what colour it was originally. Therefore, it will soak up the paint as quickly as you brush it on. You will each be given a small area for which you will be responsible. I would like you to use a scraper to remove any lumps and old dried paint that has adhered to the timber and then use the sandpaper to smooth it out again. You might also find that you need a bit of putty occasionally and although I don't have enough cans to give you one each, you will find a can of putty somewhere near you. It will take a bit longer, but we want to give the kids the best job that we can. Brush on as many layers as necessary until it is holding the colour. It would be a good idea to have a break occasionally to let the paint dry. You don't have to hurry. It is far more important to put on a good foundation before the final coat is applied, "he advised.

Some chose to paint an outside wall others preferred to paint inside where they could use a roller. Everyone was busy, and although they were not strictly tradesmen, because they were country people, painting was not new to them.

The hours passed quickly and by mid-afternoon, the house was looking stunning. Again, everyone had put in an enormous effort to give the two kids the best result that they could. Some women had helped with the painting, while others prepared the evening meal. They finished earlier than they had on the previous day and they were extremely satisfied with their weekend's effort. During the week, the carpenters, plumbers, electricians and professional painters would do their work, and if there was anything left for the volunteers, they would be back again the following weekend.

After the volunteers had gone, Mary, George, Lexie, Jack, Jeffrey and Eric sat down at a motel table with a cup of tea or coffee and a tasty snack to finish off their meal and to plan the work for the following week.

George had employed two gangs of workers for each trade. He and Eric both knew the men and were certain that they were hard workers and would do a good fast job, because they were hoping to have all of the construction finished in one week. They wanted the unit, laundry, and second toilet under the house finished and also, the veranda closed in and the new veranda completed They had asked the foreman from each gang to bring as many tradesmen and labourers as they needed to complete the work, and promised them a good bonus if they managed to do so.

The pre-built kitchen would not be delivered until the following Monday, and as they discussed what they could do in the kitchen area during the week, Mary said that she had found it to be a bit dark, especially during dull or wet days. There was only one window in the back wall and she wondered whether that could be changed.

"Yes. That wouldn't be too much trouble," Eric said. "How about if we remove that window and put a row of high louvers along the back wall?" he suggested. As he spoke, he drew his idea on the plan. "We could make them from ceiling down to adult eye level", he said.

George noticed that he had stopped the windows a short distance from a kitchen wall cupboard, and it looked wide enough to have a door there.

"Well, if we do that, I suggest that we put another outside door there and another set of steps", he said as he pointed to the space.

There was a short silence before Jeffrey, who had been listening but not participating in the conversation, spoke. "That is a great idea," he said, "but let's take it further." He had everyone's attention as he added, "Wouldn't it be nice to have another veranda along the back wall with the steps going down from it?"

Mary's enthusiasm burst out as she exploded, "Oh, Jeffrey, that would be marvellous, both for the kitchen staff to have a cool break, but also, if it joins on to the side veranda, guests will be able to roam around three sides of the house."

Everyone listened and looked at the plan. It was Lexie who joined in the conversation then. "Every farm house needs a good pantry," she said, "and that is something that is missing in this big house. The left side could join onto the side veranda, but from the other side of the doorway we could have it closed in for a big country pantry," she added. "I know how important my pantry is. Every month I go into town and stock up on non-perishable groceries. My pantry shelves are full and if we were flooded out for weeks, I could still provide good meals for everyone. This kitchen that we are waiting for is beautiful but if you have a good look, you will see that there is not much storage space." Every person's eyes were fixed on the plan as each one made a comment, then Jeffrey laughed as he said, "Let's do it. This house is growing faster than mushrooms, but I think a pantry will be a tremendous improvement. It is a fantastic idea."

Everyone agreed, which meant that once again, George would be rushing into town to get another quick permit.

They still had a lot of planning to do if the week was going to run smoothly and they were going to get the best possible result. Jeffrey reminded them that Sebastian and Belinda would be arriving the following afternoon and he asked George and Mary whether they would have time to join him when he interviewed them. Mary quickly agreed and George said that he would try to get home in time. As the friends stood up, Rex and Sylvia Brennan drove into the parking lot with Ellen and her furniture. Jeffrey gave a quiet little gasp and dashed out. He didn't admit it but he had forgotten that they were coming. Sylvia and Ellen stepped out and lifted a port and a box off the back of the truck, but as Jeffrey went to take them, they assured him that they could manage but Rex would need his help to unload the furniture. Both George and Jeffrey climbed into the cabin beside Rex and they went on up the hill to the hay barn while Mary led Ellen and her mother to her motel room.

Mary had decided to give Ellen her own small room instead of putting her in the much larger staff room with the other waitresses. On the previous day she had accidentally heard a couple of jealous remarks from the younger girls when they were talking about Bronwyn leaving. She didn't like that sort of behaviour amongst the staff and she decided that she would have to keep an eye on it.

Chapter 33

Monday was an extremely busy day at the house, but George and Jeffrey were not needed so they each went their own way. George went to town while Jeffrey went to the hospital to visit his little sister.

He hadn't told her that he was going to visit her in case something prevented him from going, so she was thrilled and gave a little scream of delight when he walked into the ward.

She was sitting in her wheelchair at the table with her three new friends and he hurried towards them.

Jeffrey had made up four little bags of treats from the motel's shelves and cleared them with the nurses before he went into the ward.

Chloe gave him a long affectionate hug and thanked him and then started to introduce her friends. As he slowly untangled himself from her hug and said hello to each little girl, he acted like a magician and produced the colourful bags. The three girls had been shyly leaning against each other, but a broad smile spread across each little face as they accepted the gifts.

Chloe had told him so much about the girls every time he rang her during the week-end, but she didn't once mention that they were aboriginal children. He felt so proud of her again. The colour of their skin made absolutely no difference. They were just three beautiful little girls and they were her new best friends. Carly, who was in a wheelchair, was eight. Rosemary was nine and Fiona was eleven.

It wasn't long before the three little girls were joining in the conversation and Chloe told Jeffrey that the girls had never had a chance to go to school and she and Lexie were trying to teach them to read before they left the hospital. She praised them highly for how quickly they were learning and picked up a pack of flash cards to prove how many words they knew already. She flashed through the words with each girl eagerly shouting out the correct answer, then she pointed to a chart on the wall. It had each girl's name on it and lots of coloured stars. The girls eagerly talked over each other as they explained how they had earned their stars.

He had allowed enough time for a two-hour visit and that time passed quickly. However, he had heard all about the accident that had injured so many people and where the families lived, and he also heard about the adults who were in hospital in Brisbane. While they were talking, he realised that, as usual, Lexie had become involved and was planning to make some big changes to their lives.

As he was saying goodbye, he promised the four happy, giggling little girls that he would try to visit them again on Thursday. He waved to them and then went down the passage to the nurses' station where he hoped to find out how Chloe was progressing and whether there were any real plans to discharge her yet.

The first surprise that he had was when two of the nurses asked him how the renovations were progressing. It was a secret and he was afraid that Chloe would hear about it. The nurses saw the shocked expression on his face and they immediately assured him that they would not spoil his surprise. They explained that their parents had been among the volunteers on Saturday and had emphasised that they must not talk about it at work because it was a surprise for Chloe. Jeffrey was relieved and was happy to tell them how much had been accomplished already, and he also told them about how much he was hoping would be accomplished by the following weekend.

"Wow. It must be a busy place," one nurse said, and Jeffrey laughed, "It looks like an ant hill today."

They told Jeffrey that the doctors were extremely pleased with Chloe and there was a small chance that she could be ready to go home on Saturday. There was one problem and that was that her doctor wanted a specialist from Brisbane to check her first and he might not be able to visit her before Tuesday.

Jeffrey had been waiting to hear those words for so long and for a moment he found himself hoping that they would keep his little sister here until Tuesday. However, a little rush of excitement brushed that thought away because, although the house could not be finished by Saturday it was looking stunning and it would still be a wonderful surprise for her, and he desperately wanted her home.

"I suppose you would like her to stay here until Tuesday, "one nurse suggested, "so that the house can be finished"

"No, not at all. It would be nice to have everything completed, but it will still be a mammoth surprise for her and she might like to watch them install the two kitchens. She will be particularly thrilled with them because she enjoys cooking and she is a good cook too. The kitchens are being made in a factory and then they can be installed in one day. Mary and Lexie chose the colours and designed them, and the house kitchen will be fabulous They chose red and white with a bit of black for the house and the unit and I can hardly wait to see them myself. However, when my little sister is ready to come home, I will be here as quickly as possible to get her."

His heart was racing and he felt like skipping all the way to the car, but he managed to control that urge.

Chapter 34

It was early in the afternoon and there were not many vehicles on the road so Jeffrey accelerated to the top speed limit of 110 kph. Sebastian and Belinda were due to arrive any time after mid-day and he wanted to be home when they arrived.

The whole area around him was flat with typical Australian bush and he was feeling extremely relaxed, happy, and peaceful. His mind was loaded with wonderful thoughts. How could he be so lucky? In the distance, he could see another vehicle which seemed to be quite long. As he closed the gap between them, he could see that it was a big four-wheel drive, towing a long caravan. He felt sure that it would be his visitors, so he didn't attempt to pass them.

When they drew level with his house, they pulled a little way off the road and stopped, so he parked behind them. He stepped out of his car and walked along the road past the caravan to the driver's door.

"Hi", he said, "Are you Sebastian?"

"I certainly am." a jovial faced elderly man said. "And this is Belinda and I am guessing that you must be young Jeffrey."

"And we are guessing that the house over there must be yours." Belinda said with a friendly smile.

Jeffrey proudly agreed and enjoyed talking about it and explaining the busy activity that was going on there right at that moment. After a short conversation he suggested that they should go on to the motel.

He told them to drive past the front and take the van around the back to where there was a large concrete slab for the van and a power pole for electricity. He said that he would be there to meet them. However, Mary saw them drive past and she went straight out to them. Jeffrey saw that

Mary was meeting them so he went into the restaurant to organise the tables in a quiet area that was reserved for little meetings. He felt that if he could judge them by their looks. he was sure that they would be very compatible, because they had such open friendly jovial faces.

They both stepped out of their vehicle and before introducing himself, Sebastian inhaled a deep breath of air and as he slowly exhaled, he said, "Oh can't you taste and feel that fresh air?"

The women gave a little laugh and Belinda said, "It's the silence that attracts me. Isn't it quiet?" Just as Belinda made her remark, a flock of thirty or forty cockatoos flew over them screeching loudly at each other, and the three new friends laughed.

"Well, they sound better than the roar of traffic," Belinda said.

No one had been introduced and already they were all feeling relaxed and comfortable. Mary spoke first introducing herself and welcoming them to the motel. After a brief conversation and a few more comments about the scenery, she suggested that they might move inside. However, Belinda and Sebastian had one more task to do before they left the van. Together they lifted some panels of fencing off the back of the van and within a couple of minutes they had constructed a sturdy little fence around the door,

and then they each went to a window on either side of their vehicle and called out, "Come on Babies, it's play time." Immediately a little dog appeared at each window and started scratching on the glass and wagging its tail furiously.

"O Dear. I had forgotten about them although Jeffrey did tell us that you had two little well-behaved dogs." While Mary continued to admire the two excited little animals Belinda stepped into the van and handed Sebastian a bowl of water, two soft bones and a large sand tray. As he placed each item on the grass, he commented that they would keep the two babies occupied while they were inside, adding that they had been taught to use the sand tray the same way as a cat would use a litter tray. Before the two visitors left the pet pen Belinda closed the security door which revealed two pet doors and then she hooked the wooden door back against the caravan wall.

"If anything frightens them, they will go through those doors like a bolt of lightning and hide under our bed," Sebastian laughed. Then, almost as though they had arrived to prove his point, Heidi and Champ trotted up to the visitors to check them out. Belinda and Sebastian were suddenly seized by fear but Mary quickly took control and made the two big dogs sit quietly and she assured her new friends that they were completely safe. Sebastian was very impressed, especially when the little elderly lady stroked and hugged the two great big animals.

"Is it safe for me to pat them?" he asked.

"Certainly. They are as gentle as your two little babies that have just disappeared, "she answered and laughed as she imagined four shiny eyes peeping out from under the bed. Soon Heidi and Champ were receiving lots of attention and both Belinda and Sebastian were beginning to believe that Poppet and Pixie would soon be enjoying two enormous playmates.

It had been a long drive from Rockhampton that morning, so the visitors said that they would like to freshen up a little before they sat down to eat.

George had also arrived home so it wasn't long before they were all seated at a round table' The waitress brought them menus and waited for their orders.

Their conversations covered many topics until Belinda asked how Chloe was progressing. Jeffrey had just returned from a visit so they were all eager to hear his latest news. When he told them that she might be home on Saturday, they were all briefly shocked and then their shock turned to excitement.

Belinda said that she would like to know a lot more about her care and current treatment before then and she wondered whether there would be any chance of meeting Chloe while she was still in hospital and, also having a talk with her doctor and other carers.

Jeffrey felt sure that Chloe's doctor would like to talk to her new nurse too and he agreed to try to arrange a meeting for Thursday when he was going back to visit her.

Mary spoke up and said "I am sure you will love her. She is one of the dearest little girls that I have met, and very independent and clever too."

"She is extremely independent, so I am certain that she will want to do as much as she is allowed to do for herself. "Jeffrey said. "You see she was very badly injured and the doctors didn't think that she would live, but she did. Fortunately, her head wasn't badly damaged, but almost every other part of her body was cut or bruised or broken. Not just her limbs but also her internal organs. It happened on that hill out there. A big vehicle hit our little car on her side and she received the full impact. She didn't have time to clip on her seat belt and as our car rolled over and over, she was thrown about inside. I can't tell you any more now, but someday I will tell you the whole story."

Belinda and Sebastian listened intently and then said that they had heard quite a lot about it on the news on TV.

There was silence for a moment and then Belinda told them that they didn't have any children of their own but she had forty-nine years' experience in nursing and most of that time was in the children's ward. She said that she always enjoyed working with children because they were so resilient and loving. Some cases were extremely sad, but it sounded as though Chloe had reached the stage where there were new rewards every day.

It was agreed that Belinda would go to the hospital with Jeffrey on the Thursday and that Jeffrey would try to arrange a meeting with all of Chloe's carers

They had discussed the nurse's duties and then both Belinda and Sebastian were interested in the housekeeping duties.

"Well, I had planned on having two women, so I hope you like house-keeping Sebastian," Jeffrey laughed.

"I am an excellent house-keeper." Sebastian replied with pretend indignation. "I have my best reference here with me."

"That is true. I have always been a shift worker and Sebastian has always been the house-keeper "Belinda said.

"How many people will be living in the house? Sebastian asked.

"Well, there will be Chloe who is eleven. Ellen who is eighteen, Dean who is eighteen and myself, and I am also eighteen, and of course both of you." Jeffrey answered and then he continued. "We each have our own bedroom and we will be responsible for keeping it clean and tidy. However, you will be responsible for cleaning the bed linen on a day that you choose, and we will bring it to the laundry for you. There is enough linen for us to remake our beds before the first set is dry. Dean and Chloe and I would like you to do our general washing and ironing too, but Ellen would like to do her own. However, there won't be much ironing from us because we don't need our daily work clothes ironed. You will also be responsible for everything in the kitchen because someone has to be in charge, but we are like a big family and some of us will always chip in and help. There is a large size dishwasher which will take most plates and dished but it is brand new and I still don't know how to use it. There is also a big washing machine and a new dryer in the laundry with two stainless steel tubs. You will also be responsible for the cleaning and tidying of all of the common areas but I don't think that it will be a big burden because we will spend most of our time in the library and on the library veranda. The library will not be open to visitors because it is where we will have our computers and each of us will have our own study nook. It will also have an abundance of books because both Ellen and Chloe love reading. There will be a huge supply of fiction and nonfiction and you are welcome to read any of them and share the library with us because we would like to make it a calm and relaxing space. You will have your own special nook in the unit but I haven't provided any equipment yet because I didn't know what you would need and I thought it would be better to let you have some input. Ellen has brought several boxes with her and during the time that we have been living here Chloe has raided the book shops and bought any book that had anything to do with nature. They are mainly animal books but also weather, rocks, farming and large outback stations and American ranches. You see she wants to turn this farm into an animal rescue farm and as a hobby, she would like to collect every type of land flightless bird. She wants every chicken, in every different colour and every different size. She will collect other animals as they are offered to her and already has the remainder of Mary's dairy cows and Ellen has brought her little animal family with her. While the volunteers were here last week-end I told them about her dream and several of the workers asked me about some of their old animals that are no longer useful on their farms. One chap asked me about a pet bull which was raised as a pet and is quiet and friendly, but he is also very old and the chap wants to add a new bull to his herd, but he can't while Ferdinand is there and he can't face the thought of destroying him. I told him that I am sure that Chloe will find a nice little paddock for him somewhere and she will make him feel loved.

Belinda was obviously interested in everything that Jeffrey said about the animal farm and Sebastian said, "I can see that you already have Belinda hooked because she loves animals too."

"Absolutely", Belinda said. "You see, I will be doing my best to get Chloe better, and then I won't have a job. I have been wondering what will happen if I fall in love with this place and then I work myself out of work."

"No. That will never happen". Jeffrey quickly replied. "If you can make my little sister better, you will have a job for ever."

Sebastian was ready to make a decision and he looked at Belinda as he spoke. "Well Love. It doesn't sound like a back-breaking job and do you remember some of the work that we considered could be offered to us when we first decided to take the plunge? I am quite keen to have a try at it. Right now, there is only one worry that confronts me, and that is, learning to live with teenagers. Have you any advice to offer us George?"

"Sebastian, if that is your only problem, you have no problem." George replied promptly. "These teenagers are some of the nicest young people that you will ever meet and I would be proud to have any of them as grandchildren. You have met Jeffrey of course, and that is Dean over there talking to the driver of that big rig. Jeffrey has worked here for twenty months and Dean has worked here for nineteen months. Before that time, I had adults doing the same jobs as they do, and I was constantly being called out to the driveway to settle complaints from the truck drivers and travellers. Since the kids have been here, I haven't had one complaint."

"We have two other boys too," Mary said. "Sam is also eighteen, but sadly he is leaving us to go to Western Australia with his parents.

However, I have assured him that his job will still be here if he ever changes his mind. He too is a lovely young man."

"George added, "Corey is slightly older, but he has fitted in well with the younger boys."

Mary quickly added, "Of course you know Ellen. She is the daughter of the people who bought your house."

"O that Ellen." They both replied. "We felt very sad leaving our house. It has been our home for all of our married life, but we both agreed that with such a nice family moving in, it did relieve some of the pain."

"Well Ellen went down on the train this morning She wasn't going to go down until next month when she will be on holidays, but after they left yesterday, she suddenly got the urge to join them, and she threw a few things in a port and went off this morning. She will be back on Sunday" Mary said.

"Until now, Belinda and I have lived a privileged and rather selfish life," Sebastian said. "We had no children, no pets and we each had a good job, so we could afford to do what we liked. However, it was too easy and there was no challenge to it, which is why we decided to set off on this journey. We have been all over the world and have seen as much as we want to see, but we have seen very little of Australia. Two years ago, we bought Pixie and Poppet, and they are our family and they go everywhere with us. Now I feel as though we have just become part of a big family and for me, it is a good feeling."

"I feel exactly the same way," Belinda said. "Now there is one more detail that Sebastian and I discussed. When we are in our own little world, we prefer the names Seb and Billy but we have never shared them with anyone else. Now we are part of a large family and we would be pleased if all of you, plus Dean, Ellen, and Chloe would use our pet names too."

"Oh, that would be so lovely." Mary said. "You are certainly welcome to join our big family."

"There is one small problem," Jeffrey said. "You haven't met all of the family yet. Jack brought us out here and his wife, Lexie has been working with the children's department ever since we arrived and they and their three girls have been Chloe's family while she was in hiding. I was fourteen and Chloe was only seven when our parents were killed in an accident, but since we have been out here Lexie has been like a mother to her. We couldn't involve Mary or George because what we were doing was illegal and we didn't want to get them into trouble with the law. Lexie was working with D.O.C.S. trying to get rid of Robinson, so she was covered.

I am not telling you who your friends should be or who you should include in your family, but will you wait until you meet them before you make your decision? Of course, it is going to be a big leap going from a family of two to a family of thirteen."

"And seven of them are teenagers," George laughed.

"We will be happy to do that," Belinda said. "I feel as though we are starting a completely new life."

They had finished their meeting and their late lunch and they each had somewhere to go.

Sebastian and Belinda had been driving since eight o'clock in the morning and they were keen to have a rest in their van.

George went up to the house to check on the progress that the men had made during the day, before they went home.

Mary went to the kitchen to select the menus for the evening meals.

Jeffrey, whose shift started at midnight, went to his room to have a sleep.

Chapter 35

George was amazed at the amount of work that the teams of tradies had completed.

"It is not just the quantity, but also the quality. The standard is superb." He told Eric as they walked around together. "I hope Jeffrey has those bonuses ready because they will easily finish by the week-end."

"Yes. I agree. It is a shame that the kitchen won't be here until next Tuesday." Eric added.

The two men talked for a while and agreed that most, if not all, of the rooms would be ready for the carpets, the curtains and the blinds by Saturday, and George promised to ring each of the suppliers, the following day. Chloe would be home before everything was finished, but what a wonderful surprise it would be, and she could join in the excitement of moving their furniture back into the house. Her room was the only room that didn't have new furniture because Jeffrey wanted her to have the opportunity to choose what she wanted and, in the meantime, she would use the same second-hand furniture that she had used previously.

It had been a busy night for Jeffrey and in the morning, he was glad to hand over to Corey and then have a shower and breakfast. While he was sitting at the table waiting for his meal, Dean and Sam came into the restaurant and joined him. He just had time to tell them about the meeting on the previous afternoon before Sebastian and Belinda came in and walked straight up to the boy's table. Jeffrey introduced them to each other and offered to bring over two more chairs but they both declined because someone had put the chairs in sets of four and they didn't want to rearrange them.

Mary appeared in the kitchen doorway and then walked over to the group. She and George had already had breakfast so he went on up to the house and hoped that the others would join him as soon as possible.

When the boys had finished their breakfast, they went across to Sebastian and Belinda and told them that they were going up to the house and they were going to put Heidi and Champ on their leads and take them for a walk. They suggested that it would be a nice walk for Pixie and Poppet too, and it would be a good opportunity to introduce the dogs to each other. They added that all four dogs had to learn to accept any new animals that were brought on to the farm.

"Yes. We would like to do that, and I am sure the babies will be excited too." Belinda said.

They had another cup of coffee while they waited for Mary, who was busy serving at the counter, to join them.

The three adults went back to the caravan and collected the two very excited little dogs and then strolled casually towards the house. The first thing that attracted Sebastian's attention was a huge vegetable garden. He liked gardening and always had a small patch of vegetables at home, but this one was as big as his whole house block. Most of it was covered with straw and two men were spreading more straw around. There was a myriad of small green plants between ten or fifteen centimetres high and he was curious as to what they were.

When the men saw them, they recognised Mary and knocked off work to talk to their visitors. She introduced everyone and then let Sebastian take over the conversation.

"I was admiring your vegetable garden," he said," I have always had a small patch at home and I was hoping to be able to make one here just for the fun of it, but I don't think that I could compete with this one." he laughed.

"Why compete? Why not join us?" Nathan said. "If you like gardening, you are very welcome to work in this one. We won't be here much longer this morning but when you see us here again come on over and we will show you how the watering system works and answer any questions that you have and then you can go your hardest and work here any time that you like."

"Oh! I would really like that." Sebastian said. Then he turned to Belinda and Mary and said "This adventure just keeps getting better and better".

When they left the vegetable garden Belinda led them across to the pen where she could see Ellen's little family. Mary explained their history as Gertie the goat began to show off to get their attention. Gertie walked over her see-saw and then stood up on her back legs and paraded around her pen. The three humans laughed and gave her a clap and she seemed to know that her performance was appreciated.

It was a simple action but once again it was a new experience for Sebastian and Belinda who had never had the chance to stroke a goat, a sheep and a pig. Pixie and Poppet were ready to play too, but when they barked at the other animals, Sebastian quickly said "Hush!" and both dogs sat down ready to listen to his next command.

The house was surrounded by a picket fence, in keeping with its date line. When they reached the gate, Mary was a step in front of the other two and she put her hand on the latch and as she did so she looked straight at Sebastian and Belinda and said in a firm voice,

"Billy and Seb, welcome to your new life and your new home."

They each had a little laugh and Billy said "Thank you Mary. That is a wonderful thing to say."

Seb looked around the front garden where he was surrounded by flowers and said, "And what a beautiful place to be entering. Who has set up this amazing garden?' he asked.

Mary told them once again how badly Chloe had been injured and how no one expected her to survive. People were shocked and disgusted with that callous brute who had tried to kill the children and when Chloe began to improve, and then fight her way back to life, they all wanted to help her. We had crowds of volunteers here replacing batons, repairing windows and stripping off paint. This garden was a gift from the local plant nursery who donated the plants and paid professional landscapers to set it up. The back yard is extra-large with just two shady trees and a couple of garden chairs, so that the dogs have somewhere to play."

"Well, I can imagine me making good use of those chairs over near the wall." Billy said.

They had all moved into the yard and Mary led them around the house to the downstairs door.

"We will have a look at your unit first" she said. "I am sure it will be very important to you, but please remember that, although it is small you have the full use of the living room, library, kitchen and verandas upstairs. This unit is just a little retreat for you when you want a bit of privacy."

They walked under the house and once again the visitors were impressed with the floor with its coloured pebble concrete.

They had a quick peep into the toilet and laundry which were attractively tiled but the plumbing was not complete. However, the washing machine and tubs were there for them to see. Mary then led them into their unit. Jeffrey had been through earlier and he had turned on the special lighting that was hidden near the ceiling. A string of little lights provided a bright white light throughout the unit.

"What a charming, cosy little unit," they both agreed. It had plenty of cupboards and plenty of floor space for them to move around.

"Oh! what a beautiful lounge suite" Billy exclaimed as she walked over and sat on it. "It is also soft and comfortable."

"I am so glad that you like it. I wanted to buy it but I didn't think it was suitable for upstairs, and then the bright idea hit me, 'Buy it for the unit'. At that time, I didn't know who would be living in the unit, but I just had to buy it because it is so pretty."

"Well, I am glad that you did," Billy laughed.

Seb said, "You know, when we made up our minds to go ahead with this adventure, we were preparing ourselves to accept shearers' sheds for accommodation. I keep expecting to wake up from this dream."

"No. It is not a dream in that sense, but it is the dream of a couple of nice kids who have had to cope with some terrible tragedies during their young lives and now they have a comfortable inheritance that is allowing them to fulfil their dreams."

"Let's go upstairs and see what other surprises are awaiting us," Mary said.

"What is this outdoor enclosure for? Seb asked.

Mary pointed upwards and explained that the floor above them was an extension of the house and someone suggested that this space would make an excellent shade-house for pot -plants. "However, I think I know what you are thinking, and yes it would be an excellent little run for Poppet and Pixie. We could still have hanging plants but keep the floor empty for the babies," she said.

As they climbed the stairs Mary told them that she expected that they would find a few more surprises upstairs. When she reached the veranda, she casually waved her right hand along the veranda and said that it wrapped around the house to the front stairs, then she looked into the long room on her left just as one of the men working in there saw her and said, "Hi Mary. We could do with some of your advice here. We were wondering how far apart we should place these shelves."

She introduced the men to Sebastian and Belinda who were stunned to hear that the long narrow room was a pantry. It was a good conversation starter and they each checked the shelves that had already been placed and made suggestions about the height of some products that would be stored there. From there they wandered into the kitchen which was finished except for the built-in cupboards which would arrive the following Tuesday.

There were no curtains, blinds or carpets but the visitors were still thrilled with everything that they saw. Their own home that they had sold was a beautiful home in a wealthy suburb but this home had a charm that a modern home could not claim.

Chapter 36

After they left the house, Mary led them on a short excursion around the farm. She could see the remainder of her cow herd down in the paddock and told them that they were very old but they would never be sent to market to be slaughtered. They would live out their lives in comfort. Although they were not producing milk, they were fed with hay and a special supplement each morning to encourage them to come down to the house fence. Chloe had insisted on that so someone could check the numbers in case one was down and couldn't get up. She is so kind and thoughtful. She is always alert to any problems.

Then Mary pointed towards the highway and said that some of their young friends were going to start a riding school over near the highway. They had sneaked Chloe out on a pony while she was in hiding and together, they decided that it might be a nice way to earn some pocket money to help them through university. They already have the ponies, so they just need a small yard fenced off and a nice little shelter shed. Because it is near the highway, it will be its own advertisement. Next to it, Jeffrey is planning to build a veterinary clinic. Ellen is qualified now, but she is going to work at a clinic in town for twelve months to gain more practical experience. The job is part time but she will also work for me in the restaurant as often as she can. Sebastian and Belinda listened with interest. This really was the beginning of a new life.

They started walking back towards the motel when the three boys caught up with them, and they had Heidi and Champ with them. Pixie and Poppet were straining on their leads trying to sniff the noses of the big dogs, but Heidi and Champ just stood there looking very alert but not at all aggressive.

"You cheeky little imps" Sebastian said, "You could get your heads bitten off."

"We will have to watch them for a while, but I don't think we are going to have any problems at all "Jeffrey said.

Pixie and Poppet were enjoying the new smells and the attention that they were receiving. When they reached the open space near the motel Sebastian and Belinda decided to let the little dogs have a free run while the boys kept Heidi and Champ on their leads. Belinda was worried, but Jeffrey felt sure that Heidi and Champ would not hurt them. At first the two little ones ran anywhere and everywhere just enjoying their freedom for the first time in nearly two days. Then one of them saw a new entertainment and raced straight up to Heidi. Poor Heidi didn't know what to do. She stepped back a bit closer to Jeffrey who was holding her lead and then she gave a playful pounce towards Pixie who pranced around excited to have a new playmate. Jeffrey kneeled down next to Heidi and placed his arm around her shoulders and talked to her. Meanwhile Champ and Poppet were also having a little meet and greet session which made the adults laugh. It was obvious that they accepted each other and everyone felt sure that they would soon become a set of odd playmates.

After a cup of coffee and a snack back at the restaurant, George and Sebastian went back to the house to clean each room that had been completed. Sam had some packing to do and Dean and Jeffrey went to work in the driveway, while Mary and Belinda did some work in the restaurant.

Chapter 37

Wednesday was a sad good-bye for Sam. He and Dean and Jeffrey had become very close friends but his parents and family were moving to Western Australia and had pleaded with him to go with them. He had been a tremendous support for Jeffrey when he was going through a bad time and would certainly have joined him in the house if he was not leaving. Dean saw Jeffrey hand Sam a cheque but he didn't know how much it was worth and Jeffrey didn't tell him. However, he did know that Jeffrey had always planned to buy Sam a car so he felt sure that it would be an equal amount.

George took the opportunity to take his new friends out on the river and introduce them to the popular sport of fishing. Mary had decided not to go but she said that she would cook them a special dinner if they brought home a good feed. George had fished in the river since he was a young boy and his father had taught him well. Some of the river was shaded, some was sunny and there were deep potholes in some areas. George knew where the fish liked to loiter and he moved down the river to his favourite spot, then helped Sebastian and Belinda put the bait on the hooks.

When Belinda felt a nibble, George helped to reel the fish in. It was a very good size and Belinda was so excited that she almost had a wet celebration.

"Now do you understand why I insisted on each one of us wearing a life jacket?" he laughed.

They sat and fished for nearly three hours, until George announced, when he pulled in number seven fish that they had enough. Mary would cook these along with an abundance of vegetables and turn it into a huge

121

feast. The two new fishermen were amazed at how quickly those three hours had passed. George explained to them that he never took more than he needed for any special occasion, and the amount that they had caught would be enough for six or seven people, even with Jack and two teenagers included.

They had each had some success and were extremely proud of themselves.

"Chalk up another new experience, "Sebastian said. "I have always been told that it is a relaxing and a refreshing past-time and I must agree, "he added.

By the time that George had cleaned and filleted the fish, Mary had the oil hot and was ready to start cooking. Belinda was keen to help so she prepared her favourite dessert. The meal was for all of the house mates but not the public so Mary wanted to have it finished before the afternoon rush of travellers started.

What a feast it had been turned into, and as the newly formed family sat around the table chatting and laughing, Sebastian reminded them once more that they would like all of them to use their pet names, Billy and Seb.

Chapter 38

When Belinda woke on Thursday morning, she lay still for a few moments planning her day. This was the day when she would meet the absolute nucleus of her work. She was being employed to care for Chloe. Everyone had emphasised that she was a lovely child, sensible, completely compliant, determined, and beautiful. However, she had heard someone make the remark frequently that Chloe had insisted on some particular plan. Could she be a spoilt little girl who always expected to get her own way? She had met similar children in hospital, and it always made it difficult to give them the correct treatment if they had different ideas. She would soon be able to judge for herself because Jeffrey had made an appointment for them to meet all of her hospital carers at eleven o'clock.

Jeffrey, Mary and Belinda arrived at the hospital at twenty minutes before eleven and slowly wandered towards the door while also glancing around the grounds which Belinda admired. They went to the first nurses' station and were directed to the waiting area in the purple section.

Right on eleven o'clock they were called into the doctor's room. There were two men, one of whom was her regular doctor and a specialist from Brisbane, as well as the three nurses who normally cared for Chloe. As they were introduced, they were greeted with friendly smiles and words of welcome.

Most of them had met Jeffrey and even Mary, but the young nurses were especially eager to meet Belinda. The doctor had phoned the head of the hospital where Belinda had worked for most of her career and found that she had an exceptionally good name and was a true legend among the medical staff.

The doctor was obviously enjoying himself as he read out loudly a fax which he had received in response to his enquiries. Then he said, "I feel honoured to meet you, and Doctor Patterson here apparently knows you quite well and he has backed every word in this fax." Belinda felt slightly embarrassed as she glanced at her friends who had enormous smiles of appreciation on their faces. They knew that they had won the jack-pot in finding such a nurse for Chloe.

Each of the staff had a few words to say about Chloe's treatment and her personality and then one of the girls went away and came back with Chloe in her wheel chair.

She didn't know that her family would be there and she gave a little squeal of delight and then started giggling. She had quite a contagious giggle and soon caused some of the adults to start laughing too.

The doctor told Chloe that he would like her to stay with them for four more days so that she could finish the physiotherapy course that she was currently working on and then she could start the second section with Belinda at home.

Belinda was really impressed when Chloe didn't complain. She could have expected the doctor to tell her that she was ready to go home when she saw her family there, but she just counted the days off on her fingers and then in a bright and excited voice added, "Can I go home on Monday?"

Her doctor didn't answer or put any mile-stone requirements in front of her, instead, he gave her a kind and understanding smile and nodded his head.

She had been in hospital for nearly three months and had to endure some painful treatment and tiresome and painful physiotherapy but she had never once complained. A couple of times she had stated the simple wish that she would like to go home, but she always accepted that her wish could not be granted. Now, home was only four days away.

Jeffrey was sitting next to Chloe who was in her wheelchair and she turned towards him with her arms stretched out for a hug and crying bitterly as she almost shouted, "Jeffrey I am coming home. Jeffrey, I am coming home."

This simple little action had such a dynamic effect that there wasn't a dry eye in the room.

A few more words of praise and encouragement were said and then the little group moved out of the room with Jeffrey wheeling the chair while Belinda stayed behind for a short talk with Doctor Patterson to renew her friendship and to ask a few questions about Chloe's abilities and limits.

They walked down two passage ways and as they turned into the third, they saw three little heads peeping around the doorway. The three of them quickly disappeared and then, just as quickly, Carly's wheel chair was pushed into the passage and then it was given a hearty shove towards the visitors causing a burst of laughter.

However, the nurse who was walking with them did not appreciate the funny side of the incident and quickly took hold of the chair and hurried towards the ward.

The family slowed down to give her a chance to reprimand the pranksters without interrupting her. Chloe was laughing and she said "I'll bet Rosemary did that." As they waited outside, they heard the nurse say, "Rosemary, I know you were just having some fun with Carly, but that was a very dangerous thing for you to do. If Carly had panicked and pulled on the brake unevenly, she could have tipped the chair over or crashed into the wall. Please don't ever do that again. If you did that to Chloe, you could jar her back and cause permanent damage."

When the family heard the nurse compare the possible damage to Chloe the funny side disappeared and they began to worry that her new friends might be too boisterous for her. However, when Mary and Jeffrey had a chance to have a conversation with the nurse later, she did assure them that, that boisterous behaviour was completely out of character and she was confident that they would not repeat it. She even smiled as she said that before Chloe had been put in the ward the girls were quite shy, but Chloe had encouraged them to play tricks on the nurses, and they had come out of their shell a lot since she had been with them. She also said that they were excited because they would probably be leaving the hospital on the following Friday to go and stay with a friend on a farm.

Mary had given her bag of sweets to Nurse Casey to share out during the weekend, but Belinda opened her bag which revealed a variety of gifts. There were pretty Chinese folding fans, handkerchiefs and little gift boxes containing powder, a comb, perfume and soap. She then took out an atlas and a globe of the world for them to share.

"Wow!" Chloe said, "We have some work to do during the next three days,"

"It looks as though someone has already done a lot of work. Who made all of these marvellous charts?" Belinda asked.

"Lexie" they all shouted at once.

Belinda had seen all she needed to see of Chloe to know that she was the lovely little girl that everyone had described and she was looking forward to working with her young patient.

Chapter 39

They took the good news home to the family and suddenly the mood of each one was full of excitement and urgency. Sebastian and George had been working hard on the house since Wednesday afternoon and as soon as the workmen were finished with a room they moved in and cleaned it thoroughly. They vacuumed, and where necessary, they mopped, and they polished the windows until they were sparkling.

As some of the rooms were completely finished, George had asked the carpet layers to start on them, because he was afraid that the whole house might be too much for them to complete in one day and then their other plans would be spoilt.

On Friday, Belinda and Mary went shopping for groceries to prepare for a big barbecue that evening and a welcome home party on Monday for Chloe. The house refrigerator and freezer were new and empty, and they were both very large, so they had ample room to store any cold food and, of course, they had an enormous pantry to store any other food.

Late on Friday the whole house was completed. Every necessary nail and screw had been inserted and every lick of paint had been applied. Once again, the men's families had arrived and all of the ladies who had been connected with the gigantic project brought plates of goodies.

It was a great celebration, and after they had made a brave attempt at eating all of the delicious food, they started on party games and dancing until midnight.

The smooth pebble concrete floor provided an excellent dance floor and it had its first experience at being the centre of entertainment.

During the day, Sebastian, George, Jeffrey and Dean had brought the old beds and some mattresses across from the barn so that Lexie and Jack and their three girls would have somewhere comfortable for them to sleep after the celebrations were over. There wasn't much of the night left but they could have a rest before the busy weekend that they were facing.

Jack and Lexie slept in a spare room but the girls chose to sleep on the open veranda where they could look up at the stars.

On Saturday, Lexie and her girls worked in the library. They were amazed at how many books Chloe and Ellen had collected and Sebastian also added a box full. It was a big room that had a massive amount of shelving and they all agreed that as time moved on and more books were added, trying to find any particular book could be very time consuming and ultimately would become a nightmare, so they decided to use the library system that the university used and teach Jeffrey, Chloe and Dean how to use it. It took the four of them the whole day to place the books, and to enter them on the computer. When they were finished, they stood at the end of the room looking at what they had created and even feeling slightly envious, although at the same time, they were delighted when they imagined Chloe's reaction. She had faced so much tragedy in her short life.

Ellen emailed Jeffrey to say that she did not need anyone to pick her up from the railway station on the Sunday morning because she was going to stay at Rockhampton for the night and then go home by car early the following morning. That had everyone puzzled because her car was out in the parking lot.

Sebastian had moved the caravan up to the house and parked it near the side fence.

The two little dogs were allowed to run loose and they were checking out all of the new smells, while Belinda and Sebastian were moving all of their things out of the caravan and into their unit. Every day had been a new adventure and now they were setting up their new home.

Jack, George, Jeffrey and Dean were loading the old furniture that had been stored in the barn, onto the farm slide and then George was using the tractor to drag it through the double gate at the back of the allotment and right up to the lift.

Mary was very tired and not feeling well so she was affectionally ordered to go back to bed and have a much-needed rest. Mary and George sometimes forgot that they were in their late sixties and they tried to keep up with the young ones.

Through the day they nibbled their way through the left-overs from the barbecue while Sebastian and Belinda kept up a supply of tea and coffee.

The house was looking magnificent with the old furniture in place. It really was quite nice and suited the age of the house. They were keeping Chloe's bedroom furniture until she was able to choose what she wanted and Jeffrey decided to keep his too. However, he did change to a queen size bed and he added a high chest of drawers. Ellen's beautiful pink lounge suite had been put into the library and it gave the room a really luxurious appearance. At the end of the day everyone was tired and they each drifted down to the motel for dinner. Jack and Lexie stayed one more night, not to work, but just to socialise and have some fun. Lexie and Belinda were so much alike in personalities that they became instant friends and Jack and Sebastian were also enjoying each other's company. When the meal was over, they said good-night to the others and went back to the house to freshen up and spend a few hours playing cards.

It had been a hard day for George who was ready for a good rest. Dean and Jeffrey were responsible for the driveway for the next two shifts and Jeffrey took the first one while Dean had a sleep, and then he took over until morning. Now that Sam had gone, they had one less worker and they were hoping that he would soon be replaced. Fortunately, Corey was always happy to do more shifts so he was sleeping at the motel and filling in as much as he could.

Because they had all worked so hard on Saturday there was nothing urgent for them to do on Sunday.

Jack and Lexie and their family went home. Mary, Belinda and Sebastian went to church and the boys enjoyed a quiet and lazy morning until Ellen arrived in her new car.

There was great excitement. She was interested in the house and they were interested in her new car. Her parents had bought it for her because her old car was not reliable and they were afraid that it might break down while she was out on the highway. However, she had no intention of selling it. Instead, she invited everyone to use it as a farm vehicle.

The day passed quickly and Corey did an extra half a shift so that they could have a family meeting.

Chloe was due home on Monday, the kitchen would be installed on Tuesday and then their normal and permanent program would begin, so it was important to understand how such a busy house-hold would run smoothly.

Sebastian began the meeting by saying, "From Tuesday onwards, Billy and I will have the responsibility of keeping this house in order, but it is important that we all know what part each of us must play. I have given it some thought and I don't see how I can provide breakfast and lunch for everyone because you will all require it at different and irregular times. Would it suit all of you to find yourself something to eat when you are ready for it? I will however try to always have something suitable for you to get quickly, and of course, this does not include Chloe. We will both look after all of her needs."

They all agreed that that would be the best way to handle it and they assured him that they wouldn't let themselves starve.

"If you will choose a suitable time for dinner, I will have a good two course meal ready at that time each evening and I will keep it hot for anyone who cannot be ready on some occasions."

Ellen spoke up then saying, "We had a family rule that if anyone used a plate or cup etc they had to rinse it off and put it straight into the dishwasher. Deirdre was our maid but that was one small way that we could help, and it really does not take very long, and it helps to keep the kitchen tidy."

Again, everyone agreed, then Billy reminded them that she and Seb had always lived on their own and their house was always spotless and tidy. "One of our fears is that we will be finding shoes or cardigans left in the common rooms and mud tramped into the house. At present this house, although it is old, it is completely clean and we would like to keep it that way. We would like Pixie and Poppet and of course, Heidi and Champ to be allowed to come upstairs but only in the kitchen and dining room where the floors are hard. Is that how you would like to have it?" Billy asked Jeffrey.

"Yes certainly. That was our rule and the dogs know that. I am amazed at how well they are getting on," Jeffrey added.

"Yes, we are too. They are like four little puppies playing together," Seb said. "I am, however, a tiny bit worried that there might be some jealousy when Chloe comes home. Heidi and Champ will certainly remember her and they will be looking for a lot of attention. At the same time our little girls will see her as a new playmate and they will also want her attention, and I know that they can be thorough little pests when they set their mind on something. Heidi and Champ are beautiful, loveable animals but one bite could do so much damage, so if everyone is watching for a change in their moods, I am sure we will find a solution at that time."

There were no further questions so Seb asked, "Well, instead of waiting for Tuesday, I have two large casserole dishes just waiting to be useful, so would you like us to cook dinner tonight?"

"Yes!" was the very enthusiastic reply, so he said "Right. Dinner will be served at 5:30."

The three young friends were sitting in the T.V. room watching a game of rugby league when Dean said, "I am so hungry I could eat a horse." Just then a very gruff voice said, "Don't you dare."

They looked around quickly and saw Sebastian coming through the doorway carrying a tray loaded with three mugs of steaming hot milk coffee and a plate of biscuits.

"Oh Seb, you are a lifesaver," Dean said. "I was just weighing up my chances of living until 5:30."

"Well, Billy and I were hungry and we didn't want you to eat one of the ponies. Seb joked.

Chapter 40

The meal on Sunday night was absolutely delicious and the artificial family began to feel a strong bond of friendship. They talked and joked with each other and even Seb and Billy who had been afraid that they could not find a common bond with teenagers were surprised at how much they had enjoyed their company.

It was Monday morning and all of the conversation was about Chloe. Nurse Casey had asked Jeffrey not to come to the hospital until one o'clock. Chloe's therapy finished at eleven o'clock and then they wanted to give their four favourite patients a special dinner.

Jeffrey was restless all morning. He fed the animals and checked their pens, then he checked Chloe's bedroom again and the library. He wanted everything to be perfect. He left home in Dean's car at twelve-fifteen which was far too early, because he wanted to drive slowly and think about Chloe. He went through the motel driveway and out on to the highway. When he drew level with the house he pulled over to the side of the road and stopped. The house looked fantastic and he smiled as he thought of Chloe's reaction. then his eyes roamed across to the hill. It had taken him several weeks to walk or ride down that hill without having a flashback to that terrible morning and he wondered whether Chloe would be haunted by it. He was thinking that he should have had that tree cut down, but then he remembered that Chloe was unconscious and she might not remember much about the smash, only Robinson's appearance at the house. He drove on slowly, trying to think clearly. It did look different now because there was a bitumen path leading down to the motel and an enormous vegetable garden. Four men were building a strong fence which would be part of Ferdinand's paddock. He hadn't discussed the position of Ferdinand's paddock with Chloe so he hoped she wouldn't be disappointed with it. His thoughts raced on and on and then he had arrived at the hospital. He sat in the car until a few minutes to one and then he moved it to the pickup spot.

As he walked through the doorway into the hospital his heart was beating madly and he couldn't stop shaking. He had waited three months for that moment, and if Chloe cried, he knew that he would not be able to control his own emotions.

He reached their ward, gave a little knock on the door and walked into an amazingly beautiful room. There were balloons, and streamers of every shape and colour, but best of all were the happy giggles and clapping from the four little patients. There was no place for tears, just cuddles and clapping and laughter. Chloe's port was packed and two large cartons containing her books and other gifts that she had received in hospital were standing next to it. Three nurses were there to see her off, so one pushed her wheel chair and the other two helped to carry her luggage out to the car. As they moved off Chloe called back to her friends, "Be good. I'll see you on Thursday."

They didn't take the wheelchair with them because there was a new manual one ready for her at home and a motorised one for her to use outside.

As they drove off Chloe almost shouted with delight, "Jeffrey, I am so happy!" then she took her phone out of her pocket and rang Mary to tell her she was coming home, then she was still excited as she rang Billy. Her very relieved brother just smiled happily. He was content to let Chloe do the talking and she didn't stop. She was half way through a word when the house came into view. She gave her typical little scream and then said, "Jeffrey the house is beautiful. It is just how we always wanted it. No. It is bigger and look at the steps. Aren't they great? Everything is so different."

He had parked the car on the side of the road so that she could have a good look at the house and all of the surroundings. There was just enough room with the tight seat belts for Chloe to wriggle around and hold out her arms for a hug and the brother and sister sat there affectionately and gratefully embracing each other. After a few more remarks Jeffrey drove on. He knew that Mary and George and Dean would all be at the house so he just gave the rest of the staff a little toot of the horn and went on up the hill.

Chloe was glancing around everywhere but her eyes were mainly focused on the house and the people who were standing at the front fence. Jeffrey gently lifted her out of the car and sat her in her new wheel chair and then the hugs and kisses started. Chloe was home!

Chapter 41

After the loud and extremely enthusiastic welcome, they all went through the gate with Billy pushing the chair.

"Oh Jeffrey! Who planted this beautiful garden?" Chloe shouted.

"That is a gift from the Bush Shack Nursery." Jeffrey answered. "They gave us the plants and provided the professional gardeners to establish it."

"I love it," Chloe said, "and there is a garden seat so that we can sit and enjoy it."

Billy and Mary and Chloe went up in the lift but the others raced up the stairs to be there to meet them.

Chloe was thrilled with her ride in the lift and she had already realised that there had been many more improvements so she was waiting eagerly to reach the veranda, but the lift was very slow.

The others had all reached the veranda before the lift did and once again, she was met with a sea of smiling faces.

Nothing could take the smile off Chloe's face as Billy wheeled her onto the new veranda floor. There were no old bamboo curtains. They had been replaced with gleaming white rails and batons. The veranda wrapped around one side of the house but was blocked by a wall on the other side. Chloe was surprisingly quiet because she was completely overwhelmed. "Are you all right Dear?" Mary asked.

"Yes, thank you Mary. It is awesome. I just can't believe that this is our old home."

"Now where will we go next?" Billy asked the group. The loudest response was, "Around the corner" so she led the way.

They went past four of the bedrooms but the doors were closed so she continued on to the back veranda. The most Chloe said was "Wow! I can't believe this. We even have another veranda and another set of stairs" There were murmurs and comments from the group but Chloe was trying to take it all in. When Billy reached the pantry and the kitchen doors, she looked at Jeffrey and asked him which one she should open. He quickly pointed to the pantry so she opened it and pushed Chloe in.

"Wow!" Chloe shouted again. "Wow. Look at all of those groceries and there are still more empty shelves." She had such a broad smile on her face that everyone else also smiled and each one began to point to some of the special treats.

From the pantry they went to the kitchen which, although it was not finished, it still looked amazing. Jeffrey quickly explained that the most important furniture would be installed the following morning. Chloe glanced around, completely mesmerised by what she saw.

The floor was an intriguing pattern of red and white tiles, a red splash back on the wall behind the space for the sink, a white freezer and a large white refrigerator. The bench tops would be white, but the stove top and sink would be black. Beautiful matching curtains covered the high louvre windows. It was a big room and Mary, who had helped Lexie to choose the design, pointed to the spaces on the wall where cupboards would be installed and then she stepped out the size of an island bench that would go through the middle of the room.

Chloe had just met Sebastian downstairs but she liked him. She liked the look of him and she liked his voice.

Sebastian said, "Mary. You and George will have to join us for our first dinner cooked in our new kitchen. If the men finish early enough tomorrow night, we will have it then. However, if they are late, I don't want to have a hurried meal so then we will have a special dinner on Wednesday night."

"Thank you Seb. We would love to." Mary answered.

"Sebastian. Can I cook sometimes?" Chloe asked.

"Of course, you can Sweetheart," he said, "and you can help us anytime you like. I have been told that you have some interesting recipes from other countries and I am eager to see them."

They went from the kitchen into the dining room which was only partially separated from the kitchen by a tall narrow cupboard which had a few ornaments and a huge bunch of flowers in a wide deep vase which was a gift from Mary and George. As Chloe admired it, Mary told her that it belonged to George's mother and that vase always stood on the same shelf on that cupboard. They had taken it with them when they moved into their little unit but now, they decided to return it to the house and its old position. Tears began to glisten in Chloe's eyes as she listened to Mary and she stretched up her arms for a hug.

Then she saw the huge table with the matching chairs.

"Wow that is a family size table.," she said as she clapped her hands together and then placed them over her mouth.

"We have a large family now." Jeffrey said with a little laugh.

As they moved out of the dining room, they entered the junction of two hallways. One went straight ahead to the front veranda and the other went to the left to Chloe's special surprise, so once again, Belinda looked towards Jeffrey for a direction, without speaking he pointed straight ahead.

Someone had been through and opened the bedroom doors. One was the entrance from the hallway and the other led on to the veranda. They also opened the windows and the curtains and raised the blinds so that the rooms were bright and airy. Once again Chloe gasped a deep breath. She recognised it as Jeffrey's room but it was so different. His furniture was the same except for a big queen-sized bed and immediately she noticed the new chest of drawers. His bedspread was grey with large splashes of black and yellow, and the carpet and curtains had been chosen to blend in with the bedspread.

It was a beautiful bright room and Chloe's memory flashed back to their first day. She looked up at her brother who was looking at her eager to see her reaction. "Isn't it brilliant?" she said, then in a more serious voice and serious face she said, "Do you remember our first days? We had to sleep in our sleeping bags until Jack brought our furniture on the Monday. And remember I was too frightened to sleep in another room. I slept in here for a few weeks until I was brave enough to sleep on my own."

\He leaned over his sister and gave her a hug as he said, "Yes Little Mate, I remember but we don't have to worry about that anymore because we have been blessed with the best friends anyone could have and Nanna and Pop have been so good to us."

Everyone was silent as Chloe and Jeffrey fought to control their emotions, but Mary could not control hers any longer and her body began to shake as she thought of this brave little girl who had needed help and company and she wasn't there to give it to her.

Belinda then quietly reminded them that people would be arriving for a party in another two hours so they moved on to the next room which was Chloe's. Sebastian excused himself because he had to go down to the motel where he had been preparing some of the party food.

When Belinda pushed her into her room her reaction was one of sheer excitement. She was back in her own bedroom. Jeffrey started to explain that they decided to keep her old furniture until she was well enough to go with him to choose some new cupboards.

"No," she said in a very firm voice. "I want to keep my old furniture because it means so much to me. I think I will need more hanging space though. The nurse who was packing my port counted twenty-three dresses I have a lot of shorts and blouses too because Lexie and Pamela brought me some new clothes nearly every time that they visited me."

Everyone laughed while Chloe was looking around her room with wide excited eyes. "It is absolutely beautiful. Who chose this beautiful bedspread and the carpet and curtains and the blind? I could never have chosen anything so gorgeous."

Jeffrey told her that Mary and Lexie had been given the job of choosing all of the accessories for the house. He said that it was a huge responsibility and they had done an excellent job and he was extremely grateful.

After a little more chatter, they moved on to Ellen's room which was full of expensive and extremely beautiful furniture.

Ellen spoke up quickly saying that she wanted to bring her own furniture and the colourful carpets, curtains and blinds in this room just set it off beautifully. It looked better than it did in her own bedroom. Chloe's room had a basic pink colour with pale grey and a touch of black. Ellen's room was mainly lilac with a touch of grey and a tiny splash of black.

As they were leaving Ellen's room Billy reminded them about the time once more. She said that she would like to show Chloe the other side of the house and then start getting ready for the guests. She looked down at Chloe and said, "Darling, "Do you mind if we leave downstairs until later?"

"No." Chloe replied with a smile, "Can we see your room first, because it is on the other side, isn't it?"

"Let's see." Billy said.

They all smiled at each other as Billy wheeled Chloe back towards the library which Chloe thought was Billy's and Seb's room. This would be her greatest surprise. They turned into the little hallway with the two bath rooms on the left and Jeffrey stepped ahead and opened both doors. Both rooms were so bright and fresh with tiles on the walls and the floor. There was a bath tub and toilet in one and a shower and toilet in the other. Mirrors ran the full length of one wall in each room, with marble top benches over cupboards and high cupboards reaching to the ceiling above the benches. Once again Chloe struggled to find the words to describe them.

The door on the other side of the little hallway was closed, but that was the room that everyone was waiting for.

Billy glanced around at the other faces and down at Chloe who was wearing a broad smile, expecting to see another bedroom. When Billy opened the door, she gave the wheelchair a gentle shove into the library.

"Wow! It's a library," Chloe said as she looked around, as though the others didn't know and she had to tell them. She rolled her chair further in and propelled herself around the room looking at everything in utter disbelief.

"I have always wanted my own library," she said, "but I thought that this was your room." she said to Billy 'Who owns all of these books?" she asked.

"You own most of them," Ellen told her, "Sebastian and Belinda own some and some of them are mine, but they are for everyone in the house to use."

Again, Belinda reminded them about the time, because people had been invited to come from 5o'clock until 8o'clock and she wanted Chloe to have time for a shower and to change into party clothes and she needed time to do the same herself.

"Who will be coming?" Chloe asked.

"Half the town, "Jeffrey laughed. "We have invited anyone who would like to come. No presents, just a plate of food."

Lexie had spread the word and with each conversation she quietly told them about Chloe's magnificent library and that it was a shame that there were so many empty shelves.

Chapter 42

As they went out of the library, they each dispersed to their own room to prepare for the party and Billy asked Jeffrey whether he had brought Chloe's port upstairs and he immediately dashed off to get it.

The shower had been specially designed for Chloe and after Billy helped her undress, she was able to cope on her own. However, she did need some help with drying herself and putting her clothes on. Billy held up the pretty blue lace frock which Chloe had chosen for the party. She had blue eyes and fair shoulder length hair which hung in long soft curls. She looked stunning and Billy said, "Oh, that is so lovely. Is this another gift from Lexie?"

"No. This one is from Pamela who also likes making clothes for me." Chloe answered.

Ellen looked beautiful and ready for a party too. She had made her hair blond and the two young girls could have passed for sisters. She told Billy to go on down to her unit and get ready because she would look after Chloe and take her downstairs to meet the guests. Lexie and the girls were the first to arrive and there were hugs and kisses and compliments from and to each one. It was a happy scene and Chloe was feeling very comfortable and safe. Suddenly she had a startled look on her face and all of the colour drained from it. Everyone glanced down towards the motel and there was a big four-wheel drive coming up the path towards the house. Lexie bent down to her and said, "It's all right Sweetheart. That is Ben and Rita Cowley. They were two of the volunteers that worked here on the first weekend."

The message was clear to all of her friends. She was still suffering from the trauma of the attack.

Ellen leaned over her and said, "You are completely safe and we will all stay with you all night. All of the pony club will be here soon and the boys will join us too, so you make sure that you stay near us. If we get careless and start roaming away, you catch up and run over us with your wheel chair and that will wake us up."

A faint smile passed over Chloe's face and she began to relax just as Ben and Rita reached them. They didn't attempt to kiss her, instead, they held out their hands to shake hands with her and she responded with a broad smile and shook hands while they told her how pleased they were to see her home. Many more guests arrived until the parking area was full and Jeffrey and Dean had to go out and direct the drivers to another area at the back of the house.

The tables were laden with food and George had hired one hundred chairs which were placed around the hall under the house. Seb took to the floor and welcomed everyone and thanked them for coming.

A table near the wall was weighed down with gifts They were neatly wrapped parcels which looked remarkably like books. Another table was loaded with flowers. Fortunately, Mary had foreseen what could happen and had brought plenty of vases which were stored in Billy's unit. All of the chairs seemed to be occupied so Seb asked the boys to go over to the barn and bring back the long stools that were there in case more visitors arrived.

It was 5o'clock so Seb invited everyone to take a plate and fill it and then go back to their chairs because there was not enough room for them to sit around the table.

It wasn't long before they were all seated and the talking was reduced to a low mumble as everyone nibbled their way through plates of delicious food and yet the table was still loaded. When the movement around the table began to slow down, Jeffrey stood up and thanked them for coming and he also thanked all of the wonderful people who had helped to renovate the house.

When Jeffrey finished, Mary stood up to talk about her favourite subject, the old house. She had prepared 150 booklets which were in much more detail than the little pamphlets that she had given to the volunteers.

One of the motel maids had helped her to produce them and to collect photos and names. They were neatly covered with cardboard and the spines were bound with tape. On the front cover there was a photo of the renovated house. When Mary finished speaking, a few people asked her questions and some of the older guests began to reminisce about some of the unforgettable events of the last century. While they were still talking about it, Jeffrey and Dean each picked up an armful of the booklets and began handing them out. Each book was very well presented and the guests were pleased with their little gift. After each person had received their own copy, it provoked much more lively talking and laughter. Ellen waited until she felt that most of the discussion was exhausted and then she picked up a bundle of papers. Three sheets had been stapled together and she began handing a set to each of the guests.

She had chosen ten popular songs, typed out their words and then, after everyone had a copy of the words, she went across to the piano and began to play Twinkle, Twinkle Little Star.

She played the first line then stopped and called out, "Are you all ready for a sing-song?" There was a very enthusiastic reply so she started again with about one hundred voices singing along.

That was followed by B. I. N. G. O. and *Little Peter Rabbit Had a Fly Upon his Nose.* Then *Waltzing Matilda, The Sunshine State, The Bear went Over The Mountain*, and many more.

It was extremely noisy and George, who had been worried about the young people who were working at the motel, stepped outside to look down at it to satisfy himself that they were not having any dramas. The party had been well advertised and he was afraid that some scoundrels might take advantage of the distraction. He doubled the staff for that shift, by having two waitresses and two driveway attendants, and for complete assurance and peace of mind he hired two uniformed police officers. Their police car was in the car park just to let any, would-be criminal know that the young workers were not on their own. He would rather prevent a crime than chase down the criminals after, no matter how trivial it might be. The car park was empty except for the police car and everything seemed to be normal so he went back inside to enjoy the singing.

When the song sheet was finished, Ellen found that the guests were not. Someone started singing *Pack Up Your Troubles in Your old Kit Bag* and everyone joined in. That was followed by *On Top of Old Smokey, For They are Jolly Good Fellows and Why Was She Born So Beautiful.* Seb was beginning to feel uncomfortable, and when he heard a lady sitting near him suggest that they should do The Hokey Pokey, he stepped out in front and held up both hands as a stop signal. He laughed as he thanked everyone for making the evening a happy and joyous party to welcome Chloe home and to wish her and Jeffrey a happy and healthy future, but he also reminded them that some guests had to travel a long way and Tuesday was a normal working day.

Jeffrey, who did not have any experience with making speeches also stood up and thanked them once again for their presence, their support and gifts that they had given Chloe and him during the last three traumatic months. He reminded them about Chloe's ambition to rescue and care for farm animals that had outlived their usefulness. He guaranteed them that every animal would have a comfortable, healthy and happy retirement.

There was a rumble of noise as more than one hundred people began to disperse and say goodnight to their friends, some of whom they had not seen for at least a year. They all agreed that it had been a fantastic night and they should organise a similar event more often.

After the last guest had gone, Billy took Chloe upstairs to bed. She couldn't help noticing how quiet Chloe was and she asked her whether she had enjoyed the evening. Her quick and happy reply left Billy in no doubt that, that was not the problem. As she turned the wheelchair into Chloe's room she clicked on the light and Chloe gave a little squeal that sounded a bit like a puppy's yelp. "Oh! I am sorry. Did that give you a fright?"

"A little bit. I wasn't ready" she said.

Then Chloe asked why the extra bed was there.

"I thought you might like some company until you settle in, so I asked Jeffrey and Dean to bring in the single bed from the spare room, and if you don't mind, I will sleep in here until you are feeling more settled" she said.

"Thank you Billy." she said as she stretched up her arms for a comforting hug and as her eyes filled with tears she added, "I am frightened that Robinson will come back again".

"You never have to worry about him again. If he or anyone else comes near you they will get more than they have bargained for. Jack has trained Heidi and Champ to be more aggressive and although they still won't bite, they will show a mouthful of sharp teeth. I have also been trained to defend myself and some day when you are stronger, I will teach you some tricks too."

Chloe began to smile as Billy went on helping her to change into her very pretty pyjamas. It wasn't long before the others came upstairs and Billy went out to say goodnight to Seb and explain that she would be sleeping in Chloe's room.

Chapter 43

On Tuesday morning Chloe woke up at 5o'clock as she had done in hospital for the last three months. As she lay there, she was making her plans for the day. She was eager to see Ellen's animal family because she had heard so much about them but she had never seen them, and now they were living on her farm. She was glad that Ellen was living with her and Jeffrey. It would be like having a big sister.

These were some of the thoughts that were running through her mind when she saw Billy swing her legs over the side of the bed and sit up." Good morning Billy," she whispered.

"Good morning Sweetheart." Billy said softly. "I didn't think you would be awake so early".

"If you help me into my chair, I will be able to take myself out. "Chloe whispered.

Billy told Chloe that Seb would be up soon and then the three of them could have breakfast together. Seb cooked a big pan of bacon and left it warming in the pan for the others while he cooked eggs and hash browns and tomatoes for the three of them.

After they had finished eating, Billy suggested to Chloe that she should choose an older frock or shorts for her farm clothes and then when they had finished feeding the animals, they could have a shower and get ready for their day's activity.

Jeffrey had already asked the groundsman to wait for them so that he could show them what to give to all of the animals. The groundsman, Courtney, had made a wooden trolley for carrying the animals' food. It was easy to push because he had used four small bicycle wheels.

Billy was as excited as Chloe was. She had hoped that when she and Seb set out on their adventure that they would find some work that involved animals and she couldn't be happier about her job. She was already very fond of her little patient and then caring for animals too was just fantastic. Courtney walked with them but they both insisted on doing the work themselves. Their first stop was at the family's pen. Gertie was showing off. She was walking around on her hind legs while Porky and Woolley were grunting and bleating against the fence to attract their attention.

Billy's and Chloe's hearts melted as they watched these animals trying so hard to communicate with them. They wanted to open the gate and go inside the pen but Courtney stopped them and warned them not to forget that they were animals who would not understand Chloe's disability. He said that Gertie might even try to lean across her lap and could hurt her badly while just trying to play with her. It made them realise that they had a lot to learn about animals. Just being kind was not enough.

Their next stop was the cow yard. There were six cows in the paddock when Chloe was home before the attack. Now there were seven because a big black and white cow had been added. Chloe was delighted. Already her rescue farm was growing. First the family and now another cow and soon Ferdinand would be joining them.

The cows really had no need to be fed because they had a lush grassy paddock that was big enough for a herd of cattle but Ellen had recommended a special diet that would help to keep them healthy and would attract them down to the house each morning. The cows were on the farm because they were very old and could not supply milk or produce calves and would have been sent to the market if Chloe did not rescue them. She needed to see them each morning so that she could check on their health and get to know each one of them.

Their last stop was the horses. These belonged to her friends who had left them in her paddock so that they could sneak her out for a ride when she was still in hiding. The pony that she had ridden each time recognised her and immediately trotted up to the fence. Chloe was thrilled that it remembered her and Billy pushed her closer to the fence so that she could stroke its nose and pat it. As they both fussed over Bimbo who was a small horse, another rather tall one moved in closer to share in the attention. "That's Locky", Chloe said "He is a real darling and he is very quiet too. I think that he is one of the horses that they will use when they start their riding school," she added.

Billy told her that she had a pony for a few years when she was a child but they had to leave it behind when they moved to the city. She said that she enjoyed riding and she would like to learn again and perhaps even buy her own horse if Ellen would help her to choose one. "It looks as though you already have a fan," Chloe laughed.

There were no more animals to visit so Billy took the yard trolley back to the feed barn and then wheeled Chloe around the yard. First, they visited the huge vegetable garden and studied the house from a distance. It looked so grand and Chloe's mind flipped back to the day that she and Jeffrey arrived. She wasn't feeling sad so while Billy sat on one of the garden seats she sat on her chair and talked to her for a long time. She told her about her childhood and her wonderful parents that were killed in the accident on the bridge, then her nanna and how Jeffrey had rescued her from the children's home. She also told her how she had filled in her time while Jeffrey was at work during their first year in the house and how his friends had crashed into their anniversary party. After that night everyone had helped her so much and sneaked her out for horse rides, shopping trips and they had even joined the church youth group and gone to the movies together. Billy listened with interest. Her little patient had been through so much trauma in her short life and yet she was still such a positive and kind little child. She was really falling in love with her. She replaced the little girl that she had never been able to have.

Chapter 44

As Billy wheeled Chloe out of the lift on to the veranda, they saw a truck go through the motel car park and travel on up the hill towards them. It was the delivery truck bringing the kitchen furniture. Billy called out to warn the others, but the teenagers had already had their breakfast and washed their dishes while Seb vacuumed the floor and dusted a couple of cupboards, which didn't need dusting, and he was about to go down to the vegetable garden and pull out a few weeds.

Jeffrey ran down the steps to meet them while the others waited on the veranda. During the next few hours, the kitchen would be turned into a beautiful modern room.

Jeffrey and Dean stayed at the house to help with directions, Ellen went to work, Seb went gardening and Billy and Chloe had a shower and then changed into fresh pretty clothes for the day's activities. Dean and Jeffrey had brought the gifts from the party, upstairs and put them in the library, so Billy and Chloe went in there after they were dressed, for the enjoyable task of opening up each parcel.

Lexie's hints had worked well and Chloe had nearly fifty more books to add to her huge collection. She also had several boxes of chocolates, jig-saw puzzles, magazines about farming and wild life and numerous flowers.

When Seb came back, he found that the electricity was turned off and he couldn't make any tea or coffee, so they packed up a couple of boxes of left-overs from the party and a large bunch of flowers for Mary and they all went down to the motel for a morning snack.

George and Mary joined them at the table and the main conversation was about fishing.

Seb was a business man. He was always thinking about new ways to make money and he said to George, "Why don't you turn your passion for fishing into a profitable hobby? You could charge a fee for lessons. Billy and I enjoyed our day on the river with you and now I'm keen to learn a lot more about fishing and I am quite certain that there would be many more duffers like me who would like to go fishing but they don't know where to begin."

"Oh, I couldn't charge for that" George said.

"Of course you could," Seb replied. "I'll bet that there are many people who envy those who can go out for a relaxing day on the water. They have never had the chance to learn how to fish and either they don't like to admit it or they simply wouldn't like to ask you to teach them, but if you are running classes, they would be happy to pay a fee. You would be doing them a favour. Some parents who are not interested themselves, might like their children to be taught. It would certainly be better than allowing the children to sit in front of a screen all day."

"I'll give it some serious thought. I will have to consider whether I could actually teach someone," he said.

They also discussed Ferdinand. He was due to be delivered at the weekend and his paddock was not completely fenced.

"Isn't he very people friendly?" Seb asked.

"Yes, I believe he is but I won't risk people going into his paddock. Jock has warned me that he is old and slightly grumpy, so I won't be allowing anyone to go too close to him." Jeffrey said.

"Have you ever watched the keepers feeding the rhinos at the zoo? They have a fence of upright logs, which are far enough apart to allow them to put their heads through but not far enough for them to squeeze their shoulders through. You could do the same for Ferdinand

How close have you been to a bull?" Seb asked.

"Fairly close at the Brisbane show." Jeffrey replied.

"Well, not everyone has that opportunity, so most of the general population would have seen one out in a paddock with its herd or perhaps not at all. Imagine if you could take a selfie of cheek to cheek with a bull or just the opportunity to stroke one. I think it would be a great attraction for the motel." Seb went on speaking and sounding more and more enthusiastic as he continued and his ideas poured out.

"Apparently he is a big fellow and quite black. Actually, I was told last night that he has won many ribbons for his size, so he is a big black bull."

"We could put bill boards down the highway on either side of the motel" Dean said.

"Yes, we could call it THE BIG BLACK BULL MOTEL" George added, "and you would need another bill board down at the river."

They were all laughing and joining in the conversation with more ideas. "We could make the bull on the bill board look savage as though he is charging someone but add smaller photos of courageous people standing cheek to cheek." Dean suggested.

It was a happy conversation with everyone throwing in a suggestion and then Jeffrey's phone rang. He stepped away from the table to answer it. The others could hear his side of the conversation and they guessed that someone was offering him another animal. When he came back to the table, he said that it was someone who was at the welcome home party the previous night, and they had a little miniature pony that needed a new home. They are obviously extremely fond of it and they are going away on a three-month cruise. He said that they didn't have any other animals and, although it would have plenty of food and water, they were afraid that it would be lonely. They also feared for its safety. There is one condition, if they want to take it home after their holiday, he wants to pay for its board for three months and then take it back. I have told him that would be okay."

Billy said "Right. What we have to do, is find a little friend for it and build them an attractive enclosure and shelter. We will make it so happy here that they will realise that it is safe and happy and hopefully, they will decide to leave it here. When we get back to the house, if you would like me to do so, I'll have a look on the internet and see what I can find."

Everyone agreed that that was a great idea. Once again, Jeffrey's phone rang. It was one of the men at the house telling him that they had finished installing the kitchen and they were packing up.

Dean and Jeffrey jogged up to the house. George and Mary were also keen to see the kitchen so they drove up. Seb borrowed a basket from Mary and he and Billy, who was pushing Chloe, walked up the path and visited the vegetable garden on the way.

Most of the vegetables were too young to harvest, but he found enough crisp young string beans and a handful of small silverbeet leaves. He also broke off a couple of sprigs of rosemary to go with the lamb roast. Nearby he found an old trellis which was loaded with young chokos and he picked five of them.

"These will do nicely to add to the other vegetables that I have already," he said. "I have a bag of potatoes, and a bag of pumpkins and some frozen broccoli and cauliflower. They will go well with my great big roast and I will make some rich gravy and some white sauce. I'll place the vegetables in large bowls along the table and put the gravy and sauce in jugs," he added as he was planning his first meal in the new kitchen.

"That sounds delicious, but there might be a problem Do we have enough big bowls?" Billy asked.

"Yes." Chloe interrupted. "Lexie gave me some last year for our anniversary party, and I already had two of my own".

They moved on to the house where they found that Mary had already made cups of tea and coffee and brought out another plate of left overs. She had also mixed up a jug of chocolate milk for those who preferred it. Everyone was moving around the kitchen or touching things and studying the whole effect of the colour scheme They all agreed that it was awesome. The main colours of red and white and the touches of black were very effective. The curtains covering the high windows were also in a red, white and black pattern.

They all sat down to eat and Jeffrey's phone rang again.

"If that is the circus with a couple of lions who need a home, tell them that we are all full up" George said.

They heard Jeffrey say "How big is the trailer? Are they comfortable in it? Well, I'll see you in about an hour."

Jeffrey walked back to the table and he said, "How did you know, George? That was the circus manager and he wants us to look after two tigers while they tour North Queensland. They have their own trailer. but there is one problem. They eat a baby goat each and every day and I don't know where to get some goats."

"No! No! No!" screamed Chloe who started to cry hysterically.

"You can't do that."

Jeffrey looked shocked and hurried to his sister's side and put his arms around her.

"I'm sorry little mate," he said. "I was just smart mouthing George. You know that I would never hurt an animal. It was the circus manager but he has two camels that he wants to leave with us. They eat grass. Beverly and Beatrice are old sisters and Beverly has hurt her leg badly and the vet thinks that she would be too uncomfortable traveling and the circus is leaving tomorrow morning. He will be touring North Queensland for six months and he was desperate to find somewhere to leave them. None of the farmers that he spoke to would help, but someone suggested that we might. He is bringing them around in about an hour."

"And where are you going to put them, Mr Smart Mouth?" George asked. Everyone except Chloe laughed. She was still snivelling and quietly crying.

Jeffrey gave her a tighter hug and a little pat on her back as he answered George. "They have their own trailer which is weather proof and they are accustomed to being tethered," he said. "We will put them up behind the barn but I want a new shelter and a fenced paddock for them as soon as possible" he added. "Beatrice is not hurt but they are old sisters and close friends and their performance is not needed. Apparently, they just run around the ring with a dog on their back and the dog performs the tricks. The circus has four young camels, so they were already considering retiring Beverly and Beatrice so this is a good time to do it. I told him

149

that we have a resident vet." Jeffrey said, "and that was a big relief for him. It was quite obvious that he is very fond of his animals"

George, Jeffrey and Dean went downstairs to decide on the exact position for the trailer and to discuss the other pens and paddocks that they needed, Seb said that he would join them as soon as he had put his big roast in the oven, adding, that he hoped he could figure out how the new stove worked. He also asked George and Mary whether they would stay for a special dinner to celebrate the new kitchen. They both happily agreed, but Mary had to go home first to organise the evening menus. Billy was going to search for a friend for Rosie and she said to Chloe, "Would you like to come with me Love? I am sure that you will know better than I will, whether a particular animal is suitable or not and this is your dream that is being fulfilled, isn't it?" Chloe, who was very quiet since her shock said, "Yes please Billy."

Chapter 45

Belinda was very efficient with the computer and she was scrolling through the ads without success. "It doesn't look too hopeful," she said, and then suddenly added, "Hey! This might be okay. How about a miniature donkey?" Then she continued, "It is five years old and extremely friendly. It gets on well with other animals. They want 350 dollars for it and they will deliver it for a small fee."

"Yes". Chloe said," Even if it won't be a suitable friend for Rosie, I want it, and I don't think Jeffrey will dare to refuse me. Do you?"

"No." Billy laughed. "I think he owes you something after the fright that he gave you. Let's go and tell them."

As they stepped out of the lift Ellen arrived home and they waited while she parked her car and then excitedly told her about the miniature pony, the miniature donkey and the camels. She was especially interested in the camels because her boss had been asked to go over to the circus to treat an animal which had been hurt. She said that she would slip upstairs and put her things away and have a quick snack and then catch up with them. As Belinda pushed Chloe over to the men she said to her, "We didn't tell Ellen about the kitchen. She is heading for a big surprise."

The men could see the cheerful look on the girls' faces and the piece of paper in Billy's hand so they guessed that they had been successful with their search.

"How many did you find?" Dean asked, and they all listened for the answer. "None." Billy said, "but we might have a substitute."

"And I am going to buy it whether Rosie likes it or not, but I want you to make the phone call." Chloe said firmly.

The others each smiled and looked at her big brother. "Absolutely" Jeffrey said "Provided that it does not eat goats". Everyone laughed except Chloe who pulled an ugly face at her brother. Then she immediately felt bad because that was the first time that she had ever done that. He was not just her brother but he was also her best friend.

Billy told them that they found an ad for a miniature donkey, but she did not know whether it had been sold. She handed the details to Jeffrey and suggested that he should ring up immediately.

As started dialling the number, Dean said, "Here comes the circus,"

They all looked towards the highway where they saw a utility pulling a circus trailer.

The donkey had not been sold and Jeffrey said that when he explained why they wanted it and where it would be housed the owners were really pleased. They had already refused a potential buyer because they didn't like the sound of how he was planning to use her. "They are going to deliver her on Sunday morning so she will be here before Rosie. The owners felt sure that she will become friends with her but they suggested that if it was possible, we should build a temporary dividing fence, so they could be near each other for a week or two without feeling threatened." Then he added, "It will also give us a chance to see whether either of them will kick or bite the other one".

Chloe was thrilled with the new addition and then turned her attention to the camels which had arrived. The driver stepped out and said, "Everyone calls me Bonzo. Which one of you is Jeffrey?"

Jeffrey stepped forward and then introduced the others.

"Well, if you come over here, I'll show you how this lock works," he said as he stepped towards the door of the trailer. "They are both sweet natured gentle camels but Beverly has had a traumatic day, and they will both sense that something is different and so, like any animal they will be a bit suspicious and afraid. Therefore, I would like the two young fellows to stay here and the rest of you to move further away, especially with the wheelchair Dear, because that could really spook them. It would be best if they have the same handlers every day. They have been with me since they were babies and they will miss me and I will miss them," he said with a slight quiver in his voice. "However, Beverly has a very nasty injury and the vet didn't like the idea of her being carried around in the trailer while her muscle and the cut are so fresh."

Ellen had joined Jeffrey and Dean and when she told the trainer that the vet who examined Beverley was her boss, he was relieved. "I can't find the words to tell you what a relief it is to know that. I didn't know how I was going to organise her treatment," he said.

"Well, you can relax," Ellen said. "I am a qualified vet but if I have any problems with her, I won't hesitate to ask Jeremy's advice or even ask him to come and check her himself."

"That is wonderful," Bonzo said, "but can you give me some idea of how much it will cost?"

"Nothing!" both Jeffrey and Ellen said. "It is all part of our care."

"Oh, you are good people, Bonzo said. "I would have given up my whole wage to pay for her treatment, but I wasn't sure whether that would be enough because we are not paid very much. The boss was talking about putting her or even both of them down but I couldn't bear the thought of that."

The three young people were shocked and assured Bonzo that they would do everything possible to heal her injury, no matter how long it took or how much it would cost. "That is what our park is all about. We save animals' lives and give them a happy and comfortable retirement." Jeffrey said. "When they have worked for people all their life they deserve to be cared for when they are sick or old."

George was holding Heidi and Champ on their leads and he took them back into the house yard so that they wouldn't frighten the camels when they came out of the trailer. Sebastian had already gone back to the kitchen to prepare dinner and Belinda reminded Chloe that she had been up since early in the morning and she told her that she would like her to have a sleep before dinner. Chloe agreed that she was tired because they always had an afternoon sleep in hospital.

She said to Billy, "Although I am tired, I feel really happy and excited. When I was hiding here, one day Jeffrey told me that Mary's old cows were retired. He said that her neighbour had added Mary's herd to his but she kept the cows that were too old to have calves and produce milk, and insisted that her neighbour would send back the others as they grew too old to be of any value, because she wanted them to die naturally of old age, and not be sent to the market to be killed. That was when I started planning my rescue farm. Nanna told us that she owned a farm in her investments and that we would inherit it, so that was how I was planning to use it. I thought that I would have old cows and some old fowls that didn't lay eggs because they were too old but I never imagined that I would have such a variety of animals. Now we have Ellen's little family, seven cows, two camels, and on Sunday we will have a miniature pony, a miniature donkey and a friendly bull. Isn't that amazing? We also have about one hundred eggs that are in the incubator."

Billy agreed with her. She told Chloe that she grew up on a farm and she had always wanted to work with animals and that this job was a wonderful opportunity.

Jeffrey, Dean and Ellen were the only ones who stayed with Bonzo and the camels, so he showed them how to attach the ramp and then quietly and gently talked to his two girls as he led them out and tethered them on the grass. There was absolutely no drama. They cooperated completely and nuzzled up against him, although Beverly was limping badly. Bonzo pointed to her injury and told Ellen that Beverly had slipped on the ramp when he was unloading them and jarred her muscles and cut her leg. He didn't undo the bandaging but he told Ellen exactly how Jeremy had treated it.

Once again, they assured him that Beverly would have the very best treatment and said that they would send him a progress report and photographs each week. Jeffrey pointed to the boundaries of the enclosure that would be prepared for them and described the shelter that would be built, so that they could roam freely without being tethered. Bonzo dragged three large hessian bags of their food off the utility and then filled their food boxes in the trailer and gave Jeffrey a written copy of the recipe for the mixture. He explained that they always provided the animals with a special diet because sometimes the grass that was growing where they had to park was not suitable for them. He then gave each of the animals an emotional hug and final pat and asked the boys to reload them while he was still there. He was still emotional when he thanked them once again for their help and their care and hurried off to his utility.

Chapter 46

Belinda settled Chloe into bed and then went into the kitchen to help Seb.

The aroma coming from the cooking roast was tantalising. Seb was peeling and cutting up vegetables, so Belinda started preparing her sweets for the evening meal and, with the special guests that were coming, she wanted it to be perfect.

Ellen and the boys checked on her little family and spent some time with them, because she hadn't had any spare time since she had returned from Brisbane. The animals showed their pleasure and excitement when they saw their own special human friend. She patted and hugged each one, with Gertie trying to push her way past the other two to claim more than her share. Jeffrey discussed the shelter that he was planning to build for them, but he wanted Chloe's and her approval first. He wanted to make it special and he was thinking of having a two or perhaps even a three-storey building with a ramp leading to the higher floors so that Porky and Woolley would be able to climb it easily. They could design it together and make it a special attraction for visitors and a play area for the animals. If George was able to find enough workers to complete the buildings and construct the fences by the weekend, they could start on it immediately.

No one had ever shown any interest in her little four-legged friends and she felt extremely pleased as she listened to the animated conversation that Dean and Jeffrey were having. The family would have two hectares to roam freely. Their shelter would look like a huge birthday cake where they could live and play. They were also trying to think of some play equipment for their paddock. Gertie was the playful clown, and sometimes the other two tried to imitate her, but they were slow and clumsy. She knew that Porky would enjoy the mud pool but she hoped that Woolley would not follow her into it.

As the trio walked back to the house, they discussed the plan for the whole park. It was Chloe's dream.

The meal was ready as soon as the three teenagers had tidied themselves and were ready to sit down. George had been down to the motel and he brought Mary back with him. Billy woke Chloe up and wheeled her out to the kitchen.

The teenagers had placed plates of sliced roast and several large bowls of vegetables along the table while Seb filled two jugs with rich dark gravy and two small bowls with white source which he also placed on the table and then, after Belinda said Grace, he invited everyone to dig in.

The meal was as delicious as Seb had hoped it would be and the compliments were soon flowing.

He humbly thanked them and then added "I like my vegetables, so your plates of food might not be as pretty as some of the meals on the TV programs, but sometimes you would need a microscope to find the vegetables on them."

His guests all agreed and then the conversations started. Stories, jokes and memories poured out but each person had his or her own individual thoughts.

George and Mary were eating in their old dining room. The house had been their home for forty years and before that it belonged to George's family. When they moved down to the motel residence, the house was almost ready to be demolished, but now these two young people who had bought it, had turned it into one of the nicest homes in the district. The really wonderful part was that they each felt completely welcome there, and they were enjoying a meal with two people who were complete strangers just over a week ago.

Belinda and Sebastian had left their own beautiful home the previous week, as they set off on an adventure into an unknown new life. Sebastian had always been the home cook and house-keeper, but Belinda was his only guest. Now he was completely motivated by this family of big eaters and each morning he had enjoyed planning his day's program. Belinda had always enjoyed her job helping sick and injured children and she had wondered whether she would find anything as satisfying in her new life. She had also feared that Chloe might be a precocious, independent child who was hard to help, and she couldn't handle that. Instead, she found a sweet cooperative pretty little girl with whom she was falling in love. She was also thoroughly enjoying her work with the animals.

Ellen had her own parents and a younger brother, and they had moved into Belinda's and Sebastian's beautiful home in the city. Her brother had gone home from boarding school and was attending the same school as a day pupil. He also had his best friend with him because his parents had been hit hard by the drought so now, he was living with her parents who were not charging them any board. They had only to supply Hugh with his weekly expenses. However, Ellen was extremely happy living with her friends and still able to keep her little animal family. She had qualified as a vet and was planning to take a year off study, but she was motivated to work for another degree because the other three young people would be studying, and she was really looking forward to the new year.

Dean also had his mother and twin sisters. He was helping Jeffrey and the fencing gang build the boundary fence. He was living board free so he was able to send more money home to help his mother. In the new year he would be going to university because Jeffrey was paying for the course to repay Dean for saving his and Chloe's life.

Jeffrey and Chloe didn't know of any other relatives in Australia except for one very unpleasant aunty and they hoped they would never see her again. However, as they surveyed the other diners, they felt that they had brothers and sisters, two parents and two grandparents. It was a wonderful safe and comforting feeling. Jeffrey had acted like a man since he was fourteen when he and Chloe went to live with their Nanna, then he had to make huge decisions about his life and Chloe's life, now he had six wonderful adults to advise and support him. Chloe had been so brave for eighteen months, now she felt as though she was mentally limp and she was happy to let Billy make decisions for her. Lexie and Jack had been wonderful but they didn't live in the same house, so they could not always help them.

Lively conversation, stories and jokes went on long after the meal was finished until the young people ordered the adults to leave the kitchen and they escorted them to the beautiful, comfortable living room. They served them with tea or coffee and then cleaned up the kitchen and packed the dirty dishes into the dishwasher. Chloe insisted on helping. She rolled her wheelchair to the sink and started washing the dishes that could not fit in the machine. With all four of them working, it was not long before the kitchen was once again, spic and span.

Instead of joining the adults, they roamed into the library where they could play board games, read, chat or play on their computers. As they walked in, the first thing that they saw was a stack of books that Billy and Chloe had unwrapped in the morning. It had been a busy and exciting day and they had all forgotten about the books.

"This would be a perfect time for me to teach you how to use the library system that Lexie has set up," Ellen said. "It is the same as the university library, so you will find it invaluable next year."

"Yes, absolutely, definitely" they answered.

It was late when the four adults came to the door. George and Mary were ready to say good-night, and then they went home. Billy had planned to suggest to Chloe that she should let her take her to bed, but when she saw what they were doing, she became curious. Both Seb and Billy were invited to help so that they would also know this strange new way of listing books. Seb also offered to work with Jeffrey and Chloe to draw up an exact plan for the park and each enclosure and shelter.

When Chloe heard Jeffrey suggest that he would like a three-storey birthday cake for Ellen's family, both she and Ellen were thrilled and immediately added a few more ideas.

All of the other shelters would be similar to each other, but they would be painted in different pastel colours. Each pen would have a two-hectare piece of land. However, some of the pens would be further divided later to suit the variety of flying birds. Those pens would need to have a chicken wire roof.

It was Chloe's project so Billy allowed her to stay until she was satisfied that they knew what she wanted. Most of her ideas were approved but some of them were vetoed by the others and many of them were highly praised by Seb who was an expert at making plans.

She emphasised that it was important to have a roadway running through the park with access to each pen's gate. and it would have to be wide enough for a tractor and other vehicles.

Chapter 47

There were no special plans for Wednesday. It would be an ordinary day like most of the days in the future and Chloe was looking forward to it because then she would truly feel that she was home.

Next morning, she and Billy were up early and found that Seb had already prepared breakfast for them.

Dean, Jeffrey and Ellen were also up early because they were eager to check on Beverly and Beatrice. Billy and Chloe promised not to go near them. They could wait until the camels were in their new enclosure and had time to settle down.

As they all went down stairs to do their work, cars started arriving. Eric and George had worked their magic again. There were many people in the district who were unemployed and Eric knew who they were. Some of them didn't have a job to go to after the house was finished so they were extremely happy to take on the new project and they had proved that they were good reliable workers.

Seb was there to meet them with his plan of the park and a detailed plan for the buildings. After explaining it to Eric and George, he left it with them and went back to his house-work.

There were four gangs, with George and Eric to supervise them, so Ellen, Jeffrey and Dean went to the camel's trailer and Billy and Chloe went about their feeding routine. The camels were very placid and accepted their new human helpers. After they were tethered and fed, Jeffrey and Dean went back to working on the boundary fence and Ellen went to work.

Chloe and Billy followed the same routine that they had followed the previous day and then went back to the house, had a shower and dressed ready for a busy day at home.

By that time, Seb had prepared a morning snack and he was waiting to share it with them.

Chloe was eager to go to her library and find a book that would tell her everything that she wanted to know about camels. She wanted to learn about their common health problems. She realised that she really didn't know very much about them at all. What is the name of a group of camels? What is a baby camel called? And what is the name of a female and a male camel? The rest of the family would tell her to refer to the computer because it would be much faster, but she was not confident with the computer and she liked her books. They were like her best friends. Once she found the correct book, she could take it out onto the veranda and sit with it and slide into her own little dreamworld. Chloe had a brilliant mind, but no one had ever tested it. She was only seven when her parents were killed and when she and Jeffrey went to live with Nanna, she had to change schools. She also changed schools when she was put in the orphanage. Then when she went into hiding in the house. Jeffrey soon realised how clever and talented she was. Chloe cooked, and cleaned the house and still had ample time to read and study. Lexie provided her with her own exam papers and Chloe answered every question to one hundred percent accuracy.

Just before lunch Billy took her downstairs where she practised walking between two parallel bars and then Billy gently lifted her down onto a mat so that she could practise other exercises that the physiotherapist had taught her. Some of the exercises were painful but she put every effort into performing them correctly.

The three of them always had lunch together but the boys would come in at any time that suited them. It didn't matter what time they came in for lunch because Sebastian always had prepared a casserole or a large shepherd pie or sometimes a tuna salad. He enjoyed preparing a tasty lunch and the boys enjoyed eating it.

Chapter 48

On Thursday morning, Chloe reminded Billy about her appointment.

"We will have to move more quickly this morning," Chloe said to Billy. "Because I have an appointment at eleven o'clock at the hospital"

"Yes, I hadn't forgotten, but I hope Gertie understands. She is always so demanding," Billy laughed. "Are you going to take the children any presents?"

"Oh yes. I had forgotten about that and they would have been disappointed because they always loved getting those bags. When we get back to the house, I will ring Mary and ask her to please make them up so they are ready when we come down."

They hurried through their morning activities and were ready to leave at ten thirty. Chloe was really excited. She was keen to see her friends again and some of the nurses who had been very kind to her. Mary took the bags out to the car and handed them over to Chloe. They contained sweets, comics, weekly magazines, sunglasses and caps. Mary said that the magazines had photographs of Prince Harry and Meghan and also George, Charlotte and Louis and she had noticed how the girls had liked those photographs when she took some magazine on a previous visit.

When they arrived at the hospital, they went straight to the waiting area outside Doctor Patterson's room. It wasn't long before Chloe's name was called and as they went in. Doctor Patterson said, "Well. How is my special little patient?"

"Good," Chloe replied with a broad smile on her face.

"Are you sure? Would Belinda agree that you are good?" he asked.

"Oh yes. Chloe is a good girl and an excellent little patient," Belinda answered. "She has been putting her best effort into her exercises and even though it has only been two days, I do believe that there is a distinct improvement."

As the doctor listened, he was feeling for sore areas. When he was satisfied, he pushed the wheelchair over to the two parallel rails. "How is your walking going?" he asked.

"Good," Chloe answered again.

"Well, let's see" he said as he helped her out of the wheelchair and placed her hands on the rails. "Try to lift your feet as you walk dear," he said.

Chloe tried hard to lift her feet but her brain didn't seem to be connected to her foot and it didn't rise. Frustrated, she swayed her body to the left and shuffled her right foot forward. The doctor watched but did not say anything. She did the same with her left foot and started to move between the rails while Belinda and Doctor Patterson watched. Then suddenly she began to lift her feet slightly and both of the adults said quietly, "Good girl!"

She continued walking until she had reached the end of the rails and then looked up at them with a happy satisfied smile. "Well done," he said. "Just keep practising that because you are almost there. Now for your new tricks," he added. He rolled Chloe in her chair over to a bed. "Now this is extremely important and a big leap, "he said to both of them. "When you can do this, you will be much more independent"

He asked Chloe to push herself up out of the chair and to hold on firmly to the arm rest "Now slide your bottom as far over the bed as you can. Make sure that you are up near the pillow." Then he turned to Billy and told her that he would like Chloe's bed to be against the wall. "Your left foot is almost on the bed so try to move it over, Good. Now try to lift your right foot up too." It was difficult and she could not lift it high enough to place it on the bed. Doctor Patterson then picked up a long wide piece of material, a little bit like a large bandage. He folded it in half and then slung it under her foot and handed her the two ends. "See whether you can lift your foot with that," he said. She leaned back against the pillow and lifted her foot onto the bed.

"Good girl" they both said and Chloe was very pleased with herself.

The doctor then helped her to get off the bed and back into her wheelchair. "I would like you to practise that every day," he told her, "But I want you to promise me that you will not attempt to do it unless you have an adult with you. It would set you back for months if you fell, so will you promise me that?"

"I promise" she giggled.

"Now are you going to visit your three little mates?" he asked.

"Yes." both she and Belinda answered.

"Well, Nurse Casey told me to ask you to please wait until after lunch. It is almost lunch time and the girls are excited about your visit and she is afraid that they won't eat their lunch if you are there."

"That is no problem. We will go over to the restaurant and have lunch ourselves and then we might be able to stay long enough to see Lexie when she comes this afternoon," Belinda said. They went to the desk and made an appointment for the following Thursday and then went to lunch.

Chapter 49

As they turned into the passage way that led to the ward, they saw a little head leaning around the door. It disappeared quickly and they went on to the ward. When they reached it, and looked in, all three girls were in bed, sound asleep.

"Shh" Belinda said. "We don't want to wake them. Perhaps we could put the bags on this table and give them a ring later. It is a shame that we have missed them because we might not have a chance to see them again."

"Yes." Chloe said "I was looking forward to seeing them too. Perhaps we should go."

As they turned and walked towards the door, suddenly all three girls miraculously, sat up and called out, "Chloe, don't go. We are awake."

That was followed by a lot of hugs and laughter. Belinda decided to leave the girls to entertain themselves while she went for a wander around the hospital.

Fiona, Rosemary and Carley talked over each other as they excitedly told Chloe that they were going to Lexie's house the following day, Friday, and that she was going to take them to school with her. Chloe also had a lot to tell them about her camels and the new animals that she would be getting on Sunday. She told them that there were many gangs working on the enclosures and trying to have them finished by Sunday. She and Jeffrey wanted to put the animals straight into their new pens and they also wanted to impress their previous owners. The owners of the pony, the donkey and the friendly bull were very fond of their pets and they wanted to put their minds at rest and show them that their pets would be well cared for.

"I wish we could come and see them" Rosemary said.

"Before you go home, I want you to visit us. We will have a big B.B.Q. lots of tasty finger food." Chloe told them.

Just then Lexie came in and she was surprised to see Chloe there, and then Billy arrived immediately behind her.

Lexie explained how she was going to teach the girls. She already had three classes. Years 4, 5 and 6. so she would put the girls into their own class with just the three of them. Chloe had a lot of questions. Lexie explained that they would be able to join the main classes for some subjects such as science and social studies physical education and music but her main aim was to teach them to read and, in mathematics, she wanted to teach them measurements such as money, time, lineal and square measure. She said that she would make up some little note books for each of them and teach the girls how to use a calculator. The girls were highly excited and continually interrupted while Lexie was talking. Chloe managed to tell her about the new animals and Lexie said, "I think you might be getting some city pigs too. The council has banned pigs from suburban back yards."

"I'd love to have some pigs, but it must be sad for their owners to part with them," she said.

"Yes. One family even sold their home and moved on to a bigger property. They have raised them from little piglets and treated them like puppies. They live in the house and sleep near a heater and go for walks on a lead, so the owners can't bear the thought of just adding them to a pig farm. I spoke to one lady at your welcome home party and then Sebastian told everyone about your dream of rescuing animals that were in trouble and she was going to contact her friend."

"Well, we have several gangs of workers there today trying to build shelters and fences before the weekend and I can hardly wait to get home and see how much they have done. It was like a beehive when Billy and I left."

Belinda joined in the conversation and said that they would really have to go because she wanted to help Sebastian prepare the evening meal. She said that George had invited him to go fishing and he would probably be running late, unless he had time to prepare a big pot of stew before he left.

Before they parted, they arranged to contact each other the following week and make definite arrangements for the barbecue.

Chapter 50

As Chloe rolled over and opened her eyes, she remembered that something special was going to happen on that day. It was a few moments before her memory kicked in and then she was aware that it was Saturday. The shelters were going to be painted. They were all finished except the three-storey house for the family. It was much more complicated. The frame work was finished but the carpenters still had to build the ramps and put on the roof and the outside sheets. When it was finished it would look amazing. She was trying to imagine how all of the others would look when they were painted. The old farm would truly look like a park. Each building had a hopper window on each side and a door at the front. The shelters did not form part of the fence, except for Ferdinand's. The others were three metres inside the enclosure so that she had to go into their pen to feed them. She wanted it that way. Ferdinand's shelter was next to the motel's car park and it was bigger than the others. Inside there were five strong poles which had been cemented into the ground. They were far enough apart for him to put his head through for a face rub or a selfie, but too close for him to push his body through. They had also built a shelf thirty centimetres wide at the level of his mouth or the bottom of his head. It was Jock's suggestion because he warned them, "The old fellow has a warped sense of humour and if a child stood in front of him, he might think it was funny to drop his head down and toss the kid into orbit. The shelf should be wide enough so that he can't lower his head."

The shelters looked like cabins. Each one had a hip roof and guttering around it with a down-pipe sending the water into a slimline tank. Every drop of water was precious so the tanks were large enough to hold the water from the greatest downpour.

Chloe had chosen the colours for the cabins. She chose water melon pink with white trimmings for Rosie and Betsy and clean hay would be spread over the floor. She really wanted to impress their previous owners.

She was happy but also a bit agitated because she couldn't do the things that she wanted to do and for one second Robinson's attack came back into her thoughts. Tears began to well up in her eyes until Billy's bright voice said, "Good morning Sweetheart. I'll bet you're excited and anxious to get out of bed."

"Good morning Billy. Can I get out of bed myself? Today, after we have finished our work, I am going to take my book out on to the front veranda so that I can watch the men painting Rosebud's and Betsy's cabin and also Ferdinand's performance shed."

"That sounds like fun so I might join you if Seb doesn't need me, and yes, you can get out of bed yourself. I am coming around there to watch you." Billy answered.

Seb was already in the kitchen and had warmed up a large pot of stew from the previous night. After they had all finished their cereal, he made toast for himself, Billy and Chloe but the teenagers made their own. The main conversation was about Beverly and Beatrice and it was clear to everyone that Ellen and the boys were extremely fond of them. Chloe was especially pleased because it would have been very awkward if the boys didn't want to look after them.

Chapter 51

By lunch time the three buildings, which included the camels' cabin had an undercoat. The men were having their lunch so Billy and Chloe also went into the kitchen to have something to eat. However, Seb was not there, he was out in the vegetable garden. It didn't take Billy long to make a few sandwiches for the three of them, then she placed some in a container and left them in the refrigerator for Seb and they took the others and some fruit juice back to the veranda. Time went by quickly and the men were back on the job. They were making such good progress that there was no doubt that they would be finished before sunset.

After a while Billy and Chloe decided to go for a walk around the garden.

They found Jeffrey mowing the pathways and Dean was clipping the edges. The flowers were a mass of colour and the vegetable garden looked lush and healthy. The whole park looked beautiful and Chloe felt extremely proud and happy.

"Wherever I look, the park is absolutely beautiful. Do you feel the same?" she asked Billy.

"Yes. I certainly do, Love. I can speak for Seb too, when I say that we are both extremely happy here. We have been here a little more than a week and we feel as though we have lived here all our life. Seb has always loved cooking and pottering away in the garden and now he is enjoying fishing with George too. I have my little patient and so many adorable animals, I think I am just as excited as you are while we are waiting for our new arrivals tomorrow."

They wandered across to Seb who was still working. He was about to knock off so he packed his tools away and then picked a few vegetables for the evening meal and they walked slowly back to the house together.

During the meal, the conversations and everyone's thoughts were about the expected arrival of the new animals on the following day.

Dean, Jeffrey and Ellen also gave an update on Beverly's condition and the camels' behaviour. Their cabin was finished but the boys had put them back in the trailer for one more night because the paint was wet.

Chapter 52

When Seb walked into the kitchen on Sunday morning, he found a note from Jeffrey and Dean asking him to wake them at six o'clock.

They had been playing games on the computer until after one in the morning and they were afraid that they might sleep through their alarm, and they had a busy morning in front of them.

Although Sebastian and Belinda had travelled the world and even worked in other countries, they had really lived a very quiet life. They had seen as much of other countries as they wished to see and now they were enjoying a completely new life. They had their two gorgeous fur babies, Poppet and Pixie, and were acting as parents to four great young people and the change had brought out two new characters.

Seb had noticed a cow bell sitting on a shelf in the pantry and he guessed that it had been taken off the new black and white cow that had been added to the little herd. He went into the pantry and brought the bell out and placed it on a shelf in the kitchen. It was still only five-thirty so he brought out a heap of bacon rashes, some sausages, some frozen hash browns, tomatoes and a dozen eggs. He had two large electric frypans and the stove top to work with and he began to cook everything except the eggs. He also set the table and placed the cereal, milk and fruit juice on it.

By the time he had done all of that, it was six o'clock, so he took the bell and walked down the hallway shaking it and shouting, "WAKE UP EVERYBODY ! WE HAVE A LOT OF WORK TO DO! Then he walked back through the hallway enjoying listening to the tired moans coming from the boys' rooms and the laughter coming from Billy and

Chloe. Before he went into the kitchen, he let out a loud evil laugh of his own.

Billy and Chloe were ready so they went straight out to the kitchen and Billy chided Seb for being a mean old man which made him laugh again.

It wasn't long before the other three joined them and all was forgiven when they saw and smelt the feast that he had prepared. Normally, the teenagers cooked their own breakfast, but Seb was cooking the eggs and all they had to do was put the delicious food that he had cooked on their plates.

After breakfast Seb and Billy were asked to go out on to the front veranda and watch for Jock who would be driving a small cattle truck with a big black bull in the back.

Ellen then took their coffee to them.

The young people quickly cleaned and tidied the kitchen and then hurried out to feed the animals. Ellen helped Chloe while Dean and Jeffrey went to feed Beverly and Beatrice.

Chapter 53

When Seb and Billy saw a small cattle truck with a large animal in the back coasting down the highway, they were sure that it was Jock with Ferdinand, so they went out the back door and down into the park where they found the four young people watching Beverly and Beatrice investigating their new freedom. It was probably the first time that they had been free since they were calves. The fence was finished and the paint on their shelter was dry, so there was no need for them to be tethered to anything. It was a new experience and they were mooching along beside the fence and having a nibble at the grass as they made slow progress. Seb and Billy clapped their hands when they saw them and Billy called out "Bravo! Doesn't that look wonderful?" The camels looked up but did not bolt. They just stared curiously at them. Seb then called out that Ferdinand had arrived.

They all hurried down to the motel where Jock had parked as near to Ferdinand's shelter shed as he could.

Several of the customers had come out to see what was happening when they saw him attaching the ramp to the back of the truck, but Jock asked everyone, including the family, to wait in the motel, and he reminded them that Ferdinand was a bull. "He is a pet," he said, "but he is a very strong animal and he can be unpredictable."

After they had all gone inside, he casually opened the gate at the back of the truck and stepped in with Ferdinand who had a short lead hanging down from a very elaborate collar. He took hold of the lead and led him down the ramp as though he was a quiet well-trained dog.

The door was extra wide and they walked through together. Jock took the lead off and walked out closing the door behind him. When he went around to the front, he waved his hand to the spectators, inviting them to join him. "I think it would be best if you go in two at a time until he settles in," he said. The first pair walked in and were surprised to find him quietly eating some chaff from his feed box. When they were close, they were intimidated by his size and changed their mind then quickly retreated. Dean and Jeffrey were the next pair to enter.

"You can go first," Jeffrey said politely.

"Thanks. You are so generous," Dean said sarcastically.

Jock was also there and he picked up a piece of pumpkin from a box full of fruit and cut up vegetables. He stepped in front of a gap between the posts and said, "C'mon Poddy. C'mon little fellow."

Dean and Jeffrey burst out laughing and Dean said "You must be kidding!"

Poddy wasn't kidding. He looked up and walked straight over towards Jock and pushed his massive head between the posts and looked surprised when the rest of his body couldn't follow it. Jock held out the piece of pumpkin and Ferdinand wrapped his tongue and lips around it as gently as a little kitten.

"There you are. He is as gentle as a kitten," Jock said.

Jeffrey had already picked up a piece of pumpkin and was walking towards Jock when he said, "Well our neighbours at home had a kitten when I was a little kid and it scratched me."

"Well, don't ever let this little poddy calf sit on your lap, because his tongue is so rough, and, if he gives you an affectionate lick on your face you will have more than one scratch to deal with."

Dean and Jeffrey laughed at the thought of this massive animal sitting on Jeffrey's lap.

Just then one of the spectators who had been watching through the window called out, "Hurry up you pair. We want a turn too."

George and Seb had come into the room and Jock asked them whether they would mind keeping an eye on the visitors and to make sure that no one tormented the bull. He said that he wanted to have a word with young Jeff.

They stepped outside and Jock said, "I see that you have a lot of work going on. Would you have enough for one more worker?"

"Who did you have in mind?" Jeffrey asked.

"Myself." Jock replied. "The drought is really beginning to bite. John and Tommy are old enough to look after the farm work, and if I can take home a wage each week, it will ease some of the pressure on Mum and the kids. It has been really hard on Joanne trying to put food on the table when I can't give her enough house-keeping money.

"How would you be at fencing? "Jeffrey asked.

"Oh, I've done plenty of that." Jock replied.

"Well, I have months of work here, so if you want some work, be here at 7-30 in the morning." Jeffrey told him.

Jock was just leaving, feeling happy and relieved, when another small cattle truck arrived with a cute little donkey riding along in the back of it. Jeffrey spoke to the driver and directed him over to the pink shelter. He, Ellen, Mary, Billy and Chloe all went over to the donkey's enclosure to meet their new guest, while the other men waited for the last of the customers to pat and feed Ferdinand.

The farm friends walked across the park but the truck had to wind around past the three-storey shelter, the house and the camel enclosure, so they arrived almost at the same time. Harry stepped out and introduced himself and his partner, Stella. She said hello to everyone although she was giving most of her attention to Betsy. As she stroked her she said, "You poor little thing that was a long ride wasn't it?" Then she reminded them that they had travelled all the way from Toowoomba and Betsy had never been in the trailer before.

Harry led her down the ramp and stopped in front of the crowd.

"Isn't she the dearest little animal?" Mary said. "I've never seen a donkey as small as Betsy, and she is so placid"

Betsy was quietly rubbing her nose against people and sniffing them while Stella let her stretch to the furthest length of her lead. "She likes people and attention," Stella said. "We are sad to part with her but Harry is a school teacher and he has been transferred to the city. We will be moving during the Christmas holidays so we wanted to find a good home for Betsy because we will probably move into a unit and we couldn't possibly take her with us."

"I like the look of your park. What do you think, Stella?" Harry added.

"It looks very nice. You said that you would have a little miniature horse too. Will she still be coming? "Stella asked.

Before Jeffrey could answer, Chloe called out, "Here comes Rosebud".

They all looked towards the highway where they saw a car towing a small cattle trailer with an extremely small animal in it. It didn't look like a horse. It looked more like a dog. It seemed to be smaller than Champ or Heidi. Both of the dogs had been quietly sitting beside Chloe's wheelchair. They were interested and alert, but also very well behaved and neither attempted to interfere with any of the activity. Billy said "I had forgotten that they were here. They are extremely well behaved. If we brought Poppet and Pixie with us, they would be going crazy and driving us crazy."

The last of the customers had finished petting Ferdinand, so George locked the door and the three men had just started making their way down towards the little pink cabin when they saw the car and trailer drive into the car park. Dean ran over to the driver and pointed to the others and then directed him through the park. They met up again at the little pink cabin where everyone, including Betsy, was watching a tiny horse being led down the ramp of the trailer.

Ian had introduced himself and Natalie and Rosie to the others and then dropped down the back of the trailer to form a sturdy ramp.

"Are you sure that is a horse?" Dean laughed.

"It looks like a horse, but I think I need new glasses," Seb said.

Rosebud was a light tan colour with a white fluffy mane and a white patch like a saddle on her back. Betsy was the opposite. Her main body was white with a couple of tan patches, and together, they looked like a selected pair.

Betsy was wearing a pink jewelled halter with a short lead attached to it, while Rosie was wearing a red jewelled halter with a short lead attached to it.

Both animals stretched their leads to try to reach the other one, so Stella and Natalie allowed them to touch noses.

Mary said, "Aren't they the most adorable little pets?" As she spoke Betsy started making a strange noise which sounded like a back to front sneeze. Then, with no further warning, she blurted out an extremely loud "Eehn haw". The people jumped and then laughed but Rosie swung around ready to make a hasty retreat. Fortunately, Natalie had a firm grip on her lead and a comforting arm around her neck. She stroked her gently while whispering quiet words to her.

Stella said to Betsy, "Oh! You are a loud mouth Betsy. That is no way to make friends."

Billy couldn't stop laughing but she managed to say, "Look at that glint in her eye and I'll swear she is smiling."

When they all recovered, Harry suggested that they should put the two of them into the shed and let them have something to eat and see whether they would settle down. Neither of them had eaten in the morning before their trip, so they were ready for a feed of their favourite mixture. Their feed boxes were back-to-back against the wire partition which meant that they were facing each other while they were eating, and it did not bother either of them. There was silence for a moment and then Natalie said, "I think they are going to be good little friends." Everyone agreed, until Stella added, "Of course, that is, if Betsy Loudmouth can control her sense of humour."

After a few more words their human friends said a slightly emotional good-bye and then Jeffrey explained to them Chloe's dream of providing a happy retirement home for farm animals. He also told them that Ellen was a qualified vet and she lived on the premises. "They will be given all the love and care and attention that they could possibly want." Mary assured them.

Both couples went away feeling a bit sad but convinced that their little pets had a good home.

Chapter 54

All of the farm friends went up to the house where they had a light lunch and a chat about the progress of the park. It was decided that George or Mary would be in charge of Ferdinand. They couldn't allow customers to visit him without supervision and both Mary and George felt quite comfortable with him because they had both grown up on dairy farms and worked their own farm for forty years. They nick-named him, The Big Fellow.

Jeffrey and Dean wanted to care for Beatrice and Beverly. They said that the sisters were already accepting them as a replacement for their friend Bonzo.

Ellen was also fond of them but her special pets formed her little family.

Chloe interrupted them as she said with a pretend frown, "Can I have some?"

"Of course!" They all replied at once and then they started to apologise. They were forgetting that it was Chloe's Park.

"That's okay. Isn't it Billy?" she said. "We will still have all of them and I am so happy that everyone likes my park. It won't be long before the chickens hatch and I still want to collect every breed of fowls and ducks or webbed feet birds. I also like to save the old cows and Jock said that several farmers were ready to cut back on their herds because they have to buy food for them. The farmers who are fond of their animals don't like the idea of sending them to market

and they are thinking of sending them to me. We have plenty of food. I also want to have some emus ostriches, and turkeys so there will be lots of animals for everyone to love."

Billy and Chloe said that they would want to continue their same routine each morning, and even when the chickens hatched, they wanted to be completely involved in caring for them. However, they did acknowledge that at some point it could become too much for them on their own. They knew that Chloe was well on her way towards being able to walk, but it would be a long time before she could do any heavy work. George suggested that he should teach Billy how to drive the tractor, and there was an old trailer in the barn that she could load up with buckets of feed for the animals and tow it around with the tractor.

"Oh, that would be great. Perhaps the gardener could put the feed into colour coded buckets, light enough for us to lift, and we could handle that. Couldn't we Chloe?" Billy added. She obviously felt extremely excited about the idea. The city girl who had arrived a couple of weeks earlier was already a happy farm hand.

Chloe said that she wanted to visit every animal every day and she felt that she was ready to start riding the motorised shopping scooter. Dean and

Jeffrey began to clear the dishes away while Ellen began to make the coffee and tea. Chloe started to move away from the table so she could help but Jeffrey told her that they could manage and what he would like her to do, was to tell them what her next plans would be

"Oh" she said in surprise, "I wasn't ready for that, but I know what I want."

"Then let's hear it." Jeffrey said.

Chloe looked towards the four adults who were sitting together and said "Will you help me with the plans and permits please?"

"Absolutely." Seb replied as he looked at Billy. She was also enthusiastic.

"You can count us in." Mary said. "I've never had so much fun in my life. I feel as though I don't want to retire yet."

"I feel the same way Kiddo. I would beg to be on your committee, "George added."

"Thank you. Everyone" Chloe said shyly.

"Well, I have had a good look at the area between the house and the motel and from the river to the highway, and I think that we could fit three, two-hectare enclosures in there, but I would rather have two enclosures and fence around the third one and plant it heavily with trees, shrubs and flowers. If I do some research to find the plants and trees that birds like, we could make it into an open wild bird aviary.

Everyone thought that it was a marvellous idea and immediately began to offer more suggestions.

"We could make paths through it with garden seats here and there, some water fountains and a lily pond," someone suggested.

"Yes, and if we choose the correct gum trees, we might get some koalas when they have to be relocated." Billy added.

"Wouldn't it be beautiful to have it full of colourful birds?" Mary said.

"One of the other areas will have a long shed, painted in rainbow colours, with long narrow pens, about three metres wide. They will be for chickens and the pens will need to have wire netting over the top to stop flying predators. The crows and hawks could easily kill some of the smaller birds.

As the chickens grow, we will watch and see which ones can share a pen, but they will be different sizes. There will be little bantams and Jap quails, and some huge speckled hens and I am sure we will need to separate them. I didn't see the parent fowls because Jeffrey bought the eggs, but eventually we will have a real variety."

Jeffrey added, "I bought them from a farm on the outskirts of Brisbane but I didn't go down, they sent them up by rail, so, as the eggs hatch, they will each be a little surprise."

"Oh! I can hardly wait" Ellen said.

"Your park just gets better and better," George said. "What else do you have in mind for this end?"

"Well, we do need at least three more motel units, some, on - site caravans and a tent area with really nice amenities. You need a good shed where you can put all of your fishing gear and spare seats from the restaurant."

"What spare seats?" George asked.

"Well. Mary said that sometimes lately the restaurant has been full and you have had to bring out extra chairs. She was thinking that she might have to tell people to book a table ahead of time, but Seb had another idea. He can tell you about it."

"Well. It was just a suggestion." Seb said "It is really none of my business, but if Mary feels she needs to book tables, the business must be growing, so why hold it back? Let's make the restaurant larger." Everyone was listening.

"First we would need to move the car park to the other side of the restaurant and make it much larger, because we are about to soar."

There was a general murmur of agreement.

"As Chloe said, we must build more units. We also need caravan parking places and a tent area. There is plenty of land on that side and if the semi-trailer drivers have to walk one hundred metres, it will be good for them."

"That is where I would like to put my sheds, so the drivers can have their own area there," Jeffrey interrupted.

"You will have more than enough room for that. "George said, "and eventually you might build a covered walk-way between your service sheds and the restaurant. It won't seem to be so far then."

Everyone was interested and ready to hang on to Seb's words again.

"After we move the car-park, we can add a large open area, with a roof over it but the sides would be low hedges. Put some colourful tables and chairs in it. However, I think you can use a bigger building. Don't extend the restaurant. Build a complete hall running at right angles to the restaurant and joined to it by a wide double glass door. Now make that hall useful and attractive. Have a low stage at the top, and if it is hired for a meeting, you will need a lot of chairs. If it is hired for a dance, you will need space so you will need to store the tables. If it is hired for a party, you will need tables and chairs, and if you can attract wedding guests, it will certainly pay for itself. To attract wedding groups, have two nice changing rooms and showers so that the couples can change into their travelling clothes and have a special room for a photograph studio."

Dean had been especially interested and said that his twin sisters would soon be teenagers and he would love to give them a party there. He also suggested that it would be nice to have a children's playground next to the hall, and that idea was well received.

Mary gave a little laugh as she said, "I remember sitting in this old house and George and I were fretting over whether a motel and restaurant would succeed. Now the young owners are going to turn it into a tourist destination."

"I like it." Jeffrey said. "We can certainly do that. Can anyone see any problems with Seb's ideas?"

There were many remarks and they were all praising the plan. The only question was from George. "Will you be willing to be the architect Seb because this will need a professional? I couldn't just turn up at the council with a simple drawing. They will want every minute detail."

"Absolutely. I would thoroughly enjoy doing it and supervising the work, and I can fit it in to my spare time." Seb answered.

"Go for it as soon as you can," was Jeffrey's enthusiastic reply.

"However, while everyone is here, I would like to hear Chloe's plans for the other end of the animal park. I'll swear that my little sister's brain never goes to sleep and I can't wait to hear what else she has in store for us mere mortals."

They all agreed and each one added a compliment.

Chloe was the brightest little girl that anyone of them had met. Her ideas were so mature and so thorough.

"Yes. Out with it, Young Chloe. What surprises are you keeping from us?" Seb said with his eyes half closed into narrow slits as though he was suspicious.

"I do have some plans, but I'm not keeping them secretly. I just have to do more research and I am afraid that you might all laugh at me."

"Never! "They answered in unison

"The cows and horses can stay in the big paddock on the other side of the old shearers' huts, and just have the lane- way to come down to the house each day. On this side of the huts, I think there would be enough space to have three enclosures. Two of them would have two hectares of land and the third one would be much bigger."

"Why?" Jeffrey asked.

Chloe replied "This is what I wanted to explore more. When we were given Beverly and Beatrice, I didn't know anything about camels, so I started reading every article that I could find in my books and on the net, and I read that camel milk is becoming popular and it is the beginning of a new industry. I don't know anything else about it, but I wondered whether some time in the future, we might buy eight or ten young milking camels and start something new. That is why I wanted to save a large block of land."

"I like the way that this kid thinks," Seb said. "She has some fantastic ideas, and I agree with Jeffrey. Her brain never shuts down."

"It is certainly worth looking into. "Jeffrey said.

"Didn't Phillip have a couple of camels?" Mary asked George.

"Yes," he answered. "Phil is my brother and he lives up in the Northern Territory. I'll give him a ring. Perhaps he can tell us some basic information."

"It sounds like a great idea, "Ellen said. "We could all do a bit of research and also ask anyone who might be interested if they can steer us in the right direction. I'll ask some of our customers."

"I have so many questions." Chloe said. "Do we need special bails for milking? What age should the camels be? Where would we send the milk?

Where can we buy some camels? We need to know all of the answers before we buy any camels".

When the new shelters are finished, we will have some spare enclosures so that we don't have a panic like the one that we had this week. Lexie is quite sure that we will be asked to have some pet pigs from the city and I would like to be ready for them. If they have lived in houses and slept on beds, I will buy some second-hand furniture for them. The house will be nice, but the paddock will be a piggy's paradise with a mud pool and wading pool and their own vegetable garden so that there is a continual supply of vegetables. We can fence each large patch off until the plants are mature and then when they devour one patch, we will start a new one.

By Tuesday, Gertie, Porky and Woolley will be able to move into their new home and the old cow shed will be vacant. I don't want to knock it down. I would like George and Mary to help us to restore it, and then it can be used for emergencies.

I would also like to buy or build some play equipment for the family.

Last week when I was watching TV, I saw a sheep jumping on a trampoline and it looked so funny, I hope that Woolley might try it."

"Yes. we could also make a wide flat swing for Gertie and put in a couple of beach balls or Gym balls for Porky to push around," Ellen suggested. The image of it amused everyone but they all agreed that it would add some interest to their playfulness.

"We could do the same for the pet pigs too. They might perform but even if they don't, it will still make their enclosure look interesting, "Ellen added. "Well, we all have a lot of homework". Billy said, "so I am going to put this writing book on this shelf. If you have some information about camels, write it down in this book. It doesn't matter how little it is. It might just be a phone number and next time that we get together we can discuss it." Then she opened the book at its muddle and said, "If you have any questions or ideas or problems with anything else jot it down here in the middle and we will discuss that too".

Chloe said, "I have one more request. Can we have a barbecue next Saturday and invite Jack and Lexie and the six girls because Fiona, Rosemary and Carly will be going home soon and they were keen to see our park".

"Of course. Absolutely. Definitely" were some of the quick responses and Billy offered to organise it.

It had been such a profitable and interesting afternoon that they decided to have another gathering in two weeks' time.

Chapter 55

On Thursday Billy took Chloe back to the hospital to see her specialist and he was amazed at her progress.

"Your active life at home is working miracles", he said. "You are two or three months ahead of our expectations," he added, after Chloe had walked. unassisted around his room and along the passage and back. "You are certainly ready to walk unassisted in your house as much as you like, but I would like you to use your wheelchair or scooter when you are out in your yard. I don't think your reflexes are working quickly enough to save you if you tripped, and a fall could still be quite disastrous."

"Can I walk to the car now?" Chloe asked.

"You can certainly walk to the door, but," he said as he looked at Belinda, "I would like you to sit safely on your wheelchair as you cross the car park. One innocent little rock might trip you and set you back several weeks. However, first I would like you to go to the desk and make another appointment for four weeks' time, and that will probably be your last appointment."

"O-k-a-y" she said with a little whine in her voice. "See Ya!"

During the drive home Chloe started singing "Pack up your troubles in your old kit bag" and Billy joined in. They were both very happy.

It was only a few days since Jeffrey and Dean had mowed and cleaned the park thoroughly before their weekend visitors arrived, but they were both working around the gardens again, making sure that it was perfect, and ready for the barbecue. on Saturday.

Seb, Billy, Ellen and Chloe worked in the house to make it spotless both upstairs and downstairs. Chloe assured Billy that she felt safe and if she wanted to go back to her unit at night that she would not be frightened.

It was a big room and they decided to leave the spare bed in her room for a few more weeks, but Belinda moved back to her unit with Seb.

On Saturday, Lexie and the six girls arrived in her old red car driven by Pamela and the new Lexus which Jeffrey and Chloe had given her as a thank you present for all of her care and help and love which she had given them when they so desperately needed it.

The three little girls jumped out first and raced over to Chloe to give her a hug. They were extremely excited and keen to explore the park immediately. Lexie had dressed them in beautiful dresses and pretty sandals and they looked lovely.

"Just wait until we take the food inside and I will come with you," Lexie called out, and then she said to Billy, "I am keen to see the park too, but I also want to go with them because I have discovered that Rosemary is fearless and a little imp too, and she might do something dangerous. She is likely to climb the bull's fence and try to pat him. Billy laughed but Lexie assured her that she was serious and she began to tell Billy about some of Rosemary's escapades. "One

afternoon Jack found her brushing Ashby, his old pony. He is extremely gentle and quiet and our daughters learnt to ride on him.

He is, however very old and stubborn these days and I don't think that you should take any horse for granted. They don't mean to hurt anyone when they kick, but they can deliver a fatal blow and Rosemary was walking under him and around behind him and stretching his tail out to comb it. If he was feeling a bit irritable, he could have killed her."

Billy agreed with her and her mind slipped back to the episode at the hospital, when Carly was suddenly pushed out into the passage in her wheelchair.

The girls beat the two adults to Ferdinand's door but they had to wait while Chloe collected the key from Mary. They all went in together and Rosemary immediately skipped up to the little fence between the poles. Lexie didn't speak. Instead, she gave Billy a gentle nudge with her elbow and walked across to Rosemary and lifted her back to the safety line.

"Everyone select a piece of fruit or vegetable and line up here," she said firmly. They all did as they were told and she took photographs of them.

After their visit to Ferdinand, they hurried off to Ellen's family where Gertie was showing off to attract their attention.

Their next stop was the camels and the girls were thrilled to be so close to them because they had never seen a live camel. The animals were curious about their visitors and walked up to the fence to have a closer look at them.

Finally, they arrived at the shelter for the miniature pony and donkey. They had never seen any animals like them and they were allowed to go into their pen and pat them.

They stroked them and hugged both of them and Rosemary asked whether she could have a ride, but of course that was not possible.

Lexie's three girls were also wandering around the park. They understood that Chloe's and their mother's time was completely monopolised and they were enjoying their little excursion on their own.

When Billy and Lexie took the girls back to the house, they walked up the stairs and allowed the girls to go up in the lift with Chloe. Although the three girls had been in a lift at the Princess Alexandra Hospital in Brisbane, they were gravely ill at the time and they didn't remember their trip, so once again this was a first for them. They were thrilled and as soon as the door opened, Rosemary was off. She skipped around the veranda and surprised Mary as she burst in through the back door. In the meantime, the other girls walked down the hallway. Mary had just finished decorating two dozen small cupcakes and she offered one to each of them.

That was not the end of their guided tour. Chloe showed them her bedroom which they loved and then took them to her library. Fiona, who had been rather quiet and shy suddenly came to life.

. "Are all of these books yours? "She asked as she stood in the middle of the room.

"Yes." Chloe answered. "Most of them are, but Seb, Ellen and Jeffrey own some of them. Do you like reading, Fiona?" Chloe asked her.

"Yes, and Lexie has collected lots and lots of books for us. I hope I can set up a library like this in one of the huts back home and then I can help some of our friends to read," Fiona answered.

"Fiona is a good reader now," Carly said. "She read a whole book last night and Lexie was very pleased.

Chloe was also pleased and she selected one of her books and said,

"Would you like to read this book?"

Fiona accepted it and flipped through a few pages and then went back to the first page and started reading slowly and slightly hesitantly, as she sounded out the words which she didn't recognise.

"Fiona, that is fantastic. A few weeks ago, you didn't even know the alphabet. You are brilliant and you can keep that book and finish it when you go home."

Just then George rattled an old cow bell and shouted out to everyone,

"Come and get it or we'll eat it ourselves." That was the signal that the barbecue was ready.

It was almost dark and two strong lights had been turned on.

The friendliness, the happiness and simple joy oozed through the group. Jeffrey and Dean were enjoying a laugh with Seb, George and Jack. Pamela and Ellen had been best friends for many years and her sisters and Chloe were also part of the group, and they had often gone horse riding together. Now Fiona, Rosemary and Carly were also included and Wendy, Christine and Fiona seemed to have formed a close friendship. Mary and Billy were sitting with Lexie who was telling them about her experience with her little guests during the past week.

They were all laughing but Lexie insisted that some of the funny side had disappeared and even patient, good natured Jack was beginning to feel a bit frazzled.

She said "Rosemary is not naughty and she is not disobedient. She doesn't continue to do something that she has been told not to do. She just thinks of something new and plunges straight in." That really cracked up Billy and Mary and they burst out laughing again.

"Fortunately, her behaviour at school is perfect and they are all great little athletes. Carly's doctor wouldn't allow her to compete in any sport, but Fiona is the fastest runner in the school, and Rosemary is the fastest runner in her age group. It is a shame that they won't be here for the inter- school athletics carnival. Fiona and even little Carly are excellent students and both of them are so keen to learn everything. Rosemary is quite bright too, but Fiona is reading so well that from now on she will be able to teach herself, and I have given her an old grammar book with punctuation and derivation and other grammar exercises. She is going to work from it and send her work to me. She is also keen to teach her friends. They are adorable little girls and I would happily foster both of them. However, Rosemary is also an adorable little girl but I think she would turn me into a nervous wreck."

The men had cooked the sausages and steak to perfection and the ladies had prepared many salads, pasta and rice dishes and a variety of sweets. With such a delicious meal and good company, they all agreed that it had been a marvellous evening.

Jack was tired after his long drive from Brisbane and he was keen to go home, but he wanted to take a couple of Lexie's passengers and he also wanted her and Pamela to travel with him, because he didn't like her to drive home along the highway, at night, without an escort.

Before the visitors left, Lexie told the family that the last adult from their bush family was due to be discharged from hospital some tine during the following week, and then they were going to give him another week to have a little tour around and a holiday before he went home. Therefore, they were having a huge barbecue and garden party at her place in a fortnight's time. She said that it was an open invitation to everyone who had helped their bush friends in any way, and she was expecting a couple of hundred people to attend.

Most of the children from the school had made the three girls welcome so they and their families were also invited.

The organisers are planning to have a variety of stalls but not for profit, it's more to repay some of the locals who have been so generous. They are all suffering because of the drought so the committee wanted to do something nice for them and give them a fun day out. "I'll give you a ring before then and tell you all about it" Lexie called back to them as she walked towards her car.

Chapter 56

Billy had always kept a close eye on Chloe when she was in the wheel chair because she knew how independent Chloe was and she wasn't sure of her abilities. She was afraid that she might stand up to reach a book and lose her balance and have a fall.

Now that Chloe was walking everywhere, it took a few days before she could shed the habit. By Monday she had decided to help Seb more and that would distract her from Chloe. On Tuesday morning he and George went fishing at five o'clock so Billy took over his morning chores. It was a successful fishing trip and George kept enough fish for him and Mary and Seb took a bucket full home for the family dinner.

During the afternoon, Chloe was in the library, Ellen was at work, the boys were working on the boundary fence and Seb and Billy were sitting on the front veranda. They were looking across the highway at the Australian bush landscape and comparing it with the view that they had from their front patio in their old home. There were a few vehicles going along the highway but the gum trees and other bushes were a complete contrast to the scene back home. From their patio back home they had to look across hundreds of roof tops to the far horizon to see a blue outline of a mountain range.

As he was watching the traffic, Seb commented on a car that looked completely out of place. Most of the vehicles were work trucks, caravans, buses, semi-trailers or ordinary sedans. There was however, one car that stood out. It was a shiny maroon Mercedes with the sun reflecting off it. "Look, it is turning into the motel," he said. Then as it passed through the motel gate, Billy remarked, "It's coming up here."

"Do you recognise it?"

"No." was her prompt reply.

"Are you sure it is not someone from church?" he asked.

"No. and I think it is time that we called the boys." she said as she picked up her mobile.

When Chloe had been so traumatised after she came home from hospital, they had chosen a signal that would summon the boys quickly if a strange vehicle approached the house. They would give three rings on the phone and then one of the boys would respond with two rings to indicate that they had heard the signal and they were on their way home.

The car had stopped in front of the little garden gate but the driver and passenger were still sitting in it. They were either talking or making a phone call.

Seb and Billy stood up and moved into the hallway where they could see but not be seen. As the men stepped out of the car, Jeffrey and Dean arrived and parked in front of the Mercedes. They both stepped out and the visitors approached them with a hand extended to shake hands.

"Good afternoon." the passenger said. "I am Doctor Mackenzie Ryan and this is my friend Doctor Cameron Lloyd. We are looking for Rohan and Ruby Connors."

"I am Rohan Connors" Jeffrey said. "But I would like to hear what your business is before I bring Ruby into it. She is only a kid."

"Is there somewhere that we could talk?" the visitor asked.

"Yes. Come with me." Jeffrey said.

Seb and Billy thought that they were coming upstairs, so they retreated to the kitchen. "There is something familiar about that passenger. I think that I know him. "Billy said. "I wish I could see his face."

Jeffrey didn't take them into the house, he took them under the house and as they walked past the cottage garden, both men commented on its beauty and also admired the rest of the grounds. "You have made an amazing job in renovating this old Queenslander too. It is about the nicest one that I have seen." Doctor Ryan said. They all sat down at a table and Doctor Ryan asked

"What do you remember about your accident in your parents' car?" It was the first question that the doctor asked and it took Jeffrey by surprise because he was expecting the visit to be about Chloe's injuries.

"Well, it was a long time ago and we don't talk about it anymore. We were coming back from a holiday at Redcliffe a beachside holiday city. We were crossing a long bridge early in the morning. It is unusual because it has three lanes of traffic. In the morning when the traffic from Redcliffe is the heaviest, there are two lanes open to that traffic. There are fewer cars coming from Brisbane so there is only one lane open to that traffic. We were in the middle lane travelling towards Brisbane, and there was a bus coming towards us. Suddenly a car pulled out to pass the bus and he couldn't get back behind it again. I think that he must have thought that he had two lanes. Dad slammed on the brakes but the car ran head on into us. When Dad braked so hard the vehicle behind us ran into the back of our car and he did most of the damage to Chloe and me. Mum and Dad were killed instantly and we were in a coma for a couple of weeks. When we came out of the coma, their funerals were over and we didn't have a chance to say good-bye."

When Jeffrey stopped speaking, the doctor put a photograph on the table in front of him. "Do you know that man?" he said. The man was lying on a bed and he had many tubes attached to him.

After looking at it for some time, Jeffrey said, "No. Should I?"

The doctor then placed another photo in front of him. It was also a photo of a man. He was sitting in a wheelchair without any tubes or wires connected to him. Jeffrey gave the doctor a stunned look and said, "That is Dad. When was that taken?"

After a pause the doctor answered, "This morning."

"How can that be?" he asked "Dad was killed."

"It is a long story and I won't go any further until Ruby is here." the doctor replied.

Jeffrey hesitated for a moment while he studied the photo and then he looked at Dean and said, "Would you run up and put Chloe in her wheelchair and bring her down Mate? Don't tell her why. You can just say that it is good news. You can tell Billy and Seb that it is good news and we will be up in about half an hour and we will tell them about it."

"I'm on my way." Dean said as he ran out of the door.

While he was away the two visitors changed the subject to admiring the house and the park again.

Seb said to Billy, "That sounds like a hint that they would like afternoon tea so I think I might whip up a batch of biscuits." Billy decided to make a tray of scones while Seb was making the biscuits. It wasn't long before the kitchen had the delicious aroma of a bakery and they both began to try to guess who the mysterious visitors might be.

Meanwhile a shy nervous Chloe had arrived downstairs. Dean pushed her over next to Jeffrey where he knew she would want to be. The two strangers stood up to greet her and they made several compliments about the park and house and Chloe relaxed as she told them about her ambition. When she appeared to be completely at ease, Doctor Ryan put the first photograph on the table in front of her. "Do you think that you might know this man?" he asked.

She studied it seriously and then said, "He looks like Daddy, but he can't be." Then he placed the second photo in front of her.

"That is Daddy!" she exclaimed. "When was it taken?"

"This morning" he answered.

"And now I have the pleasure of telling you a long story. I would just like to ask you to sit quietly and let me tell you the story without interrupting. I will answer your questions later. Could you do that for me please?

"Yes." They both said as they sat in stunned silence. "The remains of your car were among the worst I have seen. The paramedics saw that both of you were alive and you were both rushed to hospital. Your Mmum and dad had such bad injuries that no one could believe that either of them could possibly be alive, but your dad's head wasn't injured at all. His injuries were from the shoulders down because they were mainly caused by the steering column. Then one of the paramedics detected a very faint pulse. It was so faint that, out of all of the paramedics there, not every one of them could even feel it. He was rushed to hospital and Cameron and I were the leading doctors in the team that treated him in the theatre. We did absolutely everything that we could do to keep him alive. He was attached to every machine that could work for his body. They were not just supporting his body they were living for him. It is always sad for a doctor to see a patient die while he is battling to keep him alive and we expected him to die at any moment, but he didn't. He was monitored constantly, but the machines are marvellous and he kept living. He surprised us day after day. Your Nanna was making all of the decisions. The major one was whether to bury your Mum or wait for your dad, and have a double funeral. After a week she really had no choice and she went ahead with your Mum's funeral. It was not a big funeral because apparently you don't have many relatives out here and you hadn't been living in Brisbane long enough to make many close friends. The mourners who attended were asked to pray for your dad. His condition was explained to them and they were told that when he passed away, there would not be a second funeral. He would be cremated and Nanna would decide where his ashes would be preserved. He drifted in and out of consciousness, and at one time he managed to tell your Nanna that he wanted her to let the two of you believe that he had passed away immediately and was buried with your Mum.

Weeks went by, and Cameron and I suggested that we should let him go. He was still being kept alive by machines and he was in a lot of pain. Your Nanna wouldn't allow us to turn them off. Finally, she agreed on a very strict condition. We could turn some of them off, but we had to keep giving him nourishment. We could not let him starve to death if his body kept fighting. He must have been a very healthy man before the accident because when we turned them off, he not only kept fighting, but he seemed to improve.

He was conscious most of the time but he was still dangerously ill and no one would have been surprised if he suddenly passed away, so he still insisted that he wanted you to believe that he was dead. You had settled into your new life with Nanna and he didn't want you to be put through more trauma and then lose him again. He loved you dearly and I know that he really wanted to see you but he suffered that loneliness himself rather than hurt you. As he grew stronger, he and I became good friends. My wife, Josie is also a doctor and we were both ready to retire, but we didn't want to desert Greg. After many months he was strong enough to leave hospital but he had to go into an aged care home and he hated that thought. He had been given an enormous compensation, so we offered to look after him if he could buy or hire the necessary equipment that he needed. Thus, we retired and Greg came to live with us."

"Can Daddy visit us?" Chloe asked.

"He would love to visit you but he has been afraid that you might reject him because he deserted you."

"No! No! We wouldn't do that. I love Daddy. I want Daddy to visit us!" Chloe cried.

Jeffrey's eyes were full of tears as he said, "I was only fourteen when we had the accident and I missed Mum but losing Dad was like losing my best friend."

Dean also had tears in his eyes as he said, "I wish my Dad could come home."

"When can Dad visit us?" Jeffrey asked.

"How about next weekend?"

"Yes!" They both shouted.

Chapter 57

Final arrangements were made and as they walked out from under the house Jeffrey explained to the two visitors how they planned to develop the park with the extended restaurant and the workshops for him and Dean. He also told them how he and Dean were hoping to become fully qualified mechanics and they were going to specialise in trucks and any large vehicles. Chloe excitedly told them that Ellen lived with them and she was going to have a veterinary clinic down near the highway and she pointed in the general direction of where it would be built. Ellen had lent her many of her university notes and books and, although she hadn't been to high school, she was already trying to study some of the notes because she wanted to be a vet also After she finished university, she would share the clinic with Ellen. The two doctors were very impressed and said that their father knew that they had received his parents' inheritance and he was extremely pleased with how they had re-invested it.

"Studying university work before you go to high school, must be a real challenge for you," Doctor Lloyd said.

"Chloe is a little genius" Jeffrey said and, as she gave a giggle the two doctors looked at her and gave her a friendly smile.

Dean went up in the lift with Chloe while the other three walked up the stairs. "The lift will be a real asset for your dad. I'm pleased that you have that" Doctor Ryan remarked.

Seb and Billy had heard them coming and they walked into the dining room to meet them. When the visitors saw them Doctor Ryan said, "Belinda. What are you doing here?"

She answered him by saying, "I work here Mac but what are you doing here?"

"Daddy's alive!" Chloe shouted.

Belinda's and Seb's mouth dropped open and they looked at Doctor Ryan for an explanation. "It's true!" he said "and I have just come to tell the children." He hesitated for a moment and then he added, "You've met him Belinda."

She looked puzzled for a while and then she asked, "Not Greg.?"

"Yes!" he answered.

"Do you know our father?" Jeffrey asked.

"Yes. I know Greg but I didn't know that he was your father." She added, "I don't think that you have ever used his name and you said that your dad was killed, so I certainly didn't connect Greg with you."

As the others were enjoying the home cooked scones and biscuits and laughing and crying tears of happiness, one of the group, Dean, was feeling really sad. Suddenly he felt that he couldn't cope any longer and he was afraid of embarrassing himself with a flood of tears and that would spoil Jeffrey's and Chloe's amazing miracle. He excused himself and quietly went to his room. Jeffrey was the only one who understood. He stood up and said "I have been so insensitive. I forgot that Dean has lost his father too. It was only a couple of years ago, when his dad collapsed with a heart attack and died in front of him. I was so happy about our news that I didn't think about Dean. All of our talking and laughing must be bringing back some very sad memories. I'll go and talk to him." While Jeffrey was away, a new sadness overtook the happy mood and there was a haunting silence while they tried to consider how they could comfort Dean without destroying this incredible miracle. When Jeffrey returned, he said, "Dean said that he was just getting overwhelmed and he was afraid that he would burst into tears and destroy our happiness. He is feeling sad but he is happy for us and he needs a short time to sort out his own feelings and he would like to be alone for a while."

It was not difficult for everyone present to understand how the young lad would be feeling and some of the jubilation and hysterical laughter was calmed.

To help change the dull mood that had swamped the party without being insensitive to Dean, Chloe said, "I am going to ring George and Mary and ask them to come up here quickly. Should I tell them why?" Some answered "Yes!" and some answered, "No"!

"I'll just tell them that we have some good news and we want to share it with them." she said.

Cameron and Mac had already been told about George and Mary so they knew how close they were to the children, but Cameron reminded

Chloe that they would not be able to stay much longer so he hoped that they would be able to come immediately. George answered the phone and when he couldn't get any answers out of Chloe, he laughed and said, "We will be there before you can count to ten."

Chloe went to the front door to meet them and they were soon coming up the hill in their little utility. When they stepped onto the veranda, she took each one by the hand and walked between them towards the dining room, with a smile on her face, but she didn't even say hello to them.

They were met with silence and smiley faces until, once more Chloe announced, "Daddy is alive."

They were not expecting that and they looked around at the faces for an explanation. Billy took over and introduced the two doctors. As Mackenzie shook hands he said that they had the pleasure of bringing the news to the children, but they would have to leave it to someone else to re-tell it because they were running late.

They had booked a motel room in Rockhampton and had hoped to be back there before dark. He also explained that they would be bringing Greg out on Friday and they would like to book one room for Josie for Friday and Saturday night.

Jeffrey and Chloe went out with the doctors and Seb and Billy told George and Mary about Greg's miraculous return. As Chloe and Jeffrey were walking back through the hallway his phone rang. Those who were listening could hear that someone was offering him some animals. He asked them why they wanted to sell them and then waited for the answer. "I'll give you a ring back in about ten minutes," he said. When he finished, he said to the others, "Do we want ten alpacas for one thousand dollars?"

"Yes!" Billy shouted. "I'll pay for them. They are so cute and I was hoping that someone would offer us some."

"Why do they want to sell them? "Chloe asked.

"Because they have been attacked by vandals twice, and last night three of them were killed and they can't protect them any better so they are terrified that it will happen again. They have been raised as pets and are very friendly. They would like to bring them over tomorrow."

"We will buy them. "Chloe said without much thought, and then added "They will have to go in the cow yard for a few days until one of those bottom paddocks is fenced. I am glad that the family's pen is ready. We can put them in their new home first thing in the morning and then the cow yard will need to be thoroughly cleaned and new hay spread out before the alpacas arrive.".

"How will you protect the animals in those bottom paddocks if there are scoundrels that will attack harmless little animals like that?" Mary asked.

"Has anyone looked at the shearers' huts recently?" George asked"

"Yes. Dean and I had a look in through a window a few weeks ago. The door was locked and we meant to go back again, but we haven't thought of them since. "Jeffrey answered.

"How did it look inside?" Mary asked.

"We were surprised. There are still a few pieces of furniture which seemed to be in good nick, but the blinds almost cover the windows so we couldn't see everywhere. What were you considering?"

"There are five huts." George answered, "and four of them always housed six shearers each They are quite big. If we joined two together, and made an L-shaped house, it would be a family size home. We could offer it 'rent free' for some of the workers and in return they could act as security guards. Each hut is fully self-contained, with a shower and toilet but they don't all have a laundry. The hut in the middle of the line was the laundry, but most of the machines were sold or given away."

"i think that would be a wonderful idea. "Mary said. "Max and Gavin share a unit in town. They might be interested, unless it is too quiet around here because there isn't much night life. I think each hut had a common room and a small kitchenette with a sink, some cupboards, a short bench with a power point for a microwave and there was a round table that would seat six people"

"It would certainly be worth asking them. "Billy said

"I'd like to have a look at them, George. That is if you are seriously thinking of altering them in any way." Seb offered.

George laughed, "I didn't have the cheek to ask you, but I'm glad that you offered."

Jeffrey rang the owners of the alpacas to confirm that he would buy them while Billy and Chloe gave each other an excited hug. Chloe had never been up close to an alpaca and Billy started telling her what beautiful little animals they were George and Seb waited for Jeffrey and then the three of them drove down to the huts to decide on their future.

Ellen arrived home just as the men left and she felt curious about their mission until she heard about the alpacas and she was thrilled.

That news was just sinking in when Chloe told her the big story for the afternoon. It seemed impossible and too good to be true and she had many questions. She was still shaking her head in amazement and disbelief as she accepted a cup of coffee and some fresh biscuits from Billy but she also made it clear that she was delighted for them.

Ellen suggested that they could go and move the family immediately and the animals would have time to inspect their new home before dark.

"We'll put them straight into their house," she said, "and they can inspect it while there is still enough daylight."

Although Chloe and Billy fed the animals, Ellen tried to find time to visit them every day and they were always pleased to see her. She opened the gate and walked in, leaving the gate open behind her. Billy stepped up and quickly closed it fearing that one of the animals might wander out, but nothing would distract them from their human friend. After she had given each of them an affection hug, she turned around and walked out with her three babies following her.

"Aren't you afraid that they might gallop off somewhere?" Billy asked

"No". she laughed, as each one jostled the others to be closest to her Their house looked like a three-tier cake. The bottom tier was painted blue, the next one which was slightly smaller was pink and the top tier was lemon and slightly smaller again. Each tier was enclosed by a veranda with a high white paling fence The top of each paling was carved to look like a flame and it was painted bright orange. The roof was also enclosed by a safety fence.

"Isn't it beautiful?" Ellen gasped. Her two friends agreed and as they stood inside the door admiring it the animals began to mooch away and inspect each room. The floors were covered with fresh hay which gave the house a fresh farm odour. It wasn't long before Gertie found the ramp and began to climb it. Each floor was joined by a ramp and the noisy trio kept climbing while the three human friends went outside to watch them from ground level. Gertie was the first to appear and do her little victory walk on her hind legs. The three humans stood there entertained by a goat a sheep and a pig until the men arrived back from inspecting the huts. It was all good news. It might take a few weeks to organise the huts but the boys could move in as soon as they wished to do so.

There was so much happening that there would surely be a few sleepless nights ahead.

As they stood there watching the circus act on the roof of the family's house, a small group of men joined them. They had been putting the final touches to the shelter nearest to the restaurant. Gavin and Max were among them and Jeffrey told the two young lads about the plan they were considering, and asked the boys whether they would be interested in living in one of the huts rent free.

"Wow! You don't need to ask us twice. When can we move in?" Gavin asked.

"As soon as you like, depending on how much comfort you expect. There are some pieces of furniture scattered through the five huts and I am sure the girls will enjoy going into town on a spending spree tomorrow"

"Yes." Chloe shouted. "That will be fun."

Most of the men moved on while Gavin and Max remained to discuss the plan in greater detail.

"Do you have any furniture of your own?" George asked.

"No, the furniture belongs in the unit. Even the beds. How long do you think it will be before the furniture is delivered?'

"Well, we will buy new beds and linen so if Billy takes their vehicle, she could bring the mattresses home with them. The other furniture I hope we can buy from the second-hand shop and they might take a day or two to deliver it.

"It sounds like a tremendous amount of fun, shopping for all that furniture. We will leave early in the morning and do some of the shopping and then meet Ellen for lunch. "Chloe said.

Chapter 58

The following morning four of the lads started work at daybreak. They wanted to clean the cow yard before the alpacas arrived. They had just finished spreading fresh hay when they saw a cattle truck turn off the highway and pass through the motel park then continue up the path towards the house.

Jodi and Olivia introduced themselves and Jeffrey ran through the names of the excited group standing at the small gate waiting for the new tenants. However, it soon became obvious that, for the owners it was a sad occasion.

"This is a temporary home." Jeffrey explained and then he pointed to the finished shelters and enclosures around the park and also the area where the alpacas would have their permanent shelter and paddock. "We will have their permanent home ready by the week-end or soon after" he promised "and by then we will have some young men living in those huts right next to the alpacas. We will also have security lights cameras and alarms," he assured them.

While Jeffrey was speaking, Jodi and Olivia were tearfully hugging and stroking their pets and their deep sadness did not go unnoticed.

They were trying to talk but they were far too emotional and it was difficult for the new owners to understand what they were saying. Fortunately, they had written many pages of instructions in a notebook which they handed to Jeffrey. "This need not be a final good-bye," he said kindly. "If you would like to visit them, for the first twelve months, you can have a cabin or caravan free for a week-end once a month. You can watch them settle in and gradually ease your own sadness."

199

Chloe and Ellen stepped over to Jodi and Olivia and gave each of them a hug and assured them that their little pets would receive daily love and attention. They also invited them to have a wander around the park and to meet the other animals and hear their background stories.

The two young women accepted the invitation and were soon enjoying the antics of Gertie and taking selfies with Ferdinand. They thought that Rosie and Betsy were adorable and they had never been so close to camels. They even petted Pixie and Poppet who were gradually learning how to behave around the other animals. Heidi and Champ received affectionate hugs and whispers as the young ladies pleaded with them to take care of their new friends, the alpacas. Olivia and Jodi left much happier than they were when they arrived because they were convinced that the alpacas had a safe and happy home.

It was only Wednesday and so much had happened. The following day would also be busy with the women away most of the day.

Chloe was disappointed when Billy insisted that she had to allow her to push her in the wheelchair when they went shopping but the doctor had made it quite clear that when Chloe was outside, she had to be in her wheelchair.

Mary and George came over after dinner and while Seb and George played cards Jeffrey and Dean played computer games and Billy, Mary, Ellen and Chloe made a detailed shopping list. Billy convinced the others that they should cater for four tenants because there was a good chance that at least two of the other young lads could be interested in moving into the huts even if they were currently living at home.

Everyone's mind was on overload as they tried to fall asleep that night. For Billy and Mary some thought was given to Greg and such an incredible miracle but most of their concentration was centred on their shopping as they mentally scanned through their list searching for any missed details

Jeffrey's thoughts were for his father and everything that he wanted to talk about. He was a boy when he lost his father and then suddenly, he had to grow up and take on so many responsibilities.

Chloe was so happy that Daddy was coming home. She was only seven when she lost both of her parents and, although Jeffrey had been so kind and caring and had always been there for her, she suddenly missed her mother the way that she did when she was a small child. Having Daddy back brought with it a flood of memories and she began to cry uncontrollably. Billy had moved back to her unit with Seb and Chloe was on her own.

She tried to hide her crying by burying her face in her pillow but Jeffrey was still awake and he heard her. He jumped out of bed then hurried into her room and put his arms around her. All she could say was, "I miss

Mummy." The two children held each other and cried as they had never been able to cry before. They cried until they couldn't cry anymore and then they talked for a long time and cleared their heads. It had been a sad time but it also helped to prepare them for their reunion with their dad.

On Thursday everyone had an early start. Even the boys arrived early so that they could spend some time cleaning the hut before it was time for their regular work. Jeffrey would have liked to tell them that they could take the day off but there was too much work to be finished before the week-end.

The girls made an early start and arrived in town just as the shopkeepers were opening their doors. Their first target was the second-hand shop where they intended to buy as much of their list as they could. The shop was under new management and was well stocked. They were able to buy almost everything that they needed in that one shop. They even bought most of the bed linen, blankets and bed spreads because it was in such good condition and very clean. As they crossed each article off their list, they were happy and so was the shop owner. He told them that he had been very fortunate recently because he had been given the opportunity to buy all of the contents of one of the nicest homes in the district and it was all extremely high quality.

They had bought a full truck load and the grateful shop owner offered to deliver it that same afternoon after he closed his shop. The excited trio went from the second-hand shop to the cafe to meet Ellen for lunch.

She had been given the afternoon off so after lunch the four of them wandered around town for another hour, window shopping and doing a little bit of spot shopping. Their day out had been everything that they had hoped for so they finished up with a cappuccino and some rich cream cake and went home much sooner than they had expected to do.

Chloe rang Jeffrey to tell him that they were on their way home and also suggested that Max and Gavin could help with the unloading if they waited for about an hour after work.

The boys were delighted to know that their furniture was being delivered, so they bought a burger and a drink and went to their cabin to finish cleaning it.

George had set up the generator during the day and had checked the water tanks. He told the boys that the water was clean enough for general use but advised them to buy some bottled water for drinking.

Jeffrey had given Dean three days off and told him to go home to his mum and sisters for the week-end because there would be ample time in the future to meet Greg when everyone was not feeling so emotional.

At last, Friday morning arrived. There wasn't a thing out of place in the house or the park. The boys had moved into their new home and the alpacas' shelter and pen were almost ready.

Two more lads had asked Jeffrey whether they could also move into the cabin, but he was feeling quite unsure about the idea. Four young lads together might lead to parties and that was something that he did not want to encourage. His immediate answer was "I'll have to think about it."

They were surprised and appeared to be angry as well as disappointed He did think about it and discussed it with George and Seb who completely agreed with him.

Seb said, "I think you need to write out some definite rules. If they are there as security for that end of the park you don't want them having drunken parties. Make it clear that you are not banning alcohol but you are banning drunks. If in your opinion anyone is affected by alcohol or drugs, they will be given twenty-four hours to find a new residence and they will not be given a second chance."

"Absolutely." George said. "Would you like me to have a few words with them?"

"Yes. That would be good. I'll jot down some ideas and both of you can check them and add your own then we'll ask Ellen to type them up and the boys can sign it. After all, that is why they are being given the cabin rent free."

Chapter 59

It was nearly twelve o'clock when the family gathered at the restaurant, waiting for Greg and the doctors. They didn't know which car he would be driving, because the Mercedes had belonged to Cameron Lloyd, but they did know that Mackenzie would be towing a caravan.

"Yes. Here he comes," George announced.

Jeffrey dashed out to direct Mackenzie around to the caravan site because the caravan was too big to park with the cars. He could see his father sitting on the back seat and he waved to him as he walked beside the car.

Chloe hurried out propelling herself along in her wheelchair and she had a happy smile on her face as she waved to the father that she had thought, she would never see again.

Obviously, Mackenzie was experienced at parking their huge caravan and he soon had it placed squarely on the concrete site. He and Josey helped Greg out of the car and into his wheelchair, then Chloe stepped out of her wheelchair so that she could wrap her arms around him and Jeffrey hugged him from his other side. Josie was introduced and after a few welcoming words they moved into the restaurant, with Jeffrey pushing his father and Josie pushing Chloe.

The table was already set with a space for Greg at the end and Chloe and Jeffrey on either side of him. Mackenzie had met most of the people who were gathered there and of course Greg had previously met Belinda and Sebastian.

They soon had menus in their hands and were being encouraged to order a good meal.

Mary had set the menu for lunch and all of the guests gave their meal high praise. The happy chatter continued for a couple of hours, because they had been braced with several cups of coffee.

Sebastian suggested that they should walk up to the house and then they could visit the animals and inspect the vegetable garden on their way.

Once again Jeffrey pushed his father and Josie immediately stepped over to Chloe's wheelchair and with a special smile for Billy, she began pushing her towards the door.

Their first stop was at Ferdinand's cabin where they delighted in taking selfie's and stroking the big black bull.

Jeffrey then led them across to Ellen's family. As usual, Gertie was ready to entertain anyone who was watching her. They all admired her antics and gave her a noisy cheer.

Betsy and Rosie won their hearts. The two little animals had become close friends during the week and were never more than a metre apart. Sebastian left the group and went up to the house to warm the tasty savouries that he had prepared during the morning.

Beatrice and Beverly had lost their shyness and immediately wandered across to the fence where they waited for some attention. Jeffrey explained the story of their new guests, the alpacas, who were still unsettled and retreated from the fence to a safer distance. As they walked together everyone contributed to the conversation and Greg soon felt completely at ease. The three guests knew the whole devastating story of how the two children had been so viciously attacked just several months previously and they were amazed at what the children had achieved in such a short time.

Compliments and praise flowed freely from all of the adults, including those who formed part of their new family. Belinda explained how they became part of this extraordinary family and how they and their attitude to life had changed.

After visiting all of the animals the newly formed group of friends strolled back to the house where they hesitated for a short while before going upstairs. Belinda opened the door under the house and brought Heidi and Champ out and also a very excited Pixie and Poppet. The four dogs became the centre of conversation as they made their visitors welcome.

Chloe and Greg and their two helpers went up in the lift while the others walked up the stairs, and as soon as they reached the veranda, Chloe stepped off her wheelchair and walked beside her dad.

Jeffrey led everyone around the veranda to enter via the back door and enjoy the view and inspect their magnificent pantry. Josie described it as a mini-supermarket.

Sebastian was in the kitchen and Belinda joined him to help carry the food to the dining table, while the others did a quick tour of the bedrooms and living rooms but they left their favourite room for later.

Although they had eaten a delicious and filling lunch, they could not resist the tempting savouries and sweet treats that Sebastian was offering. More hours had passed and Mackenzie reluctantly commented that it had been an extremely tiring and emotional day for Greg and he felt that he would need a rest.

Jeffrey said, "It has been an amazing day and one that Chloe and I will never forget. From Chloe and me thank you from the bottom of our hearts for saving our dad and then taking care of him and bringing him back to us. Thank you very, very much." Both of the children went to their dad and hugged and kissed him, then Chloe said, "There is one more room that we want you to see before you go."

The library topped off this incredible house. Greg remembered that Chloe had loved books from when she was a small child and he was lost for words to describe this beautiful room but he looked at Chloe and said, "My little girl always loved books and she taught herself to read when she was only three years old."

Chloe gave her daddy a loving smile and said, "Jeffrey planned it and had it built for me while I was in hospital and lots of my friends gave me books to cheer me up. However, they are not all mine. Sebastian added a couple of boxes full and Ellen has added heaps that will help me next year, and of course some are Jeffrey's and Dean's." Everyone agreed that Chloe was the true reader and they had never met anyone as keen as she was, nor anyone as hungry for information.

Chapter 60

The following morning, Greg rode his motorised wheelchair up to the house and Josie and Mac walked with him. The previous day Belinda had offered to look after Greg for the morning if Josie and Mac would like to go for a country drive and they had accepted the offer. Greg had added, "I'd love to have the opportunity to just sit and talk to the children all morning and catch up on their lives. Perhaps we could spend the whole morning in that magnificent library. "And that was exactly what happened. They each filled in the years in every detail, and the children told him how Jack had smuggled them away from Brisbane. Jack and Lexie had been unable to join in the welcome but they would make sure that they were available for his next visit.

During the afternoon, George took Mac, Greg and Sebastian fishing off the bank of the river while Josie and Belinda caught up on some lady's talk. Jeffrey and Chloe spent some time with their newest tenants, the alpacas.

Olivia and Jodie had given them copious notes about their background, the sounds that they make, their breeds and behaviour, especially their habit of spitting. Alpacas communicate through body language. One example is spitting. They will sometimes attack smaller intruders with their front feet or by spitting and sometimes they will spit at humans. Their aggression towards dogs or foxes and dingoes is exploited when they are used as guard llamas for sheep. Chloe found all the information fascinating and vowed to study it more carefully, but Jeffrey, in his usual casual manner was quite bored.

During the fishing adventure Mac explained that they would like to leave at daybreak or earlier, on the Sunday morning because they wanted to have a long rest at Rockhampton and then try to drive through to Brisbane before dark. They had two drivers but neither of them liked night driving.

Seb set his alarm for three o'clock on Sunday morning, and after he had prepared a light snack for the family, he woke them up. They all roamed down to the motel where Mac, Josie and Greg were having breakfast in the caravan. Everything was packed and fastened down so they just had to say their good-byes and move into the car. It had been a fantastic wonderful and miraculous week-end which ended with hugs and promises of many more to come.

Chapter 61

On Monday afternoon, Lexie called in at the park without the children. She had left Fiona, Rosemary and Carly with Jack and her own daughters. There were a few details for the garden party that she wanted to discuss with the family and she told them that the church guild had formed a committee to organise the events for the day and they had done a marvellous job. Two semitrailers of goods that would transform the lives of the families were already packed and ready to leave. They had clothes of every size, house hold goods, water tanks, old sewing machines push bikes and even an old motor bike that was still in roadworthy condition They also had a truck load of building materials that had been donated by builders and sawmills, and some retired tradesmen were going out there for a week to repair or extend some of the huts.

She said that Pamela had been teaching the girls how to use the treadle sewing machines and Fiona had a real talent for sewing and cooking. She felt quite confident that Fiona would be able to make her own clothes and teach others how to use the machines.

"I am feeling frightfully tired," Lexie said as she tried to disguise a yawn, "but this has been an experience that I shall never forget. The girls have absolutely excelled at school, both socially and academically. Fiona is a brilliant little kid and is popular with all of her class mates. They all sing beautifully and love performing for an audience, so I am hoping that we can use them and some of their family at the party.

Lexie was excited when she explained the special treat that they had for everyone.

"Each person, even tiny babies, will be given a ticket like a bus weekly when they arrive," she said. "Printed on the ticket, there will be an ice cream, a can of soft drink, a burger or hot dog, a toy and a gift. They can collect any of them during the afternoon. Their ticket will be clicked beside each item as it is collected and it is all free.

The gifts will be their own choice. There is a list on the back of the card. It varies from an item of clothing, a box of groceries, a box of fruit and vegetables, a box of books or another toy.

The clothing is new and although some of the books and toys are pre-loved they are all in new condition. All of these items have also been donated but most of them have come from the city or towns on Jack's route, not from farmers.

There will be entertainment too, with some competitions, like flat races or goal shooting and each event will have a small money prize for first, second and third

We want everyone to relax and have a happy afternoon. The farmers are battling a severe drought but they have still been generous wherever they could. The shopkeepers who have been generous are also having a lean time because the farmers can't spend. So, this party is not just a farewell, but a thank you for the whole district.

It was a quiet week for Chloe. There were no new animals and no special visitors to distract her and all of her thoughts were on the party and meeting her friends. However, there was one thought that really worried her. She desperately wanted the freedom of being able to walk with her friends instead of being pushed in her wheelchair. She didn't want to be 'the little girl in the wheelchair' with everyone feeling sorry for her. Billy was adamant that Doctor Paterson did not want her to walk without the wheelchair when she was outside. She begged Billy to ring the doctor and when she refused to bother him Chloe tearfully announced that she wasn't going to the party.

Jeffrey heard the conversation and he knew that his little sister was not acting like a spoilt brat and just wanting her own way. During the last few years, she didn't have many special outings and nor did she have a lot of friends and he interceded on Chloe's behalf. He went to Billy and said "I know that you are protecting Chloe from hurting herself but I want you to remember that Jack and Lexie and their three daughters have been her family and helped both of us through a traumatic time. I know her well, and she would never get so upset if this occasion wasn't extremely important to her, so I will accept the responsibility and ring Doctor Paterson. I won't ask him—I will tell him that I am going to allow her to walk with her friends provided that she promises me that she won't compete in any of the events. I am sorry Billy but I do believe that it is extremely important that she is allowed to enjoy the garden party. I feel sure that both Dr Farrel and Doctor Paterson will understand. After all, when you think about it, she has been extremely patient throughout the whole terrible ordeal."

At first Billy was surprised and appeared to be a bit angry but when she thought about it she realised that Chloe had never complained or defied her before and she was obviously a very intelligent little girl and she wouldn't do anything dangerous, so she apologised to Chloe for not being more sensitive and actually praised Jeffrey for standing up for his sister. They were all friends again.

The long-awaited Saturday finally arrived and everyone was up early, eager to finish their tasks and head for Jack and Lexie.

The girls were sitting on the front veranda waiting for their friends and dashed out to meet them.

They hugged each other, but for them it was a happy and sad occasion. They were determined to stay in touch and Fiona, Rosemary and Carly were now capable of writing letters. As a final gift Chloe gave each of the girls an easy-to-use camera.

She kept her promise to walk carefully and not compete in any event but her friends competed and won a place in every competition. They each won prize money which they gave to one of the other competitors or another school friend. Because everyone had given them so much, they were thrilled at being able to give something to others.

It was nearly dark when the stall holders started giving away the last of their goods and people were packing up to go home. The time to say "Good-bye" had come. There were hugs and tears and plenty of giggling and promises. Three little girls had changed so many lives.

Chapter 62

The life of every member of this extraordinary family gradually settled into a routine. They were busy lives but never dull. Chloe had dreamed of rescuing old cattle and old fowls, but once the word spread that she would give a good home to any unwanted animal, her park grew rapidly. Jeffrey continued to build animal cabins with two-hectare paddocks and they just stayed in front of requirements. When the chickens hatched, Ellen took time off work to help some of the cute little creatures to peck their way into the world.

They had one hundred percent success with every egg producing one little chicken. Their shelter was a huge hexagonal shape building with transparent walls. As they grew, they would be separated into pens according to their size and temperament They were different sizes and different colours and with one hundred of them running around they looked adorable.

Chloe had never intended to accept cats or dogs because there were already many welfare groups that rescued them, but when one of the driveway attendants found a cardboard carton with a mother cat and six little new born kittens in it, in the car park one morning, he immediately rang Chloe to see what he should do with them. She jumped onto her motorised scooter and raced down to the motel.

Several people were standing around the box, including Mary who had already given the pretty little mother a small bowl of milk. When Chloe arrived, Mary said "We will need to get her the correct milk as quickly as we can, but I am sure she is enjoying this little drink now."

"Isn't she a pretty little animal?" Chloe said. "I've never had a kitten."

"You'll get a lot of love from them," Mary said, "We always had cats on the farm. Have we got a spare shelter ready? It won't matter about the fence for now, because she will be safer locked in the shelter, in case she takes her kittens away and hides them."

It was clear to Chloe that Mary was intending to keep them so she just agreed with all of her suggestions and let her make the decisions. "We will have to design a cat proof fence before we let her roam freely, and I am sure we have a few cans of cat food in the grocery section, but we will need to buy a lot more. "Mary said as she talked on.

"Mary, I am sure the boys finished a shelter up near the huts recently and that would be a good place The kittens seem to be very young. but I don't know anything about cats so can I leave it to you to organise a nice comfortable and safe home for them. Remind the boys that they have to be locked inside until a proper fence is built, but it can be quite small temporarily and the two hectares completed later."

Mary was delighted but she asked Chloe, with a smile on her face, whether she would make the initial introduction to Jeffrey.

Chloe was afraid that Jeffrey might have some objections, but it was her park and after telling Billy about their new tenants she whispered. "I'll pull rank on him if he starts to argue. The rest I'll leave to Mary".

The park was the busiest area in the district and definitely the biggest employer. The boundary fence was almost a never-ending job and as soon as a new shelter and enclosure was finished, new tenants arrived.

The car park was moved to the other side of the restaurant and tripled in size. The permits for the boys' service station were passed and George, Jack and Sebastian were all working on the finer details. Sebastian was a good architect and he kept a close eye on all of the plans or extra ideas. Jack had been a local and long-distance truck driver for many decades and he knew the little things that made good Service Stations and rest areas for long distant drivers. George had lived in the area all of his life. He was well liked and knew the workers and those trades men who had earned a good name. Two good mechanics were already chosen and they had recommended and selected the tools and machinery that would be needed and had agreed to take on Jeffrey and Dean as apprentices as soon as the business was organised.

Ellen's veterinary surgery was built with four comfortable outdoor areas where the animals who needed time to recover could be held for a few days. However, Ellen had kept her job with Jeremy until she had more experience and he had also told her that he was planning to sell his practice and he was hoping that she might buy it.

Pamela and Wendy had enjoyed making clothes for Chloe and the three little girls from the country and they decided that they would like to be full time dress makers.

Ellen and Pamela had been very close friends since their early school days and Ellen suddenly had a great idea. One day she said to Jeffrey,

"Pamela and Wendy are excellent young dress makers but they haven't been able to find a suitable shop at a reasonable rent. How about you build a suitable shop next to my surgery where they can sell ready-made clothes and also make clothes or uniforms to order. I feel certain that it will be popular and thus bring more customers to the restaurant."

Jeffrey thought about it for a while and then he said, "I think you are right. Have you spoken to them?"

"No. but I'll ring Pamela now."

That was the beginning of a whole new venture, because Jeffrey not only built the shop, but also a one-room living space adjoining the shop and both girls moved in.

Chapter 63

When George and Mary made the brave and daring decision to close down their farm and start a motel, neither of them knew anything about motels but gradually they learnt what people who were travelling were looking for and with their friendly and helpful personalities the whole venture became popular and grew extremely quickly. They moved out of their old home and made themselves a comfortable home in a motel unit. At first, they had older experienced staff but they gradually changed to a young staff which was at the time that Jeffrey joined the crew. Now this same little road house was more like a little village.

The animal park was a popular tourist destination. The huge service stations were almost ready for business, but best of all their beautiful old house had been restored and was one of the most beautiful old Queenslanders, and it was a tourist attraction itself.

The restaurant was extended and already there had been three well-advertised weddings held there and several more were booked over the following six months. Christmas was nearly booked out and they had actually booked the hall for their own new year party.

Chapter 64

It was a few days before Christmas, and Jack was on his last trip to Brisbane. He intended to take off Christmas- New Year and the rest of January. He had parked his big rig at a Road House out along the highway and then he went back into Brisbane to do some extra Christmas shopping.

At about 9:30 pm, Jack was walking back along Roma Street in Brisbane waiting for a taxi which he had booked, to take him back to the Highway Motel where he had left his Rig, when he saw two young boys sleeping in the closed doorway of an old shop. He stopped and looked down at the pair, wondering what he should do. They looked small and vulnerable and he didn't like to leave them there. Suddenly the taller boy sprang up and looked quite aggressive as he demanded "Who are you? What do you want?" Jack was quite aware of his own size. He was a big man and he almost laughed as this pint-sized teenager was about to challenge him, but he also saw the absolute fear in the boy's face.

"I am just wondering why two young lads are trying to sleep here in such a cold and dangerous place. I am sure I can help you." he said. As he spoke the second boy stood up and Jack said "My name is Jack and I want to help you. Have you had any dinner?"

"No." the small boy said. "Shut up Richie." the older boy demanded, "Jessie I'm hungry. I haven't had anything to eat today." The small boy complained. As he spoke the taxi which Jack had booked pulled into the curb and without hesitation Jack said as an order "Quick. Grab your blankets and pillows," and he gave the small boy a gentle shove into the taxi with a slightly more encouraging push on the bigger boy's shoulder. He closed the door and then stepped into the front seat.

215

"First we eat and then we chat and then we have a safe warm sleep in the cabin of my Rig" he said.

"Same place Chief?" the cabbie who had often driven Jack back to the motel asked.

"Yes. Andy, "Jack answered. "It's a bit cool tonight, isn't it? Would you park next to my rig please?"

As they stepped out of the taxi, Jack took the boys' blankets and pillows and placed them on the front seat of his huge vehicle and said, "Now you two slip into the toilets and make room for a big feed while I wait here." He had also noticed that the pillows and blankets appeared to be good quality. When the boys came out, he noticed how badly Richie was limping. "What have you done to your leg?" he asked.

"That's where that mongrel kicked him" Jess answered. They were near the back door of the restaurant, so Jack picked Richie up in his arms and carried him into the nearest table. He wasn't ready to ask a lot of questions although he was looking for a lot of answers. The table was quite secluded but first the boys needed some food.

"Now. How about a nice big hamburger and chips and a hot chocolate milk?"

"Yes please Jack, "They both answered politely and Jack called the waitress over and ordered the same for himself, except he had coffee.

While they were waiting, he asked Richie how his leg was feeling and Richie replied that it was fairly sore. "Does your mother ever give you Panadol to ease pain?"

"Yes." he replied.

"Do you think some would help your pain now?" Jack asked.

"Yes." Richie replied and Jack noticed a tear well up in his eyes. He took out his wallet and from the back of his folder he took a sheet of Panadol and tore two tablets off and put them on the table. "You had better leave them until you have had something to eat and then wash them down with some chocolate milk."

"Who is the mongrel?" Jack asked.

"One of the mongrels that Mum has brought home. That is why Dad doesn't live with us now." Jess said. "Dad said that he would come back for us, but he hasn't."

"We think that the mongrel might have killed him" Richie said.

Just then the food arrived and when the waitress left, Jack said "Why do you think that he might have killed your dad?"

"Because he killed our neighbour Aunty May, yesterday." Jessy said.

"WHAT?" Jack exclaimed.

"I want to find the police and tell them". Jess said.

"Tell me." Jack said in a hushed voice.

"This afternoon, he didn't know that I was home and he started telling Mum that he had shut her up. Then he thought of me and called me a dirty name and asked whether I was home and Mum told him that I wasn't, but I heard him coming towards my bedroom and I knew that he would bash me if he saw me, so I quickly rolled under my bed and he just opened the door, had a quick look and walked away. Then he told Mum that he stuffed her into a drain near the bridge and she wouldn't wash out until there was a downpour and then the sharks could have a feed, and he laughed when he said that he hoped that they didn't get indigestion from all of her jewellery. Mum was crying because Aunty May was one of her best friends and he said he'd do the same to her if she didn't shut up. That was when Richie came home and he kicked him hard on the hip as Richie walked past him.

I had already pushed the blankets and pillows through the big square safety grill on the window, but we can't fit through it. When they sat down and then called us to dinner, we were watching through the key hole, and we casually opened the door and then ran through the dining room, out the door and as fast as we could run up the street. We waited up at the corner until the dining room lights went out and then I sneaked back and got the blankets and pillows."

Jack was feeling stunned but he believed Jess. "Why would he kill her?" he asked in a whispering voice.

"Because, yesterday afternoon, Richie and I were kicking the football around in the front yard and he came out and said that we were damaging the garden and he just started kicking and punching us. Aunty May is not really our aunty, but we have always called her Aunty because she was our baby-sitter when we were little kids. When she saw what he was doing, and others in the street saw it too, she went back inside and got her stock whip and came over and started whipping him. They had a real shouting match and Mum sent us inside but he didn't come in for a couple of hours. When he came home, he told Mum that he had been at the pub."

"Do you see those three men sitting together at the other end of the dining area?" Jack asked him.

"Yes." Jess replied.

"Well, they are plain clothes police". Jack told him.

"Are they real cops?" he asked.

"Absolutely, and I am friends with one of them, so I am going to give him a ring and ask him to come and have a cup of coffee with me. Now I want you to tell him everything that you have told me but keep your voice down."

He joked with Cameron Stevens for a while and then he told him that he had two boys with him with a story that he should hear.

"Are you sure you don't want D.O.C.S.?" he asked.

"No. I'm certain, but please don't draw any serious attention to the kids. Let it appear that you and I are having a social happy conversation, but I assure you their story is not a happy one. I'll have a cup of coffee ready for you."

Cameron listened carefully to the boys and then he leaned back in his chair and looked at Jack and said" Wow. That was not what I was expecting. What do you think?"

Jack told him how he had met the boys and that he felt that their mother could be in danger and that the story should be checked immediately before there was time for the body to be moved. "I believe them," he said, "and I also fear for them, so if you can possibly keep them out of it, do so, and if you want to contact them, they will be with me."

Cameron Stevens put his hands on the shoulders of Jess and Richie and said "Be careful Boys. If what you have told me is true, and I do believe you, he is an extremely dangerous person. Jack will take good care of you. You couldn't have found a better helper. Listen to him and take his advice."

"Will you look after our Mum because she is frightened of him and she was a good mother until he forced his way into our lives."

"We'll look after her and get her out of there as quickly as we can but it might be some time before you can contact her or she can contact you." He took a notebook out of his back pocket and wrote on it "Benjamin and Bradley Livingstone from New Zealand, Blond crew cuts. Then he said "Keep them out of sight and, have you still got your friendly back-room barber?"

Jack thought for a while then he realised what he was asking and said "Oh Yes."

"Well, I suggest you use him." then he handed Jack the piece of paper.

Senior Sergeant Stevens went back to his friends and they left soon afterwards. Jack and the boys also left, but the three of them made themselves comfortable in the cabin of his huge semi-trailer.

They had been asleep for a few hours when Jack was wakened by his phone. There was a simple message, "Mission successful". Signed SSCS.

The boys were sleeping soundly. Jack was reminded of the time that he had sneaked Chloe and Jeffrey out of the city and he wondered whether these kids would have such a happy ending to their story. He liked the boys. They seemed to be two nice kids who had once been part of a good family, but they were painfully thin, the thinnest children that he had ever seen, except on T.V stories about starving people in some African countries.

They were still sound asleep when he reached his next rest area, so he parked his vehicle where he could see it from inside the restaurant and went inside and had a couple of cups of coffee and a pie. He then sat outside on a seat in the fresh air to refresh himself. He was thinking of the kids "What if he hadn't seen them? The taxi had arrived at the same time. He could easily have missed them. His next stop would be Bundaberg and he would find a pharmacy and buy some crutches for Richie, and then find a clothing shop and buy them a back pack and a variety of clothes. He would let Lexie know that they were coming and ask her to meet him in Longreach. The first thing he would have to do was to convince them to change their names and then their hair.

The shops were just opening when they reached Bundaberg and he knew the perfect place to park. It was a long parking area opposite to a large pharmacy so the boys waited in the semitrailer while he went across the road to the pharmacy and found a pair of Canadian crutches that would be just perfect for the young fellow.

Poor little Richie was stiff and sore and it was hard for him to climb down from the high cabin, but he was a brave and tough little guy and soon mastered the crutches. Jack took them around to another street, hoping that, if later, someone remembered them they would not connect them to the big rig.

As they shopped for clothes, he tried to make it sound like a Christmas outing and moved as quickly as he could without drawing too much attention. Soon they were set up with a back pack and enough clothes to keep them going for a few days and a particularly dressy outfit with sports coat and good long dark slacks. They could gradually add more. They had breakfast and set off once more. The boys were much more relaxed. They had a good sleep, a good breakfast and the cop had assured them that Jack would take care of them. Jack decided that it was time to turn on the radio and let them hear the news.

The whole bulletin was about two fishermen finding the body of a middle-aged woman floating near the bridge over the Brisbane River.

"That will be Aunty May." both boys shouted. The police were asking for help and they were not sure how she had died. She was wearing a lot of expensive jewellery but nothing to identify her.

"We have to stop and call the police." Jess said anxiously.

"That is the last thing we want to do." Jack said. "You and I both know that the police know exactly who she is. You have already told them everything, and that is Senior Sergeant Stevens way of warning you to get out of sight. Now, you saw him hand me a piece of paper at the road house." Jack put his hand into his pocket and pulled out the little sheet of paper.

"It has now become dangerous for you and he wants you to have a completely new identity. That is what he meant when he asked you to take my advice." Jack handed the boys the paper and said, "This is your new identity." As they read it Richie started to smile, "I think that will be fun," he said.

"Will we always have to be these people?" Jess asked.

"I don't know, but he also wants you to have dye your hair blond and cut it in a new style. Please say that you will co-operate. It is for your own safety. We are talking about a vicious killer who has already shown that he hates you."

"You won't know yourself when my friend finishes."

Jess partly excitedly and partially reluctantly agreed, and Jack spent most of the rest of the trip teaching them to change their identity and their thinking. "You must never admit that you know May and never try to claim any credit for finding her."

Lexie was waiting at a picnic park just outside of town and after meeting the boys and having a brief conversation with them and Jack, the boys moved into her car and she drove them to the barber shop and parked in his back garden. Jack had phoned him and given him a made-up excuse for the disguise. The two boys that went in, looked nothing like the two boys who came out. With their blond hair and new style, they could barely recognise themselves. Mark, the barber, had allowed them to use a room to change into some new and very expensive looking clothes.

Because of the hair colouring, the whole appointment had taken quite a long time and Jack and Lexie, sat in the park where they could talk quietly and Jack was able to tell Lexie the whole story. He also rang Cameron Stevens to get any special instructions from him. Cameron was pleased to hear that the boys had agreed to taking a new identity and that they were already having their hair changed. He told Jack that he would have a special officer waiting at the hospital for him and he would be posing as a welfare officer. The two boys were the victims of a high society divorce and custody battle between an Australian and a New Zealand parent. His officer would block any question that was not related to a medical problem.

The boys looked magnificent and even Jess was beginning to enjoy his role. The four of them had a good meal and then went to the hospital. The officer was waiting for them and had all the arrangements made for a thorough but private medical check. After the ex-rays they were all called into a small room where a doctor was waiting for them.

The serious look on his face told them that the news was not good. "The only good news that I have," he said. "Is that Benjamin's hip is not broken. It is very badly bruised. However, these boys each have multiple breaks that have healed. I have been told that I am not to ask questions, but I will be writing a complete report. It is one of the worst cases that I have seen of child cruelty. He wrote out some prescriptions that he wanted to be made up immediately and asked for the boys to return to the hospital the following week to see him. After a visit to the pharmacy, Jack and Lexie took the boys to their house where the three girls were waiting for them. They had often looked after foster children and they made a habit of always telling their own daughters the true story, and that was what they did as they all sat down to a nice meal.

Afterwards, the children went into the TV room to watch cartoons and Jack and Lexie went into Jack's office to have a private conversation with Billy, Seb, Jeffrey and Chloe. They talked for a long time and instead of having to repeat the same story several times they had their phones on 'speaker'.

Billy was shocked but determined to restore the two little men to good health, and Jack assured her that she would be properly compensated, not just in her wage, but through the Children's department.

Seb was keen to accept the challenge of bringing them back to perfect health, both physically and mentally.

Jeffrey and Chloe had sat there in silence as their haunted memories came flooding back. They were going to repay the fortunate chance that they had been given by giving the boys the best future that they could possibly have.

After they had made the final arrangements, they went to the children and explained that it would not be safe for them to live in their home because often they would be on their own. Instead, they were taking them to a special and unique family where they would be completely safe and live like royalty. "They are not an ordinary family. They are a group of the most wonderful people in this world, whose main aim is to help others to live a happy life.

Chapter 65

Jack and Lexie and Ben and Bradley set off once again in Lexie's car. The adults kept a happy conversation going as they pointed out landmarks along the way. The boys had never been out west and their minds were kept busy.

Suddenly, in front of them, there was a huge sign for The Big Black Bull Motel and Animal Rescue Park. Ben became excited and begged to be allowed to visit it. "Oh, you'll get plenty of chances to see it in the future," Jack said. Then the house came in sight and Jack pulled over to the side of the road and stopped.

"What do you think of that house? Isn't it something?"

"Yes. I've seen it on TV" Ben said.

By then the family had seen Lexie's car and they were starting to gather outside of the house fence and some of them were waving.

"That is your new home. Your new family has seen us and there they are waving to you. Belinda and Sebastian were hired to look after Chloe when she came out of hospital, because she had been nearly killed by a beast as vicious as your mongrel. Chloe and Jeffrey own the whole park and motel. Dean is Jeffrey's friend. Ellen moved in when her parents sold their farm, and she brought her little animal family with her. It consists of a sheep, a goat and a pig, and they were all raised together from babies, and they are confused about what they are and they try to imitate each other. George and Mary originally owned the farm and motel and they still live here and they are like grandparents.to everyone. The veterinary clinic there belongs to Ellen and Chloe is studying to be a vet. The little clothing shop belongs to our Pamela and Wendy and the big sheds are Jeffrey's and Dean's and they will be opening in the new year.

That is just a brief description of these extraordinary people. He started the motor, and said, "Well let's go and meet them."

The boys were quiet. Even Ben was almost lost for words. He just said, "Awesome! We are going to live at this park." and then continued to comment about the animals that he could see.

The whole family was home and they were keenly waiting outside the fence. When the car stopped and the boys stepped out Seb was the first to step forward. He shook hands with each boy and gave him a welcoming pat on his shoulder.

"Welcome to our family," he said. "I hope we can give you a truly wonderful future." Each one followed with a similar remark, until it came to Chloe's turn, and she put her arms around both boys and said "It's great to meet you. I hope you enjoy being part of our family".

Everyone had a welcoming remark and then Seb suggested that they should all go inside where he had some treats prepared and waiting to be eaten.

Chloe stayed near the boys and chatted all the way. When they were nearly at the foot of the stairs, Ben said, "Those stairs are high, aren't they?"

"No problem" she said and leaned across and pressed the button to open the door of the lift.

"You have a lift in the house?" they both said in surprise.

"Yes. When I came home from hospital, I was in a wheelchair, and Jeffrey had installed the lift so that I could go up and down the stairs without any help."

"Wow" was their only response, and the three of them stepped into it.

When they reached the veranda, Billy led the way through the hallway to the dining room but Jeffrey, who was carrying Ben's back pack led them to their bedroom. The boys surveyed the room with a look of sheer delight, and Jeffrey, without asking for their choice of beds, put Ben's bag on the first bed and then went across the room to open the door which led to the veranda. They both followed him and stepped out to admire the scene. Ben, staggering along on his crutches had a fixed relaxed and extremely happy smile on his face. He could see Ferdinand.

The four of the young people stayed there chatting about the animals that they could see and those that they could not see, and then they were given a loud call from the dining room. There, they found a huge table which was loaded with plates full of delicious looking finger treats and they were invited to help themselves.

Everyone was keen to help the boys relax and to feel like part of the group so some lively talk about their plans for the following week started. There were three days to Christmas, so Seb reminded the girls that he had a list of groceries that he would like them to go to town to buy on the following day. What he was really planning, was a special shopping trip to buy Christmas presents for the boys.

"What do you want to be, when you grow up?" he asked Ben.

"A vet" was Ben's quick reply.

There was a murmur around the table as many of them felt a flow of Chloe-ism pass through their veins.

"Well, if you want to be a vet, you are in good company here. We have one vet now and another one on her way, so we can get your future rolling immediately." Lexie said.

"What about you Bradley? You're very quiet. If you had a choice of anything that you wanted, what would you like to do?" George asked. Bradley went a deep shade of red and with his head bent slightly forward, murmured something that everyone except Jeffrey, who was sitting next to him, did not hear. "No way. No one here would laugh at someone's dreams." Jeffrey said. "Please share them with us"

"A chef" he answered with a slight hint of irritation.

"If anyone laughed at that, they'd answer to me." Seb announced with zest. "I always wanted to be a chef, but my father was against it and because he was paying my university fees, I had to accept his decision. Now I am head chef for this wonderful family, and I wake up enthusiastic every morning. I lie there in bed planning the whole day's menu, and even when I have completed that, I can't stop cooking. It is my absolute passion." Bradley smiled for the first time and the whole conversation turned to how they would ensure that he achieved his dream.

With the combined knowledge of all of the adults around the table, and of course, Ellen who had just completed a university degree, and Jeffrey and Dean who had just enrolled in a university course, they had quickly chosen the best subjects for both boys to study.

Chloe was already enrolled with the Distant Education, and Lexie would have the boys enrolled before the New Year. Both boys started to feel a new enthusiasm and their recent traumatic existence was already fading.

On the following morning, the ladies set off early on their shopping expedition. It wasn't very often that Chloe and Billy would allow someone else to feed the animals, but this was urgent and they knew that the boys would do a good job. Ben was delighted when Jeffrey asked him whether he would like to help and he brought out Chloe's scooter for Ben to ride.

Seb and Bradley had formed a close friendship and Bradley chose to follow him around. He even enjoyed doing basic house work and then went outside with Seb to pull some weeds out of the vegetable garden and collect fresh vegetables for the evening meal. Seb taught him the names of the various vegetables and herbs, and explained which herbs were the best flavours to add to different meats.

They spent more time cooking biscuits and scones for the morning snack.

Meanwhile as the ladies travelled down the highway, they prepared a list of ideas for presents for young lads and added it to the list that Jeffrey and Dean had given to them that morning.

Bikes and lap-tops were at the top of the list and Billy was keen to fill a stocking with many ordinary articles or possessions that most children would take for granted. Tooth brushes and paste with a container for the tooth brush, soap and container, brush and comb, shampoo, comic books, felt pens and biros, a good book each, a small model aeroplane and ship to be assembled, a packet of small chocolate bars and a packet of potato flakes. She had written down a list but as she looked around the shops many other small items were popped into her shopping bag.

The boys had arrived with a back pack and a few clothes, but she insisted that they needed to have some ordinary possessions that any child of their age would have. After filling two large shopping bags, she found a box of oil paints with six different colours and a case of water paints, so she added an art book for each and two self-teaching drawing books, one was "How to draw people" and one was "How to draw animals". After that she was satisfied until she saw some clay ornaments and she chose a white cockatoo and a pink and grey galah. Each one was about 20 centre metres tall. The other ladies and Chloe were amused but completely agreed with her choices.

As the others shopped, they bought two lap-tops, two bicycles and two large scale model cars that had to be assembled. They also bought two cricket sets with a bat and ball and three wickets, but they decided to just add them to the tree for everyone to share so they didn't put any name on them. At the base of the tree there would be a soccer ball and other coloured balls of various sizes. They would also be for sharing.

After their shopping excursion was over and they were on their way home, Chloe rang Jeffrey and asked him to take the boys up to the cat house and keep them there until they had a chance to unload their shopping.

The few groceries that they bought were taken upstairs to the pantry, but the gifts were taken under the house and hidden away in Seb's and Billy's unit.

It was the day before Christmas Eve.

Chapter 66

As the boys settled into bed that night, Ben said to his brother, "I like living here. Do you like it too, Bradley?"

"Yes, especially Seb. He is teaching me a lot about cooking, and he really does enjoy it. Is your hip still sore?"

"Yes, but those tablets that the doctor gave me are good. Soon after I have one of them, I can almost forget about my hip and what the mongrel did to me."

Seb doesn't like us calling him the mongrel. He said that he would rather that we call him a beast."

"Okay. Chloe had a beast try to kill her too, but he is in jail now. Do you think there will be any presents for Christmas? They don't have any decorations or a Christmas tree."

"Ben, Seb has cooked a lot of delicious food for Christmas and we know that everyone will be happy and we don't have to worry about what the beast is going to do to us, so even if we don't get any presents, I hope you won't be disappointed. I am glad that Mum is safe, but I never want to live with her again. I would like to see Dad again and next time that we are talking to Jack, I am going to ask him to ask Cameron Stevens to look for him. I love this family and I want to live here for ever."

"So do I Brad and I promise that I won't be disappointed."

"Good night mate. Have a good sleep."

"Good night Brad. I love you."

On Christmas Eve the usual chores had to be done and once again, Ben chose to feed the animals and Bradley stayed with Seb. He vacuumed floors, dusted shelves, and helped Seb to pack away the dishes, then they both went out to the vegetable garden. Bradley was a good worker and

Seb could already see the difference that his help was making. In the New Year he would have a word with Jeffrey about giving the boys some pocket money as a small wage.

After Billy, Chloe and Ben finished their morning chores, having fed and petted all of the animals and checked that all of the old cows had come up to their feeding area for some fresh chaff and special nutritious pellets, they had a shower and settled in to their day's activities.

Dean went home to his family. Jeffrey ran over the lawn with his ride-on mower once more. Ellen went to work for the last day before her holiday. Billy went to the kitchen to help Seb and Bradley and Ben and Chloe went to the library.

The two young ones were very much alike. Chloe taught Ben and Bradley how to use the library catalogue system and told them that they could borrow any book which they would like to read. Ben had soon chosen a book about camels and he told Chloe that they looked so interesting and he didn't know anything about them. She gave a little laugh as she told him that she had felt the same way and she quickly pulled out two more books where she said he would find a lot more facts. She then settled down in a comfortable chair on the veranda with a folder full of Ellen's university notes until Billy called the three of them to the dining room for a morning snack.

The day went by quickly and at dinner time Seb advised everyone to get an early night because he would be calling them at 5:30 in the morning for breakfast.

Once again as the boys were settling down, they had a little brotherly conversation. There was still no Christmas tree or any talk of presents but they were happy and looking forward to Christmas day.

Chapter 67

The boys woke early on Christmas morning but neither of them realised that the other one was awake so they didn't speak. Then Billy turned the record player up very loudly so that Christmas Carols were booming through the house and she shouted out in a loud voice, "Wake up everyone! Five minutes to breakfast and come out looking decent!"

The boys dressed quickly and dashed out to the dining room where everyone was offering Christmas greetings. The table was loaded with plates full of food and Seb said, "All of this has to be taken down under the house so, if we can each take one or two plates, it won't be a problem. The table down there is much bigger and we will have more room to move around." Then he looked at Ben and said, "What about you, Hoppy? Are you going to use your crutches or the wheelchair?"

"Can I use the wheelchair please?" Ben asked.

"Yes," Billy answered. "I think that would be the best idea, and you can take this tray of cutlery. Mind you don't drop it because you will have to wash and wipe it yourself."

Chloe pushed Ben through the hallway and took him down in the lift but the others went out the side door and straight down to the door under the house. They were there much sooner and as Chloe and Ben passed down the side of the house, they could hear excited laughing.

Chloe pushed him through the door and then both of them gasped and cried out as Chloe pushed Ben quickly across the room. There was a huge floor to ceiling silvery white Christmas tree and standing beside it were three bicycles. A beautiful golden coloured bike with black pencil stripes, had a large Christmas card hanging from the handle bars with "Bradley" written on it. Next to it there was an equally beautiful blue bike with a card and Benjamin's name on it, and next to it, a striking red bicycle with a pretty basket hanging from the handle bars and Chloe's name on it. Ellen was still playing "Jingle Bells".

Ben stepped out of the chair and put his hands on the handle bars and then he ran his hands along the bar and the saddle and started to cry.

George was the nearest to him and Ben looked at him and said, "Is it mine forever? Can I really keep it?"

"Yes, Little Man. It is your bicycle. It is yours forever."

There were not many dry eyes in the room as they watched the re-action and expressions of the three young people. Ellen stopped playing and Seb interrupted by calling out "Breakfast first and then Christmas presents. We must still have a healthy meal. So, there are several cereals to choose from, plenty of milk and sugar or maple syrup. Have a bowl of cereal and then eat anything you like."

"What is maple syrup?" Ben asked Chloe.

"It's yummy, but very sweet, so don't use too much until you taste it," Chloe told him.

They each chose their food and then sat down to enjoy it. The three young ones sat near each other, but Ben couldn't take his eyes off his bicycle. "Aren't the bikes great?" he- said. "I hope I can ride mine with my sore hip," he added.

"Well, if you can't ride yours yet, I won't ride mine either. I'll wait until your hip is better. "Bradley answered.

"I will too. "Chloe said.

As the eating slowed down, Seb said to George, "Do you want to be Santa or will we do it together?"

"Together" was George's prompt reply.

The both of them walked over to the tree and called for everyone's attention with a loud "Ho! Ho! Ho!" from Seb. He said "Now I will attempt to choose a variety of gifts but there are a lot to give out so I won't wait for each of you to unwrap your present."

"This big one goes to Jeffrey," and he handed him a poorly disguised guitar. Seb continued to select gifts and hand them to George who then delivered them to the recipient. Soon the air in the room was full of the beautiful fragrance of different perfumes and excited voices full of surprise.

The boys each enjoyed unloading their stockings and there were some surprised exclamations when an extremely pretty home-made stocking was handed to Chloe. None of the other shoppers realised that Billy had already made and filled a stocking for Chloe when they were on their big shopping excursion for the boys.

Everyone in this unique family was loaded with gifts, and they all agreed that they had never had a Christmas to equal it.

The floor under the house was knee deep with wrapping paper and when Jeffrey and Ellen started to pick it up Billy asked them to leave it a bit longer. "It looks so Christmassy, let's leave it there until later."

It was, however, time to feed the animals. Ellen and Jeffrey went off to feed the camels, alpacas, cows and horses while Chloe, Ben and Bradley went to the barn to get the food for the rest of their tenants.

The four adults packed the dishwasher and sat down in Seb's and Billy's unit to have a cup of coffee.

Suddenly, Billy gasped and they all looked out the back window and saw Ben travelling at top speed on the scooter and Bradley close behind him on the tractor with Chloe sitting on the big mud guard over the back wheel and the trailer being towed behind them.

Chloe's long blond hair was flying behind her and she looked as though she was thoroughly enjoying herself.

The women were shocked but both men roared with laughter.

They all went outside to watch what other mischief the trio would get up to, but when the children saw that they were being watched they settled down to do their work more carefully.

"That is the sign of three happy normal kids." Seb said, and Billy added, "It is good to see Chloe behaving like a happy twelve-year-old instead of a young business woman".

"I suggest that we don't say anything when they come in. They will be expecting to get a lecture, but we will just let their conscience bother them." Seb said. "What do you think George?"

"Well, they just set my adrenalin flowing, because that is exactly what farm kids would do. They make their own fun, and I know that there is an old motor mower in the barn and I am wondering whether I could get the boys to help me make a go-cart and put the motor on it."

"Sounds like a great idea but not today. Just act normally and let them wonder what we are thinking. I'll enjoy watching their re-action" Seb said with a wilful little giggle.

Jeffrey and Ellen were the first finished and they had a shower and a quick change of clothes before the young trio came in looking very awkward and uncomfortable.

"Hurry up kids," Billy said. "Have a shower and get into some nice Christmassy clothes for lunch. It is almost ready."Chloe went into one shower and both boys went into the other one together.

Chloe had chosen her beautiful blue lace frock and she looked gorgeous when she went down to the dinner table.

Once again it was loaded with food. Some hot food had been added, also salads and pasta or rice dishes. The boys had never seen so much food in front of them and they didn't know what to do.

"Take a plate from the pile at the end of the table and help yourself, Boys. Load up with whatever you like and if you can eat some more, come back for a second plate full. Remember, your best disguise will be to put on weight." Seb said.

It was a happy joyful meal with carols playing softly in the background.

Finally, Ellen, Jeffrey and the three young ones began to clear away the dishes and ordered the adults to find a comfortable chair and relax. They took their order for drinks and delivered them to the adults. It didn't take long and the five young people were still full of energy as they took the new cricket set outside. Ben and Bradley were delighted. They had frequently watched families playing beach or backyard cricket at festival times on television and always longed to join in.

The whole day was turning out to be absolutely marvellous.

They hadn't been playing very long when the four adults joined them.

Mary was the greatest surprise. They all decided to play "putsy out goes in".

Ellen and Chloe were given the first bat and then whoever managed to put someone out would be given a bat. It wasn't long before Mary caught Ellen's high ball and Mary was given Ellen's bat. As she faced the bowler it was clear from her stance that she had played before, and she slogged the ball hard into the back fence and ran to the other end of the pitch and back to the batter's wicket.

"Wow! You've done that before". Jeffrey said.

"Yes. I played a lot of vigoro when I was at school and I was the team captain." she answered. "Vigoro is very much like cricket but unfortunately we don't hear much about it now," she said as Seb bowled another ball at her and she gave it the same treatment. One more run was enough for Mary who was quickly exhausted and she handed the bat to Billy. The game went on for a couple of hours with everyone getting a chance to show their skill.

It had been a fantastic afternoon but they still had to let the children try out their bicycles.

Brad had learnt to ride on a friend's bike but neither Chloe nor Ben had ridden a bike before. Jeffrey was confident that Chloe would soon get her balance but he was worried about Ben's hip so he had asked the ladies to buy training wheels for Ben for safety. They each had a safety helmet and Jeffrey had brought the old bike up from the motel so that he could ride with them.

Chloe was quick to learn and the four of them went for a ride to the bottom of the park and visited the cat house where they enjoyed nursing the cats and playing with some new kittens.

Everyone voted it the best Christmas they had ever experienced, and that night they each enjoyed examining their other gifts more carefully.

Jeffrey and Ellen helped the boys to set up their lap-tops in the library and reminded them that they must never join any social media. Even the smallest slip could let someone guess where they were living. That would not only be dangerous for them, but it could also be dangerous for the rest of the family.

On Boxing Day Ellen went home to her own family in Brisbane where she intended to holiday until the New Year. Jack and Lexie arrived for a barbecue, and once again there was a busy exchange of gifts.

Chapter 68

From Christmas to New Year, it was a holiday atmosphere at the big house and the motel, caravan park and tent village were all fully occupied. The restaurant was so busy that Mary had to call in a few favours from past employees.

Jeffrey and Dean didn't want to open the Service Stations until the New Year but the whole of January was already booked out.

The drivers were booking their trucks in for a complete service and booking a caravan or motel unit for their family to have a holiday at the same time. The two new mechanics were excellent at their job and some of the truckies who travelled on the northern highway followed their favourite mechanic to his new service station.

George was busy with his fishing lessons and the rescue park was swarming with tourists roaming through to see the animals.

Jeffrey and Chloe had never charged anything for people to visit the park but they had donation boxes bolted to each gate. They didn't expect to receive much money through donations, because there were no special exotic animals, but even the old cows were very popular. It seemed that people appreciated what they were doing for these unwanted animals. Half of the money that they received, they donated to other animal shelters.

Gradually, five pigs had been added. Some of them were temporary residents, and the owners were trying to sell their home and move to a bigger property where they could keep their pets, but others were happy to give their pets over to Chloe where they knew that they would be well cared for.

Their shelter was a nice home near the restaurant where they would receive attention from the guests. It was built on two hectares of piggy paradise. Inside the home there were rugs and a fireplace for winter and air conditioning for summer. They also had soft lounge chairs where they could sleep in comfort. The paddock had soft lush grass and vegetable gardens which were rotated regularly. At one end they had a mud pond and a shallow wading pool. There were several colourful gym balls that they enjoyed rolling around and a trampoline which was set down into the ground and they often entertained their audience by standing on it and making little bouncing actions.

The new year proved to be exceedingly busy.

Jack and Lexie had taken the boys back to the hospital to be checked again. The same doctor who had seen them the previous week, saw them again. "Well, you look much happier than you did the last time that I saw you. Did you have a good Christmas?" he asked them

"Yes thank you" they answered politely. "We got new bikes and laptops and lots of new clothes and heaps of other things" Ben said excitedly.

"And you look as though you have been eating all day, every day." the doctor joked "Who is going to hop on the scales first?" Bradley stepped up first and the doctor laughed as he said, "Wow four kilos Bradley. That is amazing. Now Ben. Not quite as much but almost four. How is your hip?"

"It is much better, but I still take the tablets that you gave me and then it stops hurting"

The doctor felt his hip and as he moved it around, he found that it was still a bit tender so he gave him a prescription for another box of tablets and congratulated Jack and Lexie for the excellent care that they were giving the two boys.

They looked at each other and felt guilty accepting the praise that belonged to Seb and Billy but they decided that it was better not to tell the doctor where the boys were living.

Chapter 69

When the new school term started, the work around the house changed.

All of the young people were studying. Ellen, Jeffrey and Dean continued to work but they had to cut back on some of their hours to fit in time for study. Lexie had enrolled Ben and Bradley in their correct age level because she was confident that with help from her and Ellen and Billy, they would soon make up the time that they had lost the previous year. Chloe and Ben were doing the same lessons and they worked well together.

The library proved to be an excellent place for study and everyone respected the 'quiet' rule. After one term, the adults were absolutely thrilled with their young students. The atmosphere was contagious and it was obvious to everyone that they were all brilliant young people. They each had a dream and were giving 100 percent effort to achieve it.

Ellen continued working with Jeremy but at the same time she was working towards a higher degree.

Jeffrey and Dean were doing their apprenticeship with the mechanics who were running their Service Station and more men had to be employed to work on the park fencing.

Billy still worked with Chloe and Ben to feed the animals in the morning because she loved the work and the animals. It had become a busy time because so many new animals had been added. After they finished their morning job, they would each shower and change into neat clothes for the rest of the day. Billy had always worked in a job that required organisation and she insisted on the same diligence with their simple job.

Seb had become very fond of Bradley who enjoyed Seb's company and the work that they did together.

The three young ones each received a small wage. Jeffrey had always given Chloe an allowance which she saved in her money box, but he made it into a definite wage and he took Bradley, Ben and Chloe to town for an outing and he bought each of the boys a man's wallet and a very pretty wallet for Chloe. He then took them into a bank and opened an account for each of them. Every second Friday he deposited two-thirds of their pay into their account and gave them the other third in cash. They were amazed and thrilled when they were given their own card to operate their account, and they were asked to choose their own secret number. Neither Bradley nor Ben had ever had a cent to call their own, and having their very own bank account was beyond belief.

When Billy, Chloe and Ben were on one of their routine feeding trips, a tearful young teenage girl caught up with them and asked whether she could talk to Chloe. She said that she had a little dog and her puppies in her car and she wanted Chloe to give them a home. At first Chloe was hesitant because she had never planned to have cats or dogs, but she could see how upset the girl was and she said, "Have you tried the animal shelter?"

The girl began to cry and she said, "I haven't got time to go right over there and my father is going to shoot her."

"Well we can't let that happen, "Billy said as they all walked towards Tania's car. When she opened the door, Ben leaned in and picked up the little dog which was sitting in a box with her puppies. It licked his face and her little tail was wagging so fast that Ben said, "Hey! Slow down Whiskers or you will take off like a helicopter." They all laughed and Chloe lifted the little animal out of his arms. Chloe was given the same treatment, but what they all commented on was her size. She was the smallest dog that any of them had seen, even smaller than Poppet and its big brown eyes that were peeping through her long whiskers were pleading for help. "Where did she come from?" Chloe asked.

"I don't know." Tania answered. "She was sitting at our back door last night, so I gave her a drink of milk and put this box under the veranda and this morning she had all of these puppies. We have three farm dogs and Dad said that she would just be a nuisance. He wanted to shoot her and drown her puppies, so I put her in the car and drove away. I didn't know what to do and then I remembered your park." "We will certainly look after her," Chloe assured her, "but I really feel that someone must be looking for her. She is a dear little dog and she is just pleading for help"

Mary saw the group and went over to see what was happening. When she heard the story, she hurried inside and quickly bundled together some old towels to make a soft bed, some tins of dog food, some dry food and some puppy milk, then hurried back to the group. "Which shelter are you going to put her in?" she asked Chloe.

"I was thinking of the new yellow one. What do you think, Mary?" Chloe answered.

"Yes. That sounds perfect. It is right next to the camels but I don't think that she will worry them. She seems to be a very affectionate little pet. Let's go, so that we can get her and her babies settled." Mary said as she climbed into Tania's car.

Everyone on the staff was an animal lover. It was part of the requirements when they were employed, and they were all eager to see the little dog and her puppies.

Mary had set her up in the new yellow cabin with a large bowl of water and another bowl full of dry food, but she also gave her another bowl of puppy milk and a plate of dog food from a tin. As each visitor arrived, Whiskers, which had become her official name, greeted them with equal enthusiasm. She had a soft, safe and comfortable bed for herself and her babies, and two hectares of land to explore. Mary had also made her a separate bed where she could rest without being bothered by the puppies.

After Chloe, Billy and Ben had finished their morning's work, Chloe and Ben went to Whisker's cabin to give her some more love and attention.

As they were leaving, Billy, who was always thinking as a nurse would, reminded them that the little dog had given birth to four little pups the previous night and she needed some rest. She also told them that the puppies would still be quite frail and they should not touch them "In fact," she added, "I think you should lock the gate to deter others from bothering her for a few days. Would you mind, Chloe, asking one of the men to cut a pet door into the main door so that we can lock it, and still give Whiskers an outlet to the back yard?"

"Yes Billy. That is a good idea. Thank you. I saw Stan go down that way. I'll catch up with him and ask him now."

Chloe was so pleased to have Billy's help. Lexie had been wonderful, but she couldn't be there all the time. She loved Billy who shared the same passion for animals as she did.

Chapter 70

Life went on normally for another month. Greg and Mac and Josie had made another visit, and Greg told the children how proud he was of their investments and the pathways they had chosen for their lives. He made a fuss over Ben and Bradley who were nervous when the three strangers intruded on their new family. With Jack and Seb and George taking such good care of them and then, Greg and Mac taking an interest in their studies and dreams, they began to overcome their fears and realise that all men were not like the beast.

Chloe always made time each afternoon to visit Whiskers and throw the ball for her out in her paddock, and give her hugs and affection. The puppies' eyes were open and they were making brave attempts at pushing themselves along and rolling over each other. She had been playing with Whiskers and was ready to leave when a man standing near the gate said, "It is good to see them together again. Where did you find the clown's dog?"

Chloe looked up at him and said, "I don't understand what you mean."

"That is Tilly, isn't it?" he said. When he said 'Tilly', Whiskers stopped and her ears stood up making her look very alert.

"Where did you find her?" he asked.

"She was brought to us as a stray "Chloe replied.

The man said, "My name is Gavin and I had a temporary job at the circus when it was in town. I was the groundsman or litter man. I picked up all of the rubbish inside and outside the tent after each session, and I enjoyed watching the actors practising. I am certain that Whiskers is Matilda whom the clown called Tilly. She performed with the camels but someone stole her a couple of days before the circus left. Bonzo was heartbroken, but after the camel was hurt, Tilly didn't have an act and he thought she looked as though she was going to have puppies, so he just hoped that whoever stole her would love her and be kind to her."

When Gavin said 'Tilly,' the little dog stood up on her hind legs and walked around clapping her front paws together as though she was applauding herself.

Chloe laughed and said "Look. That proves it. Bonzo will be pleased to hear that she is safe. I'll ring him later. And she had four puppies."

Gavin looked excited and asked Chloe what she was going to do with the pups.

"That will be Bonzo's decision, "Chloe told him. He took a piece of paper out of his pocket and wrote his name and phone number on it.

"If he will sell them, please save two for me. My little daughters would absolutely love them. Now I must go or I will be late for work.

After he left, Chloe hurried home to tell the family the good news

Ellen and Jeffrey and Dean were not home so she changed her mind She decided to wait until everyone was home and she would tell them at the dinner table.

When the family sat down to dinner, and after they said grace, Seb announced that Chloe had something special that she wanted to share with them.

"What do you mean Seb? How do you know?" Chloe said with a frown on her face.

"Because I can read you like a book, and you have been fidgety all afternoon".

"You old owl," she laughed, "but you are right. I know who Whiskers is and I know where she came from.". They all stopped eating and looked towards Chloe waiting for her story.

"Seb can tell you," she laughed with an impish grin on her face. Then she continued, "This afternoon I met a man near Whiskers' gate and he told me that he had a temporary job at the circus while it was in town, and Whiskers' name was Matilda shortened to Tilly and she belonged to Bonzo and did a little act with Beverly the camel." Chloe had a very attentive audience as she told them everything that Gavin had told her. The family agreed that it certainly sounded true and the dinner conversation centred around the circus animals and Bonzo. Dean and Jeffrey both commented that they had often seen Whiskers sleeping near the camels' fence while the camels were grazing on the other side. After dinner Jeffrey rang Bonzo while Chloe rang Mary and Lexie.

"I think you should ring Tania. She will be thrilled to hear that the little dog can be re-united with her owner," Billy said.

Chloe immediately rang Tania and as the others listened. They could hear that the conversation was not a happy one. When Chloe hung up she looked around with a puzzled look on her face and said, "That wasn't what I expected. She seemed to be angry, although she was trying to disguise her feelings. I can't understand why."

"Is anyone thinking what I am thinking?" Seb asked.

"What do you mean Seb? What are you thinking?"

Billy answered before Seb had a chance. "He is thinking that Tania is the dog-napper."

"What?" Several of them shouted. Chloe, however, didn't say anything immediately, then she said very softly, "I think that you are right Seb. She seemed to be saying, "I rescued her and you have given her back to those people when you said that you would look after her. They are not her exact words, but that is the feeling that I had. I just can't understand why that should upset her."

"Some people don't like animals being trained to do things to entertain an audience. They think it is cruel. However, I would say that Tilly enjoyed the attention," Seb told them.

It was decided that they would put her in the camel enclosure the following morning and see how she behaved.

It was an excited family that locked the house and strolled up to Whiskers' cabin very early the next morning because Ellen wanted to see the action before she went to work. Whiskers was at the fence waiting for them and she leapt into Ben's arms when he opened the gate. Chloe opened the gate into the camels' enclosure and as Ben put her down, he playfully shouted, "GO! TILLY!" and that was exactly what she did. She bolted across the paddock towards the camels with her ears and long whiskers flying backwards and when they saw her coming, they trotted towards her. Some guests who were out for a stroll had joined the family to see what was happening. George and Mary had also arrived in their utility so there was a small crowd to clap them and cheer the animals on. Tilly ran around both of them prancing up and down on her hind legs and whimpering. They touched noses and one of them crouched down on the ground and Tilly ran up her front leg and sat on the camel's hump. All the spectators clapped and cheered until the camel stood up, then Tilly stood up on her hind legs and turned around in little circles clapping her front paws together as though she was applauding herself. It was a small hairy stage on which she was performing but her balance was perfect. That brought on another burst of clapping and cheering from the crowd and the camel started to trot forward.

As Beverly trotted around in a large circle Tilly sat up as though she was begging. and received another burst of cheering. Every time she changed her position, she received loud cheers and Beverly continued to trot around in circles about the size of a circus arena.

The crowd had doubled, with everyone who had heard the cheering hurrying over to see what was happening. Someone called out, "Who taught her to do that?"

Billy spoke up. She said, "Whiskers was brought to us as a stray dog, however, yesterday a man recognised her and told us that she belonged to Bonzo the clown and had performed tricks with the camels in the circus. A few days before the circus moved away Whiskers was stolen. We don't know how she became a stray after that. The camels were left with us because Beverly hurt her leg and the vet wouldn't give the owner permission to take her on their tour. It is only by a lucky chance that they have been re-united

While Billy was talking Beverly had trotted up to the fence and kneeled down so Tilly could run off her back.

Ben picked her up, but Billy stepped forward and lifted her out of his arms. Ben was small and Billy was afraid that some over-enthusiastic bystander might try to take the little dog from him.

Each person was tingling with excitement. Each one had a happy and satisfied feeling flowing through their veins. When Jeffrey spoke to Bonzo on the previous night, the little clown-man told him that he had given his boss notice that he was leaving at the end of the tour and he said that he would be looking for a new job. Jeffrey was delighted to offer him a job at the park. He was due to start at the end of the month.

Chapter 71

At the end of that same week, Chloe was given an attractive well-built cage with four rats in it. They were certainly not on Chloe's list of animals but she had promised herself that she would not refuse any pet that needed a home, except snakes and lizards. Although the cage was well built there was nothing special about it. It was just a cage and didn't fit in with the park theme. The little girls who owned the rats obviously loved them. They took them out of their cage and nursed them. Chloe felt a shudder run up her spine but she tried to disguise it. Their mother laughed and she said," You will learn to like them. They are really intelligent and I am sure that they giggle and play tricks on each other. When they are in a playful mood I could sit and watch them for hours."

As Chloe told the rest of the family while they were having dinner she said, "If they are playful and intelligent, we have to encourage them to show off when they have an audience. What can we do to make them more interesting?"

Seb as usual was full of good ideas.

He stood up and took a large sheet of paper out of a drawer and then picked up a pencil and sat down with them. He cleared a space on the table, and then he said to no one in particular, "Now that we have the rats, I'll bet we will soon have a variety of small animals, pets, in which parents or children have lost interest. Let's beat them, by planning ahead. What small pets can you think of?"

"Mice" was Ben's quick reply.

"Right" Seb said as he wrote it down.

"Guinea Pigs" Dean said.

"Yes". Seb said and wrote that down. There was silence for a while as each person was trying to think of a small pet that someone might have. Then Billy said, "How about little quails?"

"We have put them over near the bantam hens." Chloe answered.

"Yes." Billy said. "They are Jap quails, but King Quail adults are as small as an ordinary hen's two-week-old chickens, and their own little chickens are like those toy chicks that are on Easter eggs. They are really cute."

"Yes." Seb added "I remember when Donna Richland's children had some. They were so small that they could walk through the small gauge chicken wire. You don't often see them, but if no one brings some to us, we can look around for a few. They won't be too hard to find." It was agreed. There were four possible types of very small pets. "All of these animals are quick breeders, so we will have to separate the males from the females." Jeffrey said.

"It seems that we need eight pens, not cages." Seb mumbled as he started to draw a large octagonal shape. "Now, this is the roof. I'll divide that into eight sections. The whole building will be about forty metres in diameter. Each class of animal will have a big triangular pen. They must have a roof to protect them from flying predators and the partitions will be made with insect proof wire so that the young babies can't crawl through."

Ellen said, "Some small birds would be nice"

"Yes their back ground singing will make it very pleasant. Canaries, other finches and budgerigars. "Billy added.

"Those pens will be very big for mice, won't they?" Dean asked.

"Yes, and that is how we are going to make them interesting". Seb answered with a typical glint in his eyes. "We will make each section look like several little villages. There is an old retired cabinet maker in our church congregation, and at the church fete he had a stall full of miniature houses and other buildings that he makes as toy villages to suit match-box size cars. Now we could employ him to set up suitable sized buildings in each section and add parks, highways, shallow rivers railway lines and even playgrounds. All of them will be built in the right proportion to suit that particular animal. We will, of course have to put a solid lining under the floor and drain it, otherwise we will have our pets burrowing out and wild rats burrowing in."

"That sounds absolutely fantastic, Seb. We can have a path around the whole building and guests can walk around the outside and watch all of the different animals playing in their villages. I can hardly wait. It will be wonderful. We can even do something different with the bird nests." Chloe said.

After Chloe and Billy selected what they felt would be the best site for it, Jeffrey, George and Seb took over. Once again, Seb's experience as an architect was useful and George's connections with friends at the council sped up the official paper work and Jeffrey provided the finance. As soon as the council approval was received the builders were ready to start. It wasn't a huge project and progress was rapid.

Wesley, who was the retired cabinet maker, was extremely interested and visited the park to see how big the area where he was working would be. He took out a tape measure and measured each rat. then, on his rough plan he drew several buildings, a railway line, a play park and a shopping centre. After a brief conversation with Jeffrey, he went home, eager to start on the new project.

At the end of three weeks the building was completed and Wes arrived with four boxes of miniature buildings. Chloe and the rest of the family were keen to see how the rats would re-act to their new home. She even rang their previous owners to come over and watch the big event.

After the girls arrived Jeffrey and Bradley carried the cage into the much larger pen and opened the doors. There was an audience and the rats were wary. They each peeped out and then backed away. They tested the doors several times and it seemed as though they might need some extra encouragement, when one of the little girls said, "I'll bet Florence is the first to take the brave step". Next moment a pretty little black and white rat stepped right out, looked around and sniffed the air, then made a dash for the church. It was followed by three more. Each one chose a different building and then peeped back through the door.

They changed buildings frequently and then Florence, the little black and white rat, recognised their wheel from their cage and climbed in.

She soon had it turning quickly, and another rat that would like to join her ran up a ladder onto a miniature fortress that was a complete replica of the fortress in the children's park. One of the larger buildings with an open front and the word 'RESTAURANT' printed across the front had a long bowl of thick milky porridge and one of the rats found it and was soon joined by the others for a tasty breakfast. There were also pieces of fruit and vegetables on the shelves.

There was no doubt that they were enjoying their new home and were not afraid of an audience. Chloe turned to the mother of the girls and said, "You are right, I could sit and watch them for hours, but I have to try to forget about their wild relatives."

Weeks went by and no one brought in any more small pets, so, when Ellen went home for a weekend visit, she went to a pet shop and bought two pairs of pretty little mice and two pairs of guinea pigs. Each set was left together for two weeks to give them a chance to boost the population. The experiment was successful and it wasn't many more weeks before they had ten mice and eight guinea pigs but still no king quails.

Jack told Ellen where she could find a produce merchant who often had some of the less common birds. The next time that she went home, she and her brother and his friend found the business and were lucky enough to find twenty little quails so she bought all of them and some little finches, canaries and budgerigars.

Chapter 72

Friday had become a regular fishing day for George and Seb. They, and anyone who wished to join them would spend a few hours fishing until they had enough fish for a large family dinner. After they had caught the fish, the women would cook it and George and Mary would stay for dinner and then the four adults would play cards and the young people would clean the kitchen so that Seb and Billy could have the afternoon off. It was while they were playing cards, that George told Seb and Billy that he had been speaking with his brother Phillip about camels. Phillip said that he had increased his herd to ten and he was amazed at how the industry was growing It was not just milk but several other by-products. The milk was very sweet and pure white. It was a nice drink when it was cold. They also made a variety of cheeses and were working on new ones.

He had tasted a gelato that was delicious. Besides the food, some skin products had been made and they were very popular. He had installed a milking machine and the camels were quite relaxed and readily accepted it.

They had a feed box in front of them and happily munched away on their favourite food while the machine worked.

As soon as he had a chance he and his neighbour would fly across to Longreach and if George could pick him up, he would try to bring enough samples of the products for them to use in the house and sell in the restaurant. It would give them a good idea of how popular it would be and they would have to find out how far away the nearest collection point for the milk was, at present. The milk sold for nearly twenty dollars a litre.

"That really has me interested," Seb said. "However, it will be a completely new project and we will have to be fully prepared before we jump into it." He laughed and then said, "Here I am talking about it as though it is my project. It just shows how much I feel as though I am part of this family."

Mary said, "We all feel the same way, Seb. You are part of the family and I am certain that Jeffrey and Chloe would agree. We must be the most unique family in the country".

At the same game of cards George reminded them that Ferdinand was quite old and like all living things, he would have a 'use by' date. Two of the old cows had already died of old age and Ferdinand was just as old as they were. He said, "Jock told me that one of Ferdinand's daughters had a baby black bull calf that was the image of Ferdinand when he was born, and he suggested that Jeffrey should take it and start training it now. It is only one week old and will need a lot of love and attention if you are going to have another Ferdinand."

"I am sure that Chloe and Jeffrey will be interested so I'll pass it on later" Seb said.

Chloe and Jeffrey were very interested and immediately began to make special plans for the little baby. They would have to take him away from his mother so he would need a lot of care.

When they discussed it with Jock, he offered to live in a cabin with Ferdinand 2 to have the greatest impact on his character.

Matilda's cabin was the most suitable. It had been built like a small three-room house and even had a shower and toilet. One room was locked off from the animals and Jeffrey bought a king size mattress which was placed on the floor in the extra room. Matilda immediately wanted to mother the new baby, and often licked its face. Jock gave it lots of hugs and often wiped its coat down with a warm rough damp cloth to resemble its mother's tongue. It was fed whenever it called for attention and started to grow quickly.

Gavin had been given two of the puppies and the other two were delighted with their new playmate. Jock had been taken off the fencing work and his only job was to raise the baby calf. He left his bedroom door open at night and often woke up with Matilda, her puppies and Ferdinand 2 on the mattress with him. It wasn't hard for him to teach the puppies to play with the calf, and to make it easy for them to climb onto his back, he made a shelf for the pups to hop on and then the calf would go and stand near it and they would climb onto his back. His main intention was to encourage the calf and the puppies to play together without human directions.

As the calf grew his back became a much bigger stage than a camel's hump and so Jock was able to teach both young dogs to act together.

His hippo performance shed was built and Ferdinand two was taught to put his head through between the poles to receive tasty treats and attention.

With some help from Bonzo, Jock taught the two puppies to sit up back-to-back, on the ground and beg for treats, and then they taught them to do the same act on Ferdinand 2's back.

Ferdinand 2 grew into a big animal and easily filled the role of the big black bull. His grandfather stayed in his own special pen until the sad morning when Chloe, Billy and Ben found him on the ground and unable to get up again.

His shed was demolished and the space was left empty until the time when the family was ready to build a butterfly house.

Chloe had watched a program about Dubois and its beautiful gardens. They had huge mounds of straw and animal manure which would make very fertile gardens, and someday she would make any spare ground between the motel and the house into one colourful magnificent patch of flowers that would rival the gardens of Dubois.

Dubois also had a butterfly house which Billy and Seb had visited and they suggested to Jack and Lexie that it would make a wonderful short vacation that the four of them might visit someday.

Chapter 73

Five more years went by. The three youngest, Chloe, Ben and Bradley had finished high school and had gained top marks in all grades.

They were ready and keen to begin university.

Jeffrey and Ellen were married and had a loveable little toddler whom they named Stephen.

Dean and Pamela were engaged and were building a new house on the block of land that Jeffrey had given Dean. When Robinson destroyed Dean's car by crashing into it, Jeffrey offered to replace it with a better one, but Dean preferred to keep the one that the insurance had given him and he asked Jeffrey whether he would give him a block of land instead., so Jeffrey had given him ten hectares at the top of the farm. The highway swung back near the property and he and Pamela were building their house near the highway. They could use the land for a hobby farm or sub-divide it into smaller properties.

Fiona had come back to live with Lexie and Jack during school terms because she wanted to be a school teacher, and Lexie was helping her with her high school subjects.

The wild bird aviary was flourishing with pathways and seats and feeding stations for a variety of birds. There were artificial nesting boxes and little corrugated colourful sheets of corrugated plastic attached between branches to provide more protection during bad weather. The noise in the morning had turned a few guests away but others, who agreed that it was noisy, said that it helped them to relax.

One day when George, Seb, Greg and Mac were fishing, Seb said, "Do you still have hopes of going around Australia, George?"

"Well, Mary and I have talked about it but I think it might be beyond us now"

"What about you two?" he asked Greg and Mac.

"We have never really given it much thought, but we have the van and everything we need, so with some travelling companions we might be interested," Mac replied.

"I'll ask Jack and Lexie next time they are over, and I don't think that you are too late, George," he said. "If we all went, we could support each other, and I know you would only have one driver George, but I am sure that we could sort out a roster to share your driving, and make it easier for you. And we don't have to travel long distances each day."

"What about the kids? Do you think they can manage?" George murmured.

"That's the point. They are not kids anymore, and we would only be away for twelve or fifteen months. They are a sensible lot" Seb argued.

"I suppose we can give it some serious thought and think it through"
George replied.

After talking it over at home, Billy invited Lexie and Jack and the whole family around for a barbecue on the Saturday afternoon.

Both Lexie and Jack had retired but they hadn't made any extravagant plans because Fiona was living with them and Pamela, Wendy and Christine often came home for the week-end.

When Seb presented the idea, their first re-action was surprise and then they were interested.

The whole family was listening and each one had something to say.

"Don't let us spoil your plans." Jeffrey said. "We will look after the younger ones. We will make them do all of the work"

Bradley was twenty and was highly respected by the whole family, both the adults and the younger ones. He was extremely serious and sensible. "I am sure that I could cope with the cooking. Don't you agree Seb.?"

"Absolutely, Brad. You are starting to outclass me. However, I don't think that you should be responsible for the house-keeping."

"I'll look after most of that," Chloe said, "but not all of the washing and ironing."

"We couldn't leave the girls on their own for a whole year." Lexie protested. "And what about Fiona?"

"Could I come and live here with Chloe?" Fiona asked. "And I would help her with the house work. We could do Ben and Bradley's washing and ironing because Bradley will be doing all of the cooking."

"Yes!" Chloe shouted. "Ellen and Jeffrey share Ellen's room, and little Stevie 's nursery was the spare room, but now Jeffrey's old room is spare so you would be right next to me."

"Do you think that your Mum would approve?" Lexie asked.

"Yes. I am sure that she will, but she couldn't really stop me" Fiona said.

"We will be taking most of our stuff with us so Pamela, Wendy and Christine could move into the unit. They could even bring your fowls, and pony and little Larry, with them, because Champ and Heidi accepted Pixie and Poppet straight away." Billy argued.

"You make it sound easy", Jack said. "In fact, you have won me over. Have any of you got any objections?" Jack asked his family.

"No!" They all shouted. "It sounds like fun. Can we use the library?" Christine asked.

"Definitely, and there is a spare set of power points in the library for Fiona's computer and a complete set in the unit." Chloe said.

"Well, that sounds as though it has been decided, and George, you and Mary are in," Seb said firmly.

"Goody!" Mary exclaimed. "We will have to be satisfied with a second-hand van, and we could do with some advice in choosing one".

"You are not going in a second hand anything." Jeffrey said. "Tomorrow or as soon as you can all get your act together, you can go into town and buy the best one that you can find. The inside has to suit Mary and the towing has to suit George. The sooner, the better, because George can practise towing it around the park, and when you come back from your holiday, we will add it to the on-site vans, so I am going to pay for it."

"Oh, you can't --" George started to say, but Mary talked over him.

"That would be wonderful Jeffrey and I promise that we will look after it"

"I suppose it will free up a bit more money for us, and I was planning to buy a second-hand vehicle, so perhaps I can buy a new one if I don't have to buy a van or any of the accessories. We do have a nice little nest egg put aside thanks to the deal with Chloe and Jeffrey but you need to have some ready cash when you are setting out on a journey like this one," Billy said,

"I am so excited already. We were setting out into the unknown without any plan, now we will have three other vans and seven useful travelling friends with us. I just feel so blessed." After a short break and a few agreeable comments, Belinda said, "Can everyone be ready by the week-end?" That was followed by a lot of laughter and several helpful and unhelpful comments Sebastian, in his usual organised manner took a new writing pad out of the drawer and started making a list of all of the 'to do's'. The first thing we must do is contact Mac and let him know that the trip is going to happen. Who would like to do that? Right, Jack. Will you give him a ring and ask him how soon they can come out here for a couple of days so that we can plan this trip together."

Jack went out on to the veranda to make the call and Sebastian handed him a pen and paper as he left the table. There were a few sniggers around the table acknowledging Sebastian's thoroughness.

"Now, George. How confident are you driving a big four-wheel drive?"

"I would like to have a bit of practice, but I think it will all come back to me. That is what I had for many years on the farm but it was a bit rough and when we moved into the motel, we bought the new utility. I would like to have a bit of practice at towing the van too, but I wouldn't say that I feel nervous about it. You see I grew up on a farm and started driving anything that had a motor in it when I was ten or eleven years old, and I have all of the licences that are required."

In the meantime, Jack came back into the room and told everyone that Greg and the doctors are absolutely excited about the trip and they will be here on Monday at about mid-day.

"Excellent!" Sebastian said, "So, on Tuesday, all of those involved in the trip can go to town and try to find what they need locally." He suggested that each pair begin to make their own list and on Monday afternoon they could put them all together. Sebastian rubbed his hands together and gave one of his laughs and said "I am starting to feel excited too. However, for those who are not going, remember that your lives are going to change too, so you should start making some serious plans and rosters, if anything is worrying you, lets let's talk about it."

Billy and Sebastian talked about the trip and the responsibility of the park when they were in the privacy of their unit and both of them were confident that Jeffrey and Chloe, with the support of all of the others, would manage quite easily. They had already proved that they could make important decisions before all of the adults had stepped in.

Seb was confident that he could trust Hank, the chef. Bradley was not a fool and he would quickly notice if anything was going wrong. Jack had personally chosen the two mechanics and Jeffrey and Dean would be working with them. Everyone of the young people was a sensible and devoted young person and they would make sure that the park was running smoothly. They could not think of one problem that could arise and cause any serious trouble. Even the ground staff were a reliable lot. Some of them had been there since the beginning and Jock and Bonzo would be excellent foremen.

When the 'stay at home group' met they each had a few pages of thoughts that they wanted to share.

Chloe's thoughts were happy and positive. She and Jeffrey had a beautiful house and a park that was way beyond any of her dreams. The top of their property which consisted of hundreds of hectares had been divided into large paddocks and each paddock had at least one dam or lagoon. The soil that was dug out was used to build hills to protect the animals if the river ever broke through its banks There were shelters in every paddock so that the animals could find shade in hot weather and their food could be protected.

Emus, ostriches, turkeys, golden pheasants and guinea fowls roamed freely. In another area, geese swans and ducks moved through the paddocks because they could fly, and sometimes they visited the river. Their dams and lagoons were open, but for the cows and horses and other non-swimming animals the dams were fenced off and water was pumped into a trough on the outside.

The other animals in the two-hectare pens were healthy and happy with every comfort that could be provided for them. Ferdinand 2 and Toby and Tootsy were great mates. Sometimes the two dogs would go up onto their shelf and wait for Ferdinand 2 to come over to them and then they would curl up on the big bull's back and go to sleep, while he continued to mooch around grazing on the lush green grass.

Tilly still enjoyed visiting her camel friends and if an audience gathered outside, she would go through the window that was cut into the dividing fence, then climb up onto Beverly's hump and entertain them.

Jeffrey had employed a qualified chef to cook for the restaurant and special events and Bradley was apprenticed to him. Ben said that he would help Bradley prepare the meals but he thought it would be a good idea if one or two of the park groundsmen took over the care of the gardens, because they all had study to do as well as the house work. He was a very competitive young man and was keen to be the best at everything that he tried.

The young women and Dean and Jeffrey were willing to help everywhere, and just keep the park running smoothly. Jeffrey reminded everyone that without Seb and George around they would have to be vigilant and let him and Dean know as soon as they saw anything that did not look right, with the staff or the animals.

On Monday at lunch time the younger set had lunch and then returned to work or study. Both Lexie, Jack, George and Mary were at the house waiting for Mac and Cameron to arrive. Mac had told them that he and Cameron were going to be there for three days and they booked into the motel. Josie and Greg would not be coming.

When Chloe, Ben and Bradley went back to the library or their bedroom to study, Lexie commented that, in her forty years of teaching, she had never met such ambitious and committed students, not even her own family. They all agreed with her and they also agreed that it was probably because they had a rough interruption to their young lives.

Mac rang to tell them that he and Cameron were about twenty minutes away, so they re-set the table with fresh crockery and dishes full of delicious food prepared by four good cooks. Seb and Billy had prepared a meal, then Mary arrived with two more dishes and Lexie arrived with enough to feed everyone. Mac and Cameron were greeted with a very warm welcome and immediately led into the dining room. They admired the feast that was in front of them but they were more than ready to attack it.

During the meal the main topic was about the trip and it wasn't long before Mary asked Cameron whether he was interested in joining them. He was quick to thank her and to reveal that he and Nancy, his wife, would love to join them if everyone agreed with it. He made it clear that they would understand if anyone thought that the convoy would be too long. Every person agreed with enthusiasm, most of them adding that they would really appreciate another couple and an extra van. After that welcome, Cameron felt a little more confident and ready to talk about his own experience.

He and Nancy had travelled up the coast to Cape York and down as far as the entrance to the Nullarbor Plain. "However," he said, "Nancy was not keen on crossing the top on our own and we have never met anyone with whom we felt completely compatible."

Almost all of the would-be travellers were extremely excited, but not Lexie. She could not settle with the idea of leaving her girls alone for at least a year.

After enjoying their meal, they each took out their computers and began to present their ideas. Some had planned to go North first and some had prepared to go South. A lengthy discussion followed and the final decision was to go South. They would head for Redcliffe a little Beach side city just North of Brisbane. It was the first white settlement in Queensland. They would have one night stop on the way there, because they expected the first couple of drives to be strenuous for the inexperienced drivers and they didn't want to put stress on anyone at any time. They planned to stay at Redcliffe for several days. From there they could visit Brisbane and some of the nearby islands. Their next stop would be the Gold Coast, where they would spend another week. From there they would plan their trip, going slowly down the East coast to Sydney.

Sydney would also need a long rest so that they could visit the many attractions around there.

From Sydney they would plan a slow trip to Melbourne which, of course, was worth several more days. Someone suggested that they could leave their vans in a park and fly across to Tasmania, where they could hire two cars and tour around the island state.

They continued to plan their trip in the same way, across the bottom of Australia to Perth which would also deserve several days to explore the corner of Western Australia and then slowly up the Western coast to Darwin where they would then make a big decision.

They would have to decide whether to go down to Uluru and back to Darwin or go down and then go across to the Queensland coast.

All of the discussion fed their enthusiasm, especially for Mary who had always hoped to go around Australia but she couldn't believe that it would ever happen. They decided to give themselves six weeks to prepare.

Some excitement had been stirred in Lexie, but her motherly instincts were still very strong.

The girls tried to convince her that they could and they would take care of each other. Jack reminded her that they were not children anymore but she had never been away from them for more than a week, and now another pair was being added to the convoy. Lexie felt that she and Jack were a couple of outsiders and she would rather stay at home and keep an eye on everything.

Billy and Seb had become very close friends with George and Mary. She didn't know Mac very well, and now Cameron and Nancy, who were very close friends with Mac and Josie would also be part of the convoy. Jack was keen to go but he wanted Lexie to enjoy the experience too so he made a quick decision to go down to Brisbane for a week and take the whole family with him. He would buy his new vehicle while he was there and then buy the caravan and live in it for the rest of their short holiday. It would be good to give Lexie the caravan experience and it would also help them to decide what accessories they would need to make their life more comfortable. The whole family backed his idea and immediately began to prepare for it.

They would travel down to Brisbane in Lexie's new Lexus which Jeffrey and Chloe had given her as a 'thank you' for the help which she had given them when they were in hiding. Chloe was only nine years old when they arrived there and Lexie was like a mother to her.

Jack presented the idea to Lexie when they were all having a stroll around the garden after their meeting. She knew that he was eager to go on the trip and she wanted to co-operate. It would still be hard for her because they were the only parents who were leaving their own family behind.

Chapter 74

The following day, the family left for Brisbane and George and Mary went caravan and utility shopping in their local town with the support of all of the other travellers. George had always liked the Colorado and the sale yard was the first place to which they headed. After he had made a definite decision, Seb and the other men kept him talking while Jeffrey slipped into the office and wrote out a cheque for it. George wanted to argue with him but Jeffrey was very firm. He had been waiting to do that for a long time to repay him and Mary for their kindness, from when he first arrived at the motel, and their continued guidance ever since.

George, the tough old farmer, had to fight back the tears. He had always liked Jeffrey but this was the kindest act that he had ever received. Mary was also quite emotional but she was far more practical and thanked Jeffrey for his amazing generosity. She knew that he could easily afford to pay for it, whereas she and George were just retired dairy farmers who had managed to put a few dollars aside plus the money that they had received from the sale of their farm. Going around Australia in a caravan had been her dream for a long time although she had never expected it to become a reality.

Jeffrey was also giving them the Park caravan to use so they would have enough money to thoroughly enjoy such a wonderful adventure.

Seb drove the Colorado while George went along as his passenger.

The next stop for the travellers was the caravan yard on the other side of town.

The vehicle was the men's purchase. The caravan was Mary's and Billy's choice. Mary said that she didn't want a big van.. She would like a bit of luxury in the bedroom, the kitchen and the dining area. She also needed a shower and toilet but not a washing machine. She didn't need a lot of cupboard space because she intended to pack carefully. As they all walked around, every van seemed to be exactly what Mary wanted and she was having a difficult time choosing. The men who were experienced travellers began to help by quietly pointing out advantages and disadvantages until Mary was left with a choice between two. She decided to let the men make the final choice because George would have to set it up and tow it.

It was time for them to have a break so they all went along to George's and Mary's favourite cafe where they enjoyed a good Australian feast and once again gave a short history lesson about the pioneers in the district.

After lunch the men went their own way and Billy and Mary went shopping for some of the little bits and pieces that they thought would be handy on the trip and to enjoy themselves. The men would also have their own fun and then, Cameron and Mac would go home in Cameron's car and Seb and George would tow the caravan home with the Colorado.

Chapter 75

Meanwhile Jack had found his favourite vehicle, a Nissan Navara. The girls wanted a bright red one but he had spotted a luxurious one that looked like black velvet. The salesman told him that it had been a special order but the buyer had changed his mind. It was Jack's vehicle and he insisted on choosing its colour, saying, "You can choose any caravan that you like. I don't care if you choose a moon buggy, but the ute is mine."

They were fortunate because there was a caravan show on, at the Redcliffe show grounds on that weekend and they had a large variety to choose from. They had a wonderful time, walking among the vans checking each one out, but Lexie had her own special requirements. It had to be big enough for five people to sleep comfortably. That reduced the selection but they finally found one which had loads of cupboard space. The dining seats converted to a double bunk and the lounge sofa made another comfortable bed. The main bedroom which was divided off with a pleated curtain was sheer luxury, and their minds were made up. It had a well set out kitchen, a toilet, a shower and a small washing machine. Jack, who had no voting rights described it as an absolute master piece. It was huge but that didn't bother him because he had driven his big rig for many years and Lexie also had a licence to drive it and had driven his rig on several occasions. The deal was done and Jack proudly towed it back to the park where he had already booked a space.

They hadn't taken any crockery or linen with them so the ladies went off on another shopping excursion. The girls insisted that everything for the van had to be new and Lexie chose red as her basic colour for the kitchen and gold for the bedroom.

Jack also went shopping for outdoor furniture and electronic equipment that would give them the best recording of their trip and would keep them in close touch with their family. None of them had ever bothered to keep up with the latest mobile phones but Jack invested in two of everything that they needed to have the best and closest contact with their family and the unique family also.

Fiona had already settled into the bedroom next to Chloe and seemed to be happy with her new life, and it was obvious that the girls were looking forward to being independent and living in the unit with their friends in the big house in the BIG BLACK BULL ANIMAL RESCUE PARK.

It was their second night at Redcliffe and Lexie was beginning to feel excited and in charge of her life. The following day they all went to a tourist centre where the guide was a tremendous help. He seemed to know every detail about every kilometre of their trip and handed them a set of six pamphlets for every 'must see' attraction on the way. They had one for each of the vans and one for the whole family back home.

That night, their second night in the van, Wendy set one set up in a scrap book in their correct order with other details that the guide had told them about distances, rest areas and good caravan parks while the rest of the family enjoyed watching television. Lexie's excitement had reached top level. She was, by nature, a leader, and although she was never a bossy person she had to feel in control of her own life and she had an extremely strong maternal instinct and both of these feelings had been satisfied. They enjoyed a couple more days swimming and relaxing on Suttons Beach before heading home. Jack's mission had been a complete success.

Jack was a big man—a gentle giant—and he adored his Lexie and she was very much in love with him, and now that Lexie was excited about this amazing adventure, he was bursting with happiness.

They had one night's break on their way home and then went straight to their friends.

They called Mary when they were about half an hour's drive away, so everyone was there to meet them. Lexie parked in the normal car park but Jack took the van around the back so that anyone who wanted to have a close scrutiny of it would have more room.

It made George's and Mary's van look small but Mary was still extremely happy with her own compact little van. When Seb stepped out after spending the longest time in it studying every detail, he said to Jack, "Have you ever seen our van?"

"I remember you were parked outside the fence for a couple of days when you first arrived," Jack replied. "I think it was quite long too."

"Yours is seven years younger, otherwise they are almost identical. This is our van with a few modern touches," he laughed. "I suppose you chose a big one for your family. We chose a big van because we expected to live in it."

Billy and Lexie joined them and when they heard about the coincidence, they too had a laugh.

The remainder of the time slipped by quickly. They each had their own friends to notify and some reading to do. Jack and Lexie brought their pets over to the park and the girls carefully selected and packed the things which they wanted to take with them. The unit would be empty when Seb and Billy moved their own things into their van, although there were a few things which they decided they wouldn't need. Pixie and Poppet knew something was happening and they stayed close to their human family. They skipped in and out of the van and were especially excited when their own beds, sand trays and food dishes were put back in their usual position.

When Jack was at Redcliffe he booked five places side by side for their stay at the little beach-side city. He wasn't sure how long they would stay so he booked for the whole week. It was their first major stop and near Brisbane.

George, Seb and Jack and their wives would have one overnight stay on their way down to Redcliffe and there would be many attractions to visit in that local area. Cameron Mac and their wives and Greg would join them at the park and they would launch their adventure from there. Their next stop would be at the Gold Coast and then they would move slowly down the coast towards Sydney.

That special day eventually arrived. Jack and Lexie arrived at the motel at four in the morning with Pamela following close behind in the Lexus which was packed tightly. She was followed by Wendy who was driving Lexie's old red car, and Christine and, of course Little Larry. He was an old fluffy white dog like a mop with two shiny black eyes.

The travellers were ready to leave and a huge crowd was there to see them off. Dean and Jeffrey had bought a box full of toy trumpets and kettle drums. The girls had a bag full of blown-up balloons.

After plenty of hugs and kisses, tears and promises the little convoy moved out onto the highway. The 'stay at home' crowd then began to blast their trumpets, bang their drums release their balloons and shout their last messages to the melody of horns.

Ruby, whose name was changed to Chloe, and Rohan Connors, whose name was changed to Jeffrey, stood side by side with their arms around each other's waist watching Seb's van disappear around the bend. Jeffrey could feel the vibration of Chloe's body as a wave of emotions spread through her nerves. "Don't be upset Little Mate," he said. "The time will pass quickly and we will all be here again waiting for the first van to come around the bend when they come home"

"But what if something happens to them?" she asked. "Well, I can't promise that it won't." he answered, "but I can assure you that they are all good drivers and are not risk takers, and they have Jack who is a good mechanic, George who is also pretty good, and Dad who can't do much but could give good advice. They also have two specialist doctors who brought Dad back to life when everyone had given up and of course, Josie is also a doctor and Billy is a top-class nurse so I don't think we should worry because they all deserve a wonderful holiday."

As he spoke, he saw two sad young men trying to get their last glance at the caravans too and he led Chloe over to them. Clearly, they were quite upset. Two tall, solid, handsome young men whose names were once Jess and Ritchie. They were no longer two skinny frightened young boys. Jeffrey unashamedly stood between them and put his arm around Bradley's and Ben's shoulders and gave them the same little encouraging speech that he had given Chloe. Then he added, "You are a valuable and loved part of this family and you always will be. You are my young brothers"

"And my big brothers." Chloe interrupted. Jeffrey continued, "If anything, anything at all is worrying you, you must tell me. I would be happy to employ someone to help you in the kitchen if you need help, although you will still be in charge. Perhaps someone is bullying one of you or you have money problems, please talk to me. There isn't any problem that we can't solve together."

"Thank you." they both replied, then the four young friends walked up to the house together each telling their own story of how Jack had saved their life and the others had turned their life around.

For the rest of the day there was a slight anti-climax but the animals still had to be fed and Jeffrey and Dean went back to work. Chloe Ellen and Fiona helped the girls move into the unit while Ben helped his brother Bradley prepare the food for a great Aussie B.B.Q. that afternoon.

Dean's mother and twin sisters gave their little dairy herd to Jeffrey and Chloe and moved into one of the cottages in what had been affectionately named "Shearers' City."

Twelve months later the friends were all gathered at the restaurant waiting for that first caravan to come around the bend in the highway.

Pamela and Dean's house was finished and they were married one month later.

Chloe's little dream was an amazing success.

ABOUT THE AUTHOR

Born in Toowoomba in 1937, Bluey Rogers (Ada Kusters) is a retired primary school teacher. With five children, ten grandchildren and nine great-grandchildren and a passion for writing, she is now living her 'golden years' in Queensland, Australia.

OTHER BOOKS

Home Before Dark